MIND FIELDS

by
Thomas Garlinghouse

Published by Open Books

Copyright © 2021 by Thomas Garlinghouse

Interior design by Siva Ram Maganti

Cover image © Lysenko+Andrey shutterstock.com/g/romantitov

ISBN-13: 978-1948598507

To Lauren

Who always believed in me and was the first to hear the good news.

Author's Note

Deriving specific details and statistics regarding the Chinese annexation of Tibet is a task fraught with the obstacles of controversy, misinformation, and propaganda. Though the basic facts and data cited in this novel are as accurate as can be verified, all names, characters, and novel scene incidents portrayed in this production are fictitious. No identification with actual persons (living or deceased), places, buildings, and products is intended or should be inferred.

"One must know how to protect oneself from the tigers
to which one has given birth."

—Old Buddhist saying

Prologue
The Tibetan Plateau, 1951

AN ICY BLAST OF wind roared down the high mountain gorge. It whipped at everything in its path, including the two men struggling up the steep, narrow trail. Dressed in tattered parkas and threadbare woolens, they plodded along in single file, bent forward under the weight of heavy backpacks.

The man in front, the younger of the two, stopped to catch his breath. He stood for a moment, breathing hard, frozen breath swirling around his head. His thick, smudged-stained glasses immediately fogged up so that he had to take them off and wipe the lenses with gloved fingers. He put them back on and glanced anxiously over his shoulder.

The professor, a man in his early thirties, was falling farther and farther behind. His right leg bandaged and encased in a makeshift splint, the man limped along using a pine branch as a walking stick, his face a mixture of pain and exhaustion.

The young man let out a frustrated sigh. They couldn't linger here; if they did, they'd soon die of exposure. The professor needed to move faster. There was simply no other option. But the young man wasn't in much better shape than the professor. His head pounded from dehydration and his wind-burnt features ached to the touch. The non-stop hiking through this harsh, unforgiving environment was beginning to take its toll.

He turned his face back to the wind, grimacing against the biting cold, and continued plodding forward. He had walked several paces before he realized his companion wasn't following. When he looked over his shoulder, he saw that the older man had slumped to the ground. He spun around and rushed over, stumbling on the rocky trail, his backpack bouncing up and down on his back.

"Professor!" he shouted over the roar of the wind. "We have to get moving!"

The older man grunted in agreement but made no effort to stand. Instead, he sat slumped over, his head hanging between his legs, his breaths coming in ragged gasps.

In despair, the young man drew himself up against the wind and took a moment to study the surrounding terrain. His blue eyes traveled along the sharp-ridged summits of the great mountains that rimmed the horizon on all sides. He shivered. The stark immensity of the massive Himalayan peaks never failed to make one feel puny and insignificant. And that was how he felt now as he gazed at the huge walls of gray granite surrounding him like indifferent giants.

At 15,000 feet elevation, this was the most forbidding landscape he had ever encountered—a frigid, wind-scoured land of rock, ice, and snow. It was an environment as hostile and remote as another planet.

He turned away from the wind and looked back the way they had come. Far below, the valley floor was a patch of fertile green in a swirl of gray and white. They had climbed a considerable distance and the young man was amazed they had gotten this far, especially with the professor's leg turning septic. If they could just reach the high pass, they might have a chance of eluding their pursuers. The Nepalese border wasn't far beyond the pass; if only the professor would get up.

Sudden movement in the valley below caught his attention, jarring him back to reality. He brought up a hand to shade his eyes and squinted. Several figures were beginning to ascend the trail. He felt his breath catch as recognition set in. They were the Chinese soldiers who had been following them with dogged determination the last two days. Dressed in green fatigues and sturdy boots—and armed with machine guns—they were a troop of People's Liberation Army soldiers, sent to arrest the meddling foreigners.

He stood frozen in place, uncertain about what to do, his eyes riveted on the soldiers below. Then, all at once, he snapped out of his paralysis. He spun back around and grabbed his companion's shoulder.

"Professor," he shouted, "we have to get going! They're coming up the trail!"

But the older man made no move to get up. He just hung his head and mumbled incoherently.

He shook the professor's shoulder vigorously. "We have to get going now!"

The professor's head seemed to sag even lower. "Go on," he croaked, his voice hoarse and thick. "Leave me here. I don't think I can make it."

"I'm not leaving you!" he shouted. "We're going to make it together."

This time, as if shaken out of a stupor, the older man glanced up, turning watery eyes to his companion. Then, feebly, he extended an arm. The young man took it and hauled the professor to his feet. He stood unsteadily, swayed slightly, but didn't fall.

The young man turned to face his companion, his gloved hands gripping the man's shoulders tightly. "Professor," he said, his eyes a mixture of deep feeling and compassion, "it's now or never. We can't linger."

The professor stared at the young man for a moment, his face deathly pale. But, gradually, as the younger man's gaze bore into him, he suddenly felt a surge of resolve and optimism run through him. He drew a deep breath and, grimacing from the pain that lanced through his leg, nodded.

The young man draped the professor's arm over his shoulder and pulled the man close against him. "Let's go," he said.

They started off, struggling against the violence of the wind, the fierce gusts whipping at their clothes. They hunched against it, plodding forward, feet stumbling on the rocky ground. The narrow gorge seemed to amplify the sound of the wind, raising it to a constant shriek. Soon the sky darkened, and needle-like sleet began to pelt them.

The trail grew steeper as they ascended so that they were soon picking their way over boulders and loose rock. The pass loomed in the distance, half obscured by mist and snow. It seemed so far away. The young man hoped to God they would make it.

Chapter 1

Humboldt County, California, Modern Day

TAYLOR HAMILTON SLOWED HIS Jeep Cherokee and turned off Highway 101, pulling onto a quiet country road marked Madrona Lane. Stepping on the gas, he drove east, the coastline receding in the distance behind him.

The surrounding countryside was thicketed with towering redwoods, spruce, sword ferns, and Douglas-fir. Scattered patches of coastal fog clung stubbornly to the hollows of the nearby hills. As he drove farther east, the fog began to dissipate, revealing blue skies and bright sunlight.

After battling through thick fog for most of the way up from San Francisco, Taylor let out a sigh of relief. He rolled down the window and draped his arm over the sill, feeling the sun warm against his skin.

He'd been driving since six that morning and now, five hours later, was finally nearing his destination. He felt a tingle of excitement. He was looking forward to moving in for good this time. The trips back and forth from the city over the last several months had been exhausting and time consuming. It would be good, finally, to settle into the new house; indeed, to settle into his new life.

Taylor and his wife, Kate, had bought the house, which was located just east of Oceanport in Humboldt County, less than a year ago. In fact, it had been almost exactly five months. They had initially used it as a weekend getaway, but Taylor had increasingly fallen in love not only with the house but also with the area—a region of coastal fog, redwood forests, and wind-swept coastline. He was a mystery writer who had recently published his first novel, which, to his surprise, had

1

won an Edgar Award for "outstanding debut novel," and was selling well. The proceeds from sales, along with the generous advance from his publisher for two more novels, had allowed Taylor to purchase the house. His creative side was stimulated by the rain-soaked setting of extreme northern California, and their weekend stays had succeeded only in whetting his appetite for longer stays. Finally, he had proposed they relocate to Oceanport full time.

At first, Kate was reluctant to uproot her life. She didn't want to be too far away from San Francisco, where she worked as an attorney. Nor did she want to move to what she considered some "backwater" part of the state. But Taylor had been particularly persuasive in extolling its virtues and downplaying its negatives. He honestly believed they could make it work. He could stay in Oceanport full time—and write—while Kate could spend part time in the city and part time in Oceanport. She only needed to be in the office three days a week; the rest of the time she could conduct business via phone and email. She had finally agreed, so they sold their house in the Sunset District and rented a small apartment near downtown, where Kate could stay for those three days.

Presently he came to a fork in the road. The lane branching off to the left led up a slight rise to the house of his nearest neighbor, an older man whom Taylor hadn't yet met. Slowing the Jeep, he turned right onto a very narrow road, which was lined on both sides with thick-trunked redwoods. He drove through what seemed like a dim tunnel framed by overhanging and twisting boughs. Through the foliage up ahead he caught occasional glimpses of the house.

It sat on a low hill and overlooked a vast expanse of green, forested hills, pastures, and wetlands. Freshly painted and stark against the blue sky, it was a majestic old structure with an elaborate façade, a four-columned portico over the doorway, pointed bay windows, and a large central gable—the quintessential northern California Victorian mansion. To Taylor it felt isolated from the outside world, a fact that pleased rather than repelled him, though in reality, Oceanport was only a fifteen-minute drive away.

He turned onto a gravel driveway and rolled to a stop in front of the house. Killing the engine, he sat for a moment, listening to the symphony of metallic pops and clicks as the Jeep cooled from the long drive.

A sense of deep satisfaction spread through him as he gazed at the house through the windshield. It was hard to believe he actually owned this magnificent house, this jewel set amid some of the most spectacular scenery on offer in California. The thought almost made him giddy.

He opened the door and climbed out, his leather sandals crunching on the gravel that lined the driveway. The air was crisp, but the sun was warm. He took a deep breath, filling his lungs with the pleasant dampness. Several white puffy clouds scudded by on a light breeze and birdsong emanated from the nearby trees. He closed the door with a firm hand. The sound echoed in the calmness of the day.

Dressed in faded jeans and a T-shirt, he looked lean and fit. Few would have guessed he was entering his fourth decade of life. His face was tanned and lined from many years spent out of doors, and his hair, though he had less of it than he'd had in his twenties, was still relatively thick and wavy.

He took a moment to stretch, bending forward and then backward at the waist, loosening muscles that had been knotted up during the long drive. Straightening, he went around to the back of the Jeep and flipped open the gate. The rear of the vehicle was crammed with gear, mostly file boxes, but also duffel bags and various other odds and ends. Most of the furniture had been delivered weeks ago so that most of the stuff he was now bringing to the house was his personal belongings—or personal "crap" as Kate had so indelicately put it. Lying diagonally across all this was his prized possession—his surfboard, a six-foot-six, three-finned "thruster." It was encased in a sturdy canvas board bag with a shoulder strap.

He carefully backed his board out of the vehicle tail-first and placed it gingerly on the ground. Then he walked to the front of the house and hopped up the steps. He took a moment to fish in his pocket for his keys and unlocked the door. Instead of stepping in right away, he stood at the threshold and peered inside. The house was quiet and light from the large bay windows spilled into the foyer, creating a latticework pattern of dark and light on the floor. He lingered there for a full minute, not wanting to mar the picture spread out before him, feeling his presence might somehow disturb the tranquility.

He reached around and flicked the light switch. Returning to the car, he started to unload the boxes, stacking them on the ground next to his surfboard. As he reached for another box, he happened to look up and noticed a man and his dog coming down the road. Even from this distance, Taylor knew it was an older man. Though he was tall, he was stooped, and he carried a cane. He walked slowly and with a limp—his right leg trailing slightly behind the left. But what really caught Taylor's attention was the dog padding alongside the man. It was huge—huge and black, with massive front paws that slapped at the ground with each ponderous step.

Taylor stopped what he was doing, put his hands on his hips, and stared in amazement. To call the animal a dog didn't quite do it justice. It looked more like a big trundling bear. It was a mass of thick black hair and muscle. Its face was broad and its muzzle blunted, its eyes set back deeply in its head.

The old man came to a stop. The dog mirrored its master's actions, stopping at the same time the man did and sitting down on its haunches, its tongue lolling out in a pant, white canines flashing in the sun. Taylor noticed it had neither leash nor collar. The man shifted his cane to his left hand and put up his right in greeting.

"You must be the new neighbor," he called out. His voice was pleasant, well-modulated, with a touch of what Taylor imagined was east coast Brahmin, either Boston or New York.

Taylor tore his eyes away from the dog. "Yes, that's right."

The old man smiled, showing a row of yellow-stained teeth. He was extremely thin and gaunt with an angular face and sharp features, including a prominent, hawk-like nose. He looked to be well into his eighties, perhaps even his nineties. His hands were large and gnarled with prominent veins. He wore a tattered sweater and underneath a black beret, wavy, silver hair fell to his shoulders. Despite his age, his eyes were warm, intelligent, and lively.

"My name's Havelock Rowland," he said. "I live in the house just up the road. Saw you pull up and thought I'd come over and say hello."

"Nice to meet you," Taylor said. "I was wondering who lived up there." He paused, turning his attention back to the dog. "I gotta say, that's the biggest dog I've ever seen."

The man grinned and cast the animal an affectionate glance. "This is Dorje," he said.

"Dorje?"

"It's a Tibetan word," the man explained, looking back to Taylor. "It means 'thunderbolt.'"

"Aptly named," Taylor said. He studied the animal, still amazed at its size. "What kind of dog is it?"

"A Tibetan mastiff."

"Are they all that big?"

The man chuckled but didn't answer. "You here by yourself?"

Taylor nodded. "For the moment, but my wife's coming later this evening. She had to stay in the city this morning."

"I understand you're a writer," the old man said.

"Yes, I am."

"Anything I'd know?"

"You like mysteries?" Taylor asked.

"Not a huge fan, I'm afraid, but I like a good Sherlock Holmes once in a while. Is that what you write? Mysteries?"

Taylor nodded.

"Well," the man said, glancing around, "if you're looking for solitude and inspiration you came to the right place."

"That's exactly what I'm looking for."

"That's why I came up here, too," the man admitted, glancing at the surrounding trees and foliage with a contented smile. "I love the peace and quiet of this place."

"Have you lived here long?"

"Ever since I retired. About fifteen years."

"What did you do?"

"I taught physics for thirty years."

"Really?" Taylor was suddenly interested. "Fascinating subject. I've always been interested in physics, but I never had the math skills to understand much of it. What branch did you teach?"

"Astrophysics. I worked at NASA before I got my permanent teaching job at Berkeley."

Taylor was impressed. "No kidding? When did you work at NASA?"

"The 1970s."

"During the moon missions?"

Havelock nodded and gave a self-deprecating grin. "But it sounds more exciting and romantic than it actually was. Frankly, I did a lot of data crunching on crude computers. When I got my Berkeley job, I exited the place as fast as I could."

"Still," Taylor said, "it must have been an interesting time to work there. When all that was going on. Armstrong and Aldrin, and all those guys."

"Yes, it was an interesting time, but I've always preferred teaching."

The two men fell silent after that. A breeze rustled the branches of a redwood tree towering above them.

Havelock pointed at Taylor's board bag with the end of his cane. "I see you brought your surfboard." He chuckled and shook his head. "You're a braver man than I am, Gunga Din. The water up here scares me. Always looks so cold and ominous. Can't imagine going out into it for fun."

Taylor chuckled along with the older man. "Yeah, well, I spent years surfing Ocean Beach in the city. That place gets pretty big and scary as well, with all the shifting sandbars. Good practice for up here."

The two men paused again. Havelock rubbed his weathered face and nodded, grinning slightly. "Well, I'll be off." He snapped his fingers and the dog immediately leaped to its feet, like a soldier coming to attention. "See you around." He trundled off down the road, leaning heavily on his cane, Dorje following dutifully alongside.

Taylor's gaze fell instinctively on the lumbering rise and fall of the dog's massive shoulders. He shook his head in amazement, and then turned his attention back to the boxes.

———————

Taylor stood by the large bay window and gazed out, watching the sun set on the horizon. As it faded, leaving a brief but intense afterglow, the clouds were illuminated by brilliant swathes of orange and red. These gradually turned to purple before fading altogether, leaving only an all-encompassing night.

"How was your day?"

Taylor turned at the sound of the voice and looked across the room. Kate was seated on the couch, holding a full wine glass. Dark, shoulder-length hair framed a well-shaped nose and two wide-set, dark eyes set behind a pair of stylish black glasses. She was dressed in her "work clothes," a dark skirt and matching sweater over a white blouse. She had gotten to the house only an hour ago, and too tired to change into something more casual, had simply kicked off her shoes and plopped down on the couch with an exhausted sigh. The only thing she'd wanted to do was open a bottle of wine and relax.

"Pretty uneventful," he said, "but at least I got all the boxes moved and most of the stuff put away."

"That's something."

"How was your day?"

She shrugged. "Considering I worked for half of it and then spent the other half driving, it was okay. I listened to a podcast on the way up."

"Which one?"

"On patent law."

"Good God," Taylor said, making a face, "that sounds...so boring."

Kate laughed.

Taylor crossed the room and crouched down in front of the blazing fireplace. He jabbed at the logs with a poker, sending a swirl of sparks into the air, and glanced over his shoulder. "Ran into our neighbor today."

"Which one?"

"The old man who lives in the big house at the top of the street."

Kate settled down on the couch and took a sip. "How was he?"

"A nice old guy. Used to be a physicist."

Kate looked up, surprised. "Really? That must've made your day."

"He told me he used to work for NASA," Taylor said. He put the poker down, straightened, and crossed back to where she was sitting. He poured himself a glass and eased in beside her.

"I wonder how he ended up here?" she said.

Taylor shrugged, taking a sip. "Not sure. But he had the biggest dog I've ever seen. You should've seen it."

Kate laughed.

"What's so funny?"

She eyed him over the rim of her glass. "Dogs and physics—your two favorite subjects. Is this your way of telling me you still want a puppy?"

"I'm serious. It was huge. The thing must've weighed well over two hundred pounds, I'd say."

Kate raised her eyebrows and let out a whistle. "That is big," she said, impressed. "What kind was it?"

"He said it was a Tibetan mastiff."

"I've heard of that breed. But I don't know much about it." She took another sip of wine and stretched her legs out in front of her, letting out a tired sigh.

"God, I'm so glad to be home," Kate said.

He smiled at her. "So, you're beginning to see this as home, eh?"

Adjusting her glasses, she took a moment to glance around the room, her eyes taking everything in with a cool appraisal. The firelight cast a warm glow on her face as she nodded approvingly and then turned back to him. "Yes, I think so."

"I'm glad," he said, reaching over and giving her arm a gentle squeeze. He held up his glass. She clinked it lightly with her own.

They were both silent for a time, listening to the crackle of the fire, and enjoying the wine, the evening, and each other's company. The light from the fireplace flickered against the walls, and the stillness of the night seemed to radiate a pleasant ambiance.

"You going to surf tomorrow?" she asked.

Taylor nodded.

"Are there supposed to be any waves?"

"Not really. It's supposed to be pretty meager but I'm itching to go. I haven't surfed in a week."

"A week?" exclaimed Kate with playful sarcasm. "That must be horrible for you." She reached over and patted his knee in a motherly gesture. "Poor boy."

Taylor chuckled and raised his glass to his lips. He was about to take a sip when Kate laughed suddenly. He lowered his glass and looked at her, his brow furrowing. "What's so funny now?"

"It's just that you're so predictable."

He paused for a moment and then grinned. "But that's why you love me, right?"

Chapter 2

TAYLOR'S JEEP CRUISED ALONG the narrow, two-lane road through the early morning fog. As he neared the coast, the fog grew thicker and wetter so that he had to use the wipers. They thumped back and forth monotonously.

He had a busy day ahead of him. He figured he'd surf for an hour or so, and then meet Kate for a late breakfast in Oceanport. After that, he and Kate planned to do some shopping for the house. She'd seen some bathroom mirrors at a second-hand store down by the wharf that had caught her fancy. Depending on what time they got back to the house, he planned to spend the rest of the afternoon setting up his office and computer.

Taylor drove cautiously, taking the curves that led to the coast with care. The road was known to locals as the "White Knuckler." It dipped in and out of ravines and jogged around hair-pin curves. It had, over the years, claimed its share of unsuspecting drivers.

Rounding a final bend, Taylor sighted his destination, Humboldt State Beach, just as the sun was rising over the forest-clad mountains to the east. It was a long stretch of open coast, one of the few stretches of sandy beach in the area, scattered with driftwood and fronted by coastal dune. Importantly, it was also graced with a series of offshore reefs that on the right combination of swell and tide produced rideable surf.

The Jeep's tires grinded against gravel as he pulled into a dirt parking lot set on a bluff above the beach. He rolled to a stop and peered out the window. The fog was rapidly dissipating, and he got a good look at the waves. As predicted, conditions weren't great; in fact, the ocean was wind-blown and choppy with a steady onshore breeze blowing. He rubbed the back of his neck and frowned. It looked even worse than he had expected, and he felt his initial enthusiasm sag. Still, he told himself, he'd managed to drag his ass out of a warm bed this morning and drive all this way. It seemed a waste to turn tail and head home.

He pushed the door open and stepped out. Immediately the cold, damp air bit into him and he shivered. He contemplated retreating to the warmth of the driver's seat and blew into his cupped hands to warm them. He continued to gaze out at the water, studying the waves. To his surprise, he noticed that occasionally a set would roll in that had potential. He watched one wave in particular. It hit the reef and squared up. But instead of dumping, it peeled at an angle. Taylor perked up, lifting an eyebrow. The wave had considerable wobble, but it was rideable.

That decided it. Gritting his teeth, he stripped out of his clothes and began to suit up, squeezing into his thick 5-mm wetsuit. He stepped into his neoprene booties and pulled on his hood. Then he extracted his board from the back of the car and squatted down on one knee. He rubbed a bar of wax across the deck with the practiced ease of someone who had done the procedure a million times. Straightening, he thrust the board under his arm and plunged down the trail that led to the beach. He sprinted across the sand, leaving deep footprints behind him. There was a flock of gulls down near the water's edge that took to the sky at his approach, lifting off the ground with a mad flapping of wings. They hovered in the air, screeching and squawking, as he waded into the shore break and paddled out, a black-clad figure amid a swirl of gray water and white foam.

An hour later, Taylor emerged from the ocean, carrying his board under his arm. His face was flushed from the salt and cold, but a smile lingered on his lips. The session had been worth it. Although the waves hadn't been anything to write home about, he'd caught a few fun ones. That was all he required.

He ascended the bluff and was startled to see a young man standing near the front of his car. He stood quietly, his arms held stiffly at his sides, smiling at Taylor with a goofy, lop-sided grin. Taylor stopped, assessing the situation, his eyes narrowed. For a moment, he thought the man might be trying to break in but had been halted in the act by Taylor's sudden appearance. He cast a quick, appraising glance at the car but it looked fine. He turned his attention back to the young man. Strangely, he was dressed stylishly, in a black long-sleeved turtleneck shirt, well-pressed pleated black trousers, and black polished dress shoes. His face was boyish and crowned by a mop of unruly, long blond hair, which was slightly lifted in the breeze. He had on a pair of small round glasses through which two exceptionally blue eyes stared out with a look Taylor could only describe as eager excitement.

The young man stepped forward. "That was you in the water, correct?"

Taylor was startled by the abrupt way he had asked the question. He nodded curtly. "Yeah."

"I have never seen that before," the young man went on. There was an odd cadence to his voice; he spoke without contractions and each word was delivered with a slight pause. "That was amazing."

Taylor stooped to place his board on the ground, and then straightened back up. He took off his hood and dragged a hand through his hair. He eyed the young man guardedly. "Never seen what?"

"What you were doing. Out there in the water."

Taylor blinked, baffled at the man's statement. He stared at him. "You've never seen surfing before?"

"Is that what it is called?"

Taylor was dumbfounded. But before he could add anything to the conversation, the young man squatted down on one knee near the board and reached out his hand. He stopped, his palm hovering over the deck, and looked up at Taylor.

"You ride on this? This conveyance?"

"It's called a surfboard."

"A most interesting craft, to be sure." He paused. "May I touch it?"

Taylor didn't know what to make of this guy. He stared at him for a long moment, looking him up and down, and then nodded reluctantly. "Yeah, I guess."

The young man placed his hand flat on the board's deck, fingers splayed. He stayed in that position for a minute or so, not moving. Taylor noticed he was staring at the board wide-eyed, as if it was the most fascinating thing he'd ever seen. Finally, he looked back up. "Yes," he said, nodding enthusiastically, "a truly amazing craft. Of what is it made?"

"Polyurethane and fiberglass."

The young man's eyes lit up. "Polyurethane!" he exclaimed. "A polymer composed of a chain of linked carbamates."

"Come again?"

The young man blinked, and his expression went blank for a second, obviously not understanding Taylor's question. After an awkward moment, he asked, "May I hold it?"

"The board?"

"Yes."

Taylor was beginning to get irritated now. This guy was too weird. "Look," he said, unzipping the back of his wetsuit, "no offense, but I'd rather you didn't. It's actually a little more delicate than it looks."

The young man stood up abruptly and took a deliberate step away from the board. "I understand." He let his arms fall to his sides and lowered his gaze, as if embarrassed. "I have, as they say, 'transgressed the boundaries of polite convention.'"

Taylor tried to be diplomatic. "No, no, it's nothing like that. I just don't want you to drop it. It might get damaged."

"Yes, I see that now," the man said, nodding. "I must apologize sincerely and ask your forgiveness."

"Don't worry about it."

"No, I will not succumb to worry. But you will have to excuse me, for I sometimes get a little too eager. It is a fault that my person is always pointing out."

"Like I said, no problem."

"You see," the man continued, the look in his eyes one of almost pleading earnestness, "there is so much in this world I need to learn."

"Yeah, I guess so," Taylor said.

The sarcasm in Taylor's response was apparently lost on the young man. He was silent, his blue eyes wide and unblinking.

Taylor went around to the back of his car and began to strip out of his wetsuit. He put on a pair of blue jeans and a T-shirt and grabbed a hooded sweatshirt. As he slipped it on, he glanced over his shoulder to see if the young man was still there. He was; in fact, it looked like he hadn't moved at all. He continued to stand with his arms at his sides. The embarrassed look on his face had passed, replaced again by his goofy smile—aimed directly at Taylor.

"Is there something I can help you with?" Taylor asked, stepping into his sandals. The tone of his voice this time was less than diplomatic. He was beginning to get irritated again. There was something weird about this guy, something vaguely creepy behind his boyish exterior; something Taylor couldn't quite put his finger on.

But the young man seemed blithely ignorant. "No, thank you. I am perfectly fine. I do not require any assistance."

Taylor stowed his board in the back of the car and got into the driver's seat. He was eager to get out of there. That was one of the strangest conversations he'd ever had. He turned on the ignition and pulled onto the road. As he drove off, he glanced in his rearview mirror. The young man was still watching him, an awkward, goofy smile on his lips.

"What a whack job," Taylor muttered to himself, shaking his head.

———————

"How was surfing?" Kate asked.

Taylor sat down across the table from her and massaged his right shoulder, giving a slight grimace as he kneaded the muscles. "The waves were kind of mushy. But it was good to get wet."

"You okay?" Kate asked, observing him.

"Yeah," he nodded. "Just a little sore from paddling. I'm not as young as I used to be."

"Join the club."

"What did E.B. White say, 'in a man's middle years there is scarcely a part of the body he would hesitate to turn over to the proper authorities.'"

She chuckled. "Cute. That the guy who wrote *Charlotte's Web*?"

He nodded. "Have you ordered?"

"I just did. Your favorite. Eggs Benedict."

"And coffee?"

She grinned. "That goes without saying."

They were seated at an outside table of a café in Oceanport. Kate was dressed casually but warmly against the chilly coastal breeze that now blew in from the water. She had on a fleece jacket, a multi-colored scarf, long cargo pants, and a wool beanie, from which her hair cascaded downward over her shoulders. Taylor thought, at the moment, she looked positively un-lawyer-like. The only accoutrement that hinted at her profession was her black glasses.

Taylor, for his part, looked exactly like someone who had just gotten out of the water after a long surf session. His eyes were red and scratchy from the water and salt encrusted his hair.

"I was hoping after breakfast we could go check out that store I talked about earlier," Kate said. "The one down by the wharf."

Taylor nodded, taking a drink of water and crunching an ice cube pensively.

Kate noticed the look on his face.

"Something wrong?"

Taylor set the water glass down on the table. "I just had a weird experience."

Kate raised an eyebrow and pushed a loose strand of hair behind her ear. "What happened?"

Taylor proceeded to tell her about the young man. How he seemed completely out of place, dressed as he was and loitering about the parking area. But he hadn't been homeless; far from it, his clothes looked expensive and tailor-made. He told her how he had seemed completely ignorant of surfing, almost like a child seeing it for the first time.

"He actually called my board a conveyance," he said.

"A conveyance?"

He nodded. "The whole thing was pretty weird."

Kate scratched her chin. "You think he was trying to break into your car?"

"That crossed my mind." He shook his head. "But I don't think so."

"Maybe he was autistic."

"No, I don't think that either." He paused. "He reminded me of—" His voice trailed off into thought.

"Of who?"

He furrowed his brow. "He was like a genuine Harold Skimpole come to life."

Kate squinted at him, frowning. "Who?"

"He's a character from Dickens. In the novel *Bleak House*. This totally naïve, childlike young man."

"Do you think he was on drugs?"

"That crossed my mind, too. But no, I don't think so." He shrugged. "Like you said, maybe he was autistic, or something."

Kate took a drink of water. "Well, I wouldn't worry about it. Probably just some random weirdo."

"You're probably right," he said. "I just thought it was odd."

When their breakfast arrived, Taylor forgot all about the strange young man.

Later that morning, they wandered down to the wharf and strolled along the boardwalk, passing a colorful array of shops and restaurants. The weather was still overcast and the sky a metallic gray, but it hadn't rained yet. The wind, though, was blowing harder, in fiercer gusts. Gulls wheeled over the water and dived for scraps of food in the harbor.

Despite the blustery weather, there were a lot of people out enjoying the day. Tourists mingled in front of shops, peering into windows, bundled against the chilly air, while fishermen clomped by in heavy boots and chest-high waders stained with fish blood. College students from nearby Humboldt State University, many arrayed in faux tie-dye and Birkenstock sandals, wandered about, darting in and out of shops and pubs.

As Taylor understood it, Oceanport had once been a major whaling port. With a well-protected deep-water bay, it was one of the best situated whaling ports in all of Humboldt County. Whaling had been a thriving enterprise for several decades, all the way up to about 1920. When whaling ceased, the town turned to lumber but the Depression hit hard so that Oceanport fell on difficult times. Over the next several decades, however, the small commercial fishing fleet staged a brief comeback only to collapse again in the 1980s and 1990s. Now, Oceanport had reinvented itself as a tourist spot—a place of quaint Victorian buildings, antique shops, restaurants and brew pubs, all surrounded by rugged and breathtaking coastal scenery.

They came to a small shop situated at the end of the wharf. Above the entrance was a hand-painted sign that read *Hsing's Second Hand*.

"This is the place," Kate said. She pulled her wool beanie down to just above her eyes and tugged Taylor's arm.

They darted inside, the wind blowing the door shut behind them with a bang. The store was cluttered with various bric-a-brac, and every available space was occupied. But as Taylor looked around more carefully, he noticed the items weren't just cast-off pieces of junk; many, in fact, though used, were in good condition.

Kate touched his arm. "Here, this is what I wanted to show you."

Taylor followed her down an aisle. At the end was a large, full-length mirror propped up against the wall. Around the mirror was an ornate gold painted frame.

"What do you think?" Kate said, gesturing at it.

Taylor scratched his chin and inclined his head. "It's kind of showy, isn't it?"

"I thought so at first. But it's growing on me. I think it'd be perfect for the house. I was thinking we could put it in the master bathroom."

"You're back again, I see."

Taylor looked over his shoulder at the sound of the voice. A short Asian man was standing behind them, an accommodating smile on his face. He was wearing a button-down sweater and glasses.

Kate turned around. "Yes, I'm back. Good to see you again."

"Still interested in the mirror?" he asked.

Kate nodded.

The man smiled. "It's still a bargain. Only a hundred bucks."

She turned to Taylor, her eyes more than a little pleading. "I'd love to have it. What do you think, hon?"

He looked at it again, folded his arms, and shrugged. "If you think it'll work. For the bathroom, I mean."

"I do."

Taylor turned to the proprietor. "A hundred bucks, you said?"

The man nodded.

He thought for a moment but then nodded. "Okay, we'll take it."

As the man rang up the sale, he asked, "So, are you folks in town for a few days?"

"Actually, we're in town for good," Taylor told him. "We bought the place at the end of Madrona Lane."

"Really?" He looked up in surprise. "The old Victorian? I was wondering when someone was going to buy that place."

"Just moved in for good yesterday."

"Well, welcome to the neighborhood." The man put out his hand. "I'm Ed Hsing."

"Nice to meet you," Taylor said, shaking.

The man hesitated, eyeing both of them cautiously. "Have you met your neighbor yet?"

"The old man?" Taylor nodded. "Met him yesterday when I was moving in. He has the biggest dog I've ever seen."

"Frankly, that dog of his kind of scares me. There's something not right about it. It doesn't act like a normal dog. It's unnatural."

Taylor chuckled at the man's hyperbole. "It is pretty big and intimidating," he agreed.

"He has a bit of a reputation in town," Ed Hsing said. "Havelock, I mean. As a recluse. Used to work for NASA, apparently."

"Yeah, that's what he told me."

Ed Hsing paused for a moment. "I've never really cared for him," he added.

"Really?" Taylor was surprised. "He seems like a nice old man. A bit eccentric, maybe. But friendly."

The proprietor just shrugged.

Chapter 3

OVER THE NEXT MONTH, Taylor fell into a routine of writing, surfing, and working on the house. He soon discovered, however, the latter task was taking up a lot of his time. Though solidly built, the house nonetheless required a million little fixes, and Taylor spent several hours of each day engaged in one of these: fixing a faulty pipe, repairing a light fixture, or repainting a patch of wall.

It worked out that Kate was able to conduct much of her practice from home, though at the same time, she continued to work in the city for three days, spending the beginning of the week in San Francisco and the remainder in Humboldt with Taylor. As predicted, Humboldt County proved conducive to Taylor's creative side; in fact, by the end of the month, despite all the work on the house, he had finished a big chunk of his new novel and was already making notes for the next one. He'd also run into his neighbor Havelock, and Havelock's dog, several times. Usually, he encountered the old man on the road, walking Dorje. He'd learned over the past month that the man was quite regular in his habits. He walked Dorje twice a day, once in the morning and once in the late afternoon. It was a schedule that hadn't varied, at least in the time Taylor had been around to observe.

The old man was an interesting character—eccentric, opinionated, and highly intelligent. The two men got along well, despite their obvious age and generational differences. Taylor was amazed at the elder man's breadth of knowledge; he could, for example, converse about the Higgs boson one moment and then shift gears to discuss something entirely different, like the *Tibetan Book of the Dead* or the finer aspects of Provençale cooking. It was obvious Havelock had led an interesting and varied life.

But it was equally obvious the old man fit the stereotype of the "scatter-brained professor." He would frequently lose his train of thought while discussing some subject or abruptly jump to another topic if the latter proved more interesting. Sometimes Taylor found it difficult to keep up with the man's rapid-fire thought processes. He nonetheless thoroughly enjoyed talking to the old man, though he suspected Havelock lived a rather lonely existence in his big house with few visitors or friends. Taylor wondered whether he had any children, but the old man never mentioned any, though he did, in passing, mention his wife who had died several years ago.

Taylor also got to observe Havelock's mastiff, Dorje. It was the oddest dog he'd ever come across. It was incredibly well-behaved and obedient, almost to a fault. When Havelock wanted Dorje to do something he would say the command out loud and snap his fingers and the dog would immediately spring into action. It was almost as if the dog understood language, or could even, seemingly, read the old man's mind. Most of the time, however, Dorje was perfectly content to lie around and do nothing; indeed, except when Havelock gave it a command, it was the laziest dog in the world. Taylor considered himself a "dog person" and normally had a good rapport with dogs, but Dorje was different. Taylor had tried on a few occasions to make friendly overtures but had gotten nowhere. Dorje was completely indifferent and uninterested. The most Dorje would do was give Taylor a cursory sniff of the hand before turning its head and looking away, as if bored. It wasn't that the dog was particularly unfriendly; it appeared to be a simple case of the dog's complete devotion to Havelock. Dorje's sun rose and set with Havelock. Nothing else mattered.

But there was no doubt Dorje was a good guard dog. The sheer size of the animal, its huge paws and massive shoulders, were enough to put the fear of God into anyone dumb enough to break into the house or threaten Havelock. And the animal had a bark—when he wanted to use it—that could chill the blood of any intruder. It was naturally protective and fiercely loyal to Havelock and highly territorial. Havelock had commented on several occasions that he felt his house was safe from break-in with Dorje patrolling the premises. Taylor could well believe it.

———

Two evenings later, when Kate was in the city, Havelock invited Taylor to his house. When Taylor got there, he was amazed to find that the inside of the house was a veritable museum devoted to Tibetan culture and antiquities. Taylor wandered about for a bit, fascinated by all the exotic artifacts, from small Buddha icons to Tibetan textiles, jewelry, musical instruments, weapons, and various other items, some made of metal and others of stone. There were several *thangka* paintings on the walls, and the photograph of a brilliantly colored Tibetan sand mandala held a prominent position above the fireplace.

Taylor walked over to the photograph and inspected it. It was sharp in detail, the colors vivid and contrasting. He turned back around, scanning the room in amazement. "How on earth did you acquire all this?" he asked.

"Over many years and many visits to Tibet," Havelock said. "I was first there in 1951. I'd just finished my doctorate and was on a scientific expedition in Nepal. We crossed the border into Tibet."

"What kind of expedition?"

"We were there to observe and photograph the transit of Venus across the Sun. The viewing was spectacular at that altitude."

"I'll bet." Taylor scratched his chin, trying to remember his history and gazed back at the photograph. "Wasn't that around the same time as the Korean War?"

"It was," Havelock said. He paused for a long moment. "It was also the time when China invaded Tibet."

"I recall reading a little bit about that," Taylor said. "But I don't know that much about it." He paused and turned to look at Havelock. "You were there during that time?"

"Yes." The single word response was uttered with a bitterness that surprised Taylor and a sudden tense silence fell over the room. Taylor watched as Havelock stared up at the mandala, not saying anything for what seemed like several minutes. Taylor suddenly wished he hadn't asked the question.

The old man continued to stare at the photograph, but his eyes were moody and faraway, as if he had withdrawn into some private domain of memories. For a moment it looked as if something like anger flashed in his eyes. "Many of my Tibetan friends were killed."

"I'm sorry."

Another silence fell between the two men until Havelock broke it.

"The world was focused on the Korean War at the time," he said, "so no one paid any attention to what was going on in Tibet. It played no critical role in world affairs, so its loss was considered no big deal. It was sacrificed to the Communists." He turned to face Taylor. "But, make no mistake, it was a bloodbath. The Chinese were determined to eradicate the entire Tibetan social fabric. And they just slaughtered everyone—men, women, and children. If you were Buddhist, you were considered subhuman and therefore not worthy of living. And if you were a monk you were tortured until you died." He paused, looking at Taylor evenly. "Do you know what the preferred method was?"

Taylor shook his head, afraid to know the answer.

"They would string the victim up and repeatedly beat his testicles until he passed out. Then they'd revive him and do it again. Sometimes they used a hot poker and applied that to the testicles. Or up the anus."

Taylor just stood listening, aghast, not sure what to say. He watched as Havelock got increasingly red in the face as he spoke, and his fists clenched at his sides.

"I blame all the Reds in the State Department," he hissed. "They just handed Tibet over to the Chinese on a silver platter. They—" He stopped, drew a breath, and drifted into silence, his rant over. He looked down at the floor and slowly unclenched his hands.

"I'm sorry," he said, looking back up. His eyes were clear now; the anger that had overtaken him, that had burst upon him in a white-hot torrent, was now gone. "I'm sure you don't want to hear an old man lament about his past."

Taylor was at a loss for words. He wanted to say something that might dispel the awkwardness that had descended but couldn't think of anything.

Havelock walked over to a table and picked up a small, four-sided metal cylinder to which was attached a long, well-used wooden handle. He handed it to Taylor. "Know what this is?"

Taylor held it by the handle and scrutinized it. It appeared to be some type of miniature club, but it was too delicate for that. He noticed that the cylinder rotated and that a small metal chain dangled from it. At the end of the chain was a smooth pebble. He looked at Havelock and shook his head. "I have no idea."

"It's a prayer wheel," the old man explained. "The Tibetans believe that by spinning it, you send prayers out into the air. There's a small parchment with Tibetan prayers inside the metal cylinder." He paused. "The Tibetans are an interesting people. Their whole lives are suffused with religion. Very different from us Westerners."

"I don't know much about Tibetan culture," Taylor admitted. "But I've read a little about the Dalai Lama. Sounds like a real interesting guy."

Havelock gave a snort of disapproval and a dismissive wave of his hand. "A mere figurehead. An amateur."

"Really? But don't the Tibetans see him as an important figure?"

"They do. They believe him to be a living Buddha. But the real lamas are the ones in the remote monasteries. The ones who rarely see a foreign face their entire lives. What they can do with their minds is incredible." He gave an amazed shake of his head. "If you'd seen half of what I've seen..."

His voice trailed off.

Taylor handed back the prayer wheel. "How many times have you been there? To Tibet, I mean."

Havelock carefully placed the prayer wheel back on the table. "Many times. The first time I had the opportunity to spend several months in one of the monasteries. I studied with the head lama."

"That must have been amazing."

"It was." A faint smile of reminiscence crossed the old man's face. Without missing a beat, Havelock suddenly rubbed his hands together. "Would you like some *raksi*?"

"What's that?"

"Tibetan rice wine," Havelock explained. "It's good but pretty potent."

"How potent?"

Havelock grinned. "Just wait and see."

Taylor regarded the old man for a moment. "Am I going to regret anything tomorrow?"

"Quit complaining, for Chrissake, and try it."

"Sure, why not?" Taylor relented, shrugging. "It's not like I need to drive home tonight."

Suddenly animated, Havelock spun around and shuffled off to the kitchen. A minute later he returned carrying a clear bottle and two glasses. He set the glasses on a table and uncorked the bottle with a grand flourish. He proceeded to pour a healthy splash into both glasses.

With a chuckle, Taylor watched the old man and wondered how many of Havelock's guests received the same strong-arm treatment.

He figured a visit to Havelock's house necessarily required at least one glass of *raksi.*

Havelock handed over one of the glasses. Taylor held it up to the light and swirled the liquid around. It was clear and reminded him of vodka or gin. He held the glass under his nose and took a sniff. It smelled slightly antiseptic.

"What did you say it was made out of again?" Taylor asked. "Fermented rice?"

"Sometimes they use millet. And sometimes they flavor it with rhododendron."

"Rhododendron?" He made a face. "That sounds horrible." He continued to swirl the liquid around in the glass, suddenly reluctant to give it a try.

"Don't be shy," Havelock said, eyeing him with impatience.

Taylor took a sip. The liquid seared his throat as it went down and he coughed, his eyes watering. "You weren't kidding about its potency," he gasped.

Havelock chuckled and, without bothering to ask whether Taylor wanted it, topped off his glass. Then he lifted his own and, throwing his head back, swallowed the contents in one gulp.

"So, what did you learn from that lama?" Taylor asked. "The one you studied with."

A very slow smile spread across the old man's features. "Many things," he answered, setting aside his glass. "Things that would blow your mind."

Chapter 4

TAYLOR AWOKE THE NEXT morning feeling horrible. He lay in bed, his head throbbing with a dull ache. Havelock had been overly generous with the *raksi* and Taylor had been reluctant to stop the man. He hadn't wanted to seem impolite or ungracious, so had let Havelock keep pouring glass after glass. They had managed to kill the bottle between the two of them.

Now he was paying for it. He groaned and buried his head in the pillow. But this did nothing to stop the throbbing. It felt like his head was being squeezed in a steel vise. Rolling onto his back, he gazed up at the ceiling, his eyes blinking against the glare. From the angle of the sun filtering in through the window, he knew it was late morning. He swallowed and turned away from the brightness. His throat felt like sandpaper and his tongue tasted bitter and gummy. With a sigh, he sat up and swung his legs over the side of the bed. He sat for a moment, rubbing his face with his hands.

Some crows started up outside the window, their raucous cries echoing through the morning air. Taylor couldn't help imagining they were mocking him, mocking his lack of restraint.

He got up and shambled into the kitchen. He felt dehydrated so he drank several glasses of water. Then he started brewing a pot of coffee. When it was done, he poured himself a cup and stood by the window, gazing out, his vision slowly coming into focus. It had been very damp the night before, and now, with the sun's rays penetrating the canopy, a gauzy mist rose up from the ground and swirled among the tree trunks.

With several sips of coffee in him, Taylor began to feel better, the headache lessening, the nausea retreating. He turned back from the window.

His conversation with Havelock, at least the bit he remembered, was intriguing and he was curious to learn more about the Chinese invasion of Tibet. He knew a little, but had to admit, was overall ignorant on the subject.

After showering, dressing, and eating a banana, he went into the study to do some research. Navigating onto the Internet, he typed "Chinese invasion Tibet" into the search engine, found a website that discussed the country's modern history, and was soon reading about the event. It began in 1950 when the People's Liberation Army crossed the Yangtze River and marched into Chamdo, a region in eastern Tibet. A ragtag Tibetan army, many of the troops wearing chainmail armor and carrying nineteenth century muskets, met them but was immediately crushed by the superior Chinese force, estimated at 80,000 troops. The Tibetans were forced to sign what came to be called the Seventeen Point Agreement, which effectively handed the sovereignty of Tibet over to the communist Chinese. Relying on assurances from the Chinese that Tibet, despite being incorporated into communist China, would remain autonomous, Tibetan officials, including the Dalai Lama, believed Tibetan culture and traditions would continue as they had for hundreds of years. From the very beginning though, the officials in Beijing had other plans. Over the next ten years, the communist Chinese launched nothing short of a complete reorganization of Tibetan society—aimed at eradicating Tibetan culture.

Monasteries were razed, monks killed and tortured, and the elite of Tibetan society, especially the intelligentsia, either murdered or thrown into prison. The Chinese encouraged immigration into Tibet and implemented forced land redistribution. This latter process involved turning the most productive and arable land over to individuals deemed most useful to the Chinese overlords. Finally, in 1956, armed rebellion broke out. With covert help from the American CIA, the rebellion was initially successful. But China cracked down hard in 1959, leading a force into Tibet's capital, Lhasa, and killing between 10,000 and 15,000 Tibetans in three days. Mass killings continued; by one estimate nearly 90,000 Tibetans died because of this crackdown. However, the Tibetan estimate placed the number at over 400,000 people. With the help of the CIA, the Dalai Lama fled to India.

Although resistance continued, the next several years were

devastating for Tibet. A terrible famine hit the country and lasted for three years. Tens of thousands perished. But it was the Cultural Revolution in China that unleashed the most devastating chapter in Tibetan history. Over 6,000 monasteries were razed, and an untold number of people were murdered, jailed, thrown into "re-education" camps, or simply disappeared. It was a holocaust, in the truest sense of the term.

Taylor finished reading. He logged off and sat back in his chair, his arms crossed over his chest. He shook his head sadly. The devastation and death wrought in Tibet since 1950 was horrific—a largely unknown and forgotten story. And Taylor suspected the website's version was only the tip of the iceberg; it was only a generalized recounting of the story. An entire country, indeed, an entire society and culture, had been devastated while much of the world had turned a blind eye, impotent or unwilling to help.

―――――――――

Two days later, Taylor was outside, hacking away at the berry bush that twisted its way up the side of the house. It was a mass of thorns, vines, and branches, and seemingly impenetrable. He'd been at it for two solid hours, but it was still dense and tangled. He'd made a dent, but only a small one.

Taylor lowered his pruning shears and let out a tired sigh. He stepped back to survey his handiwork and wiped sweat from his brow with the back of his hand. Berry vine clippings lay in neat piles at his feet. His arms were scratched and red from the thorns and the front of his shirt was damp.

Nonetheless, despite the hard work, he felt good. It was a feeling, as he gazed around, he might have attributed to the day. There was a languid, unhurried quality to it, exactly the quality Taylor liked best. The morning haze had burned off and now the sky was clear and blue, with only an occasional wisp of cloud. It was one of those exquisite days that simply could not be ignored. It seemed to pour its essence out into everything. There was a harmony to it. It was one of those days, in fact, that gave one the impression that everything—life, the universe, indeed, everything—was proceeding along as it should.

He looked up and saw Havelock and Dorje coming down the road. Glancing at his watch, he noticed it was a few minutes after four o'clock.

The old man was right on time for his afternoon walk. Taylor waved.

Havelock waved back and veered across the street, coming forward. As always, he moved slowly, limping along, his cane tapping at the ground with each step. "Good afternoon," he called out. He came to a stop, the big dog right at his side. Shifting his weight, he leaned forward on his cane, and eyed the tangled berry vines. After a moment he transferred his gaze to Taylor and winked. "Looks like you've got your work cut out for you there."

Taylor nodded. "It's a jungle. It's obvious these haven't been cut back in ages."

"They haven't. The previous owner just let them run riot."

"What was he thinking?"

"He wasn't," Havelock said. "He was an idiot. Didn't deserve that house."

Taylor chuckled and eyed the older man with a look of amusement. "I hope I can prove worthy."

Havelock grinned back. "I guess we'll have to wait and see."

Havelock seemed particularly jovial today, Taylor thought; although he was decked out in his normal attire, a somewhat austere ensemble which consisted of dark slacks, a warm fleece jacket over a dark shirt, and his ever-present beret, there was what Taylor could only describe as a twinkle in his eye.

"How's your day going?" Taylor asked.

Havelock gazed at the scratches on Taylor's arms. "Better than yours apparently. At least mine's devoid of sweat and toil."

"A little sweat and toil are good for the soul," Taylor said. "Isn't that what they tell us?"

Havelock snorted derisively. "And we're fool enough to believe it's true. 'Work will set you free,' and all that, right?"

Taylor chuckled.

The *clip-clop* of horse's hooves coming up the road interrupted their conversation. They turned and saw a blonde girl riding a brown mare. She was wearing knee-length riding boots and an equestrian hat with a tight chinstrap. She tossed a wave as she drew near.

Taylor waved back. He recognized her as the daughter of the man who owned the house near the turnoff from Highway 101. It was a ranch style house with extensive horse stables. He had seen her on a few occasions before, riding through the hills.

As the horse trotted by, Dorje turned his head. The horse stopped suddenly, backtracked a few paces, its hooves clopping nervously against the asphalt. It tossed its head and emitted a shrill whinny. Taylor could see that this action surprised the rider, who urged the horse forward. But the animal wouldn't go any further.

Taylor glanced at Dorje, who seemed to be the cause of the horse's fear. The dog was completely unperturbed, almost oblivious.

The rider kicked her horse forward, but the animal was stubborn. It wouldn't budge.

"What's wrong, Elsie?" the girl said, reaching down to pat the horse. Then she kicked its sides. "C'mon."

Instead of going forward, the animal reared up, whinnying in fright, its forelimbs thrashing the air. The sudden movement caused the girl to lose her hold on the reins. She threw her arms around the animal's neck, desperately holding on. Its forelegs came crashing back down, but somehow the rider managed to stay in the saddle.

Taylor dropped the shears and came rushing over. He grabbed the horse's reins. It backtracked several paces, and Taylor was dragged stumbling along. Finally, the rider managed to regain control of the animal. Its eyes were big and round, and it continued to emit a series of fearful whinnies.

Taylor handed the girl back the reins. "Are you all right?" he asked.

The girl swallowed and nodded, obviously shaken. She tightened the chinstrap of her helmet with a shaky hand. "I don't know what got into her. She nearly threw me."

Taylor turned back and eyed Dorje. The dog was sitting on its haunches quietly. He turned back to the girl. "Maybe you'd better turn back," he said.

The girl nodded, sitting astride her horse, and taking slow, deep breaths. The animal pawed the ground and snorted with nervous energy. She stroked its mane with a caressing hand.

"You sure you're okay?" Taylor asked.

She nodded.

"Need help back?"

She shook her head. She got down from the horse and, taking its bridle, turned the animal around and led it off.

Taylor watched her disappear down the street before turning and walking back to where Havelock and Dorje were standing. He stooped down to pick up his shears.

"That was weird," he said, shaking his head. "The horse seemed scared of Dorje."

Havelock shrugged but didn't say anything. He reached down and stroked the dog's head, moving his hand over the fur in an even, deliberate manner.

Taylor gazed at Dorje. The dog was quiet and still, as if nothing had happened, its eyes deep, unfathomable pools. He thought for a moment and then turned back to Havelock.

"I've always been curious about Dorje," he said. "Where did you get him?"

"From a breeder."

"Did you raise him from a puppy?"

Havelock nodded. Before Taylor could ask another question, Havelock said, "I wanted to mention how much I enjoyed your company the other night."

"That was fun," Taylor said. "Thanks for having me."

Without missing a beat, Havelock kept the conversation going. "I was impressed you actually took an interest in an old man's stories. Usually I can't interest anyone."

"Not at all," Taylor replied. "In fact, you spurred me to do some reading about Tibet. Pretty fascinating stuff. I learned a helluva lot about the Chinese invasion." He paused. "I had no idea it was that bad."

"No, nobody does," Havelock said. "It was a holocaust. And no one seems to care."

Taylor could only agree, nodding. But he didn't want to say anything else, for fear of setting the old man off again.

"Anyway," Havelock said, "I thought we might do it again some night."

"Get together again, you mean?"

Havelock nodded.

"Sure," Taylor said. He gave a self-deprecating grin. "But I think this time we might go easy on the *raksi*. That stuff gave me a kick-ass headache."

Havelock grinned back. "Fair enough."

Chapter 5

TAYLOR ZIPPED UP AND flushed. Havelock's old porcelain toilet gurgled and clanked as he washed his hands in the sink. Toweling off, he left the bathroom and made his way down the hall. As he walked past one of the rooms, he heard what sounded like footsteps behind the closed door. He stopped, and the footsteps seemed to stop as well. He stood listening but didn't hear anything else. That was odd, he told himself, he thought Havelock lived alone. Curiosity got the better of him and he considered opening the door and looking inside. But he soon decided against it; it was none of his business. He lingered for a moment longer, listening. But there was silence. Perhaps he'd simply been mistaken.

He descended the stairs and came back to the living room. Immediately Havelock took up where he'd left off.

"Tibetan Buddhism is a complex subject," the man said, continuing the conversation they'd started an hour ago. He paused to fill two shot glasses with *raksi*, and handed one to Taylor, who had seated himself on the couch. Dorje was lying near the fireplace, sleeping. The dog's chest rose and fell but no noise issued from its mouth. Taylor almost felt as if the dog was hibernating, or in some type of suspended animation, rather than sleeping. He glanced at it for a moment, but his attention was directed back to Havelock when the old man spoke again, in what Taylor suspected was his best lecture voice.

"Tibetan Buddhism is really a hybrid of Mahayana Buddhism, which came from India, and the old Bon religion."

"What's that?" Taylor asked. "The Bon religion, I mean."

"The old indigenous religion of Tibet. It's a shamanistic religion filled with nature deities and demons. Bon practitioners were supposed to have the ability to summon demons, control the weather, and change into animals."

"So, the two blended together?"

Havelock nodded. "Yes, that's probably the best way of putting it."

Taylor paused. "Do Tibetan Buddhists believe in demons?" he asked.

"Well, no, but—" His voice trailed off.

Taylor looked at him, awaiting an answer.

"It's a bit complicated, you see," Havelock said. He paused to take a sip of *raksi*. "They don't believe in demons, but such things do have a prominent place in their culture."

"I'm not following," Taylor said. "Do you mean as symbols?"

"Yes, certainly as symbols. But it's even more complicated than that." He looked at Taylor evenly. "Have you ever heard of the term *siddhis*?"

Taylor shook his head.

"It means supernatural powers," Havelock explained. "What we'd probably call psychic abilities."

"Do you believe in that?" Taylor asked.

A smile played at the corners of Havelock's mouth. He tossed back the remainder of his *raksi* in one gulp and eyed Taylor. "I take it you don't."

"I'd like to think I have an open mind. But those kinds of things are hard to believe. They make great fodder for novels, of course, but—"

"Have you ever heard of *tummo* breathing?"

"No. What's that?"

"A Tibetan breathing technique that generates heat in the body. It's used to stay warm in the cold. I've seen monks use it to survive in sub-zero temperatures."

Taylor furrowed his brow, trying to follow. "How is the heat generated?"

"Through mental processes. Through intense visualization."

"You mean imagining it?"

"Basically, yes. But the process involves visualizing a hot fire in one's belly. The key is to hold the image as long as possible with as much detail and clarity as possible."

Taylor paused, studying the old man. "You said you've seen this done?" he asked.

Havelock nodded enthusiastically. "Yes, indeed. Many times."

Taylor took a sip of *raksi*. He was quiet for a long moment. "But you're a scientist. I don't see how you can believe any of this."

"I didn't at first," Havelock said. "But I've seen and experienced too many extraordinary things to be a skeptic anymore. The world is simply much more fantastic than we realize."

"Look," Taylor said, "I'll grant you the world is a strange place. There are a lot of unexplained phenomena out there. A lot of strange coincidences. But, I have to tell you, I just find it hard to believe that people can do these amazing things with only their minds."

"You do realize there have been numerous scientific studies of psychic phenomena, right? And that many of these have demonstrated statistically significant outcomes."

"I don't know," Taylor shrugged. "Have they? I mean, you read about things occasionally, but are they legitimate? Who knows? Nothing's been conclusively proven, has it? As I understand it, the scientific community is pretty much in agreement that psychic abilities are completely unproven. That most of it is a hoax."

"So, you're a 'hard science guy,' eh?"

"A 'hard science guy?'" Taylor looked at him, puzzled. "You mean—"

"I mean if you can't taste, touch, smell, or measure it, it doesn't exist, right?"

"I wouldn't necessarily say that," Taylor replied. "I mean, you know as well as I that quantum physics has some pretty interesting things to say about the physical world. Or what we perceive to be the 'physical' world. But that doesn't mean I'm ready to take off on a wild flight of fancy. I'd like to think that someday science will find answers to all our questions."

Havelock grinned but it was a grin that carried a hint of condescension. "I used to be like you. I used to demand the world follow logical, coherent patterns."

"But you don't anymore?"

"Let's just say I've discovered that the subjective is more real, more powerful than the objective. It's the only thing that really exists. And the subjective is notoriously messy and illogical. What did Heisenberg say? 'Not only is the universe stranger than we think, it is stranger than we can think.'"

Taylor was quiet, considering this. It simply didn't make any sense to him. He studied the older man for a moment. "You sound like a bit of a mystic," he said at length.

Havelock chuckled. "I've been called worse."

"Still, it's pretty hard for me to accept what you're saying. I do think an objective world exists."

Havelock sat back, regarding Taylor thoughtfully, almost as if scrutinizing a small child. "What if I were to demonstrate something the Western mind can't rationally explain?"

"Such as?"

"You've heard of PK, right?"

"PK?"

"Psychokinesis."

Taylor furrowed his brow, trying to remember the term. "That's moving objects with your mind, right?"

Havelock nodded. "Correct."

"Are you saying you can do this?" The look on Taylor's face betrayed severe skepticism.

The corners of Havelock's mouth seemed to twitch in some private amusement. "Why don't I let you be the judge? You can see for yourself and then decide."

The old man got to his feet slowly and with some effort. He shuffled off to the kitchen. In a moment he came back holding a metal spoon and sat back down.

Taylor looked at the spoon, and then at Havelock.

"Spoon bending?"

Havelock nodded. "Have you ever witnessed this?"

"No," he shook his head. "But I've read about it."

"Well, now you'll get to witness it," the old man said.

Taylor made no comment, only watched as Havelock settled himself more comfortably in his chair. Presently the old man closed his eyes and took a deep breath, which he let out with an audible sigh, his chest rising and falling. He held the spoon upright in front of him, with the handle pointing downward.

Taylor watched closely, intrigued, but not really expecting to see anything extraordinary. He had the feeling Havelock may have convinced himself he had this ability but that he was only fooling himself. Either that or Taylor was on the receiving end of some sort of prank— soon to be revealed. Still, he remained quiet, his eyes riveted on the spoon. For several minutes nothing happened.

Bored, he stole a quick glance at his watch, noticing it was a little after eleven o'clock. He should probably get back to the house soon; still, he didn't want to be rude. He'd allow Havelock to have his little "demonstration" and then make up an excuse and bolt.

When he turned his attention back to the spoon, however, he was surprised to see it vibrating ever so slightly. He blinked, thinking it must be Havelock's hand shaking, but the old man was holding the spoon stable. Soon the spoon began to vibrate faster.

All at once, as if some unforeseen force—or some invisible presence—suddenly took hold of the utensil, the spoon began to bend. Taylor watched in amazement as the top curved downward, almost as if it were melting in Havelock's hand. In seconds, the spoon had completely bent double so that the top of the spoon was parallel with Havelock's knuckles.

Taylor was utterly stunned; he didn't know what to say. He clamped his eyes shut and shook his head, as if to clear it. Regaining his composure and opening his eyes, he sat back and stared at Havelock.

"How'd you do that?"

The old man's eyes flashed open. "If you've been listening, I told you already."

Taylor paused. "With your mind?"

Havelock put a finger to his temple and tapped it. "Exactly."

"C'mon, Taylor," Kate said. "That's the oldest trick in the book. Magicians do it all the time. It's just sleight-of-hand. An illusion."

"It looked pretty damned impressive to me. Not like an illusion at all." There was a slightly defensive tone in his voice. "I have no clue how he did it."

Kate gave an exasperated shake of her head and took a drink of iced tea. "Sometimes you can be so gullible."

It was midday and they were in a seafood restaurant on the boardwalk having lunch. They were sitting at a table that faced a large plate glass window, giving them a view of the boardwalk and the Pacific Ocean beyond. Puffy white cumulus clouds stood up against the horizon, and a brief rain had glistened the boardwalk outside.

"I watched the spoon bend right in front of me," Taylor went on. "It moved of its own accord. He didn't bend it with his hand or thumb."

"It only proves he's a good illusionist," Kate said. "Look up 'spoon bending' on YouTube. You'll see tons of people bending spoons. Some of them even tell you how to do it. It's not magic."

"I didn't say it was magic, I just said I have no idea how he did it."

She eyed him appraisingly. "But you think he might have some sort of psychic ability, right?"

"I don't know."

Kate looked at him. "I can't believe you're taken in by this."

Taylor was silent. He moved the last piece of fish around on his plate with his fork. He sighed and glanced out the window, watching a woman pass by walking her dog, a young German Shepard.

"Look," Kate said, "I know he's your friend, but I think he's duping you."

Turning back, he said, "Why would he do that?"

"I don't think he's doing it out of malice. I just think he's lonely and wants attention. You're probably the first person who's paid attention to him in years."

He nodded, realizing she was probably right. "Yeah, I suppose so. But it looked impressive."

"Like I said, it just means he's a good illusionist."

They finished lunch and paid the bill. Leaving the restaurant, they walked along the boardwalk hand in hand, their shoes clomping against the heavy wooden timbers underneath. A stiff onshore breeze was blowing, carrying with it the heavy smell of salt. Gulls screeched overhead, gliding on the blustery currents. Occasionally the pair stopped to peer into a shop window, commenting on the merchandise inside. Other times, they stopped and leaned against the galvanized iron railing, looking out to sea, their faces turned directly into the cold wind so that they had to squint. Waves were breaking far out toward the horizon, their crests white against the gray sea blown back like horses' crests. A miniature lifeguard boat—or what looked like one—bobbed up and down, challenging the surf.

As they strolled along, Taylor's mind kept drifting back to the events of last night. He couldn't stop thinking about it, couldn't stop obsessing over it. Still, truth be told, he was hard pressed to disagree with Kate. He knew she was probably right, that the spoon bending demonstration was likely just a well-executed illusion. What else could it be? But he nonetheless kept entertaining the tiniest sliver of a possibility that what he had witnessed was exactly what Havelock had said it was: the power of the mind over matter.

A part of him wanted that to be true. A part of him wanted to believe that the world was a much stranger and more complicated place than people typically assumed. He supposed this wish, this desire to believe in the strange and wonderful, stemmed from a deep-seated desire to experience what Einstein had called, "the mysterious"—the most beautiful thing one can experience.

The wind steadily increased until a series of chilly gusts were blowing off the ocean, cutting and severe. Kate snuggled up next to Taylor as they walked, and he slipped his arm around her waist.

"What do you think about painting the solarium yellow?" Kate asked suddenly. The breeze caught her hair as she spoke and whipped it around her face. She brought up a hand to corral it, but only succeeded in placing a few errant strands behind her ear.

"Huh?"

"The breakfast nook," she said. "I was thinking we could paint it yellow."

"That would be okay," he said absentmindedly.

She stopped and looked up at him. "You're not listening to a word I'm saying, are you?"

"Yes, I am. You said you wanted to paint the breakfast nook yellow."

"Well, what do you think?"

He paused, considering her question for the first time. "Maybe off-white would be better."

"You don't like yellow?"

"Too bright."

"A breakfast nook is supposed to be bright. Bright and cheery."

They continued along the boardwalk, arguing about colors as the wind gusted stronger.

Chapter 6

TAYLOR SPENT THE FIRST few days of the following week finishing his new novel. By Wednesday, he had a draft to his liking, and he sent it to his agent in San Francisco. But there wasn't time to rest. The second of the two new novels his publisher had commissioned was due by the end of the year. So, Taylor broke out the outline for the second novel and began writing. This task obsessed him for the remainder of the week, and he ended up doing very little work on the house.

That Friday night, however, Taylor received a phone call. He didn't recognize the incoming number and was about to ignore it—let the caller leave a message—when some insistent inner voice made him answer it.

"Hello?"

"Mr. Hamilton?"

"Yes, speaking. Who's this?"

"Mr. Hamilton, my name is Debra Rowland. I'm Havelock Rowland's daughter."

"Oh, nice to meet you." He paused, surprised. "What can I do for you?"

"I'm sorry to call you at this late hour, but I'm a little concerned about my father. I've been trying to reach him on the phone all day but haven't got a hold of him. It's probably nothing, and maybe I'm being a little paranoid, but I was wondering—"

"I could check on him right now, if you'd like," Taylor suggested.

Her tone brightened. "Could you? I mean, if it's not too much trouble."

"Of course not. I'll go over there now and call you right back."

"Thank you."

Taylor hung up the phone. He grabbed his coat and a flashlight and went to the front door. Just as his hand touched the knob, he heard Kate's voice behind him.

"You going out?"

He turned around. She was standing in the foyer, dressed in a bathrobe.

"Yeah, but I'll be back," he said. "Just going over to Havelock's."

"Who was that on the phone?"

Taylor explained it was Havelock's daughter and that she'd been trying to reach her father all day.

"I didn't know he had a daughter," Kate said.

"I didn't either."

"How'd she get our number?"

Taylor put on his coat and shrugged. "Not sure. Maybe Havelock gave it to her."

"You think he's all right?" Kate asked, worry in her voice.

"I'm sure he is. Probably just got preoccupied and forgot to return her call. Either that, or he had too much *raksi.*"

She furrowed her brow. "What's that?"

He chuckled. "I'll explain later. See you in a bit."

Taylor stepped out and closed the door. A heavy fog swirled wraith-like about him, and the penetrating dampness in the air sent a chill up his spine. He shivered and zipped up his coat. Switching on the flashlight, he descended the steps and started off down the road toward Havelock's house. The fog was so thick the beam only penetrated a few feet in front of him.

It suddenly occurred to him he hadn't seen Havelock all day, either. Nor the previous day. He usually ran into him while the old man was walking Dorje. He hoped nothing had happened to the old man, but he soon realized he was being overly dramatic. The last time he'd seen Havelock, which was a few days ago, the old man had seemed fine. And there were any number of reasons why the man's dog walking schedule might vary. There was no point in jumping to conclusions.

The fog grew thicker as he trudged up the road to Havelock's house. The sound of his shoes crunching against the asphalt seemed magnified by the stillness of the night. This, along with the cloying mist and the eerie atmosphere, seemed to play on every irrational fear that lurked in his subconscious. He admonished himself for being silly but found himself, from time to time, glancing around quickly and almost involuntarily, as if expecting some demon, or some homicidal maniac, to spring from the dark.

The sudden howl of an animal tore through the air, the sound echoing from somewhere distant. Taylor stopped, startled. The sound seemed unnaturally loud in the stillness of the dark and fog. It rose to a resounding pitch, piercing the air, and then died off. Silence followed in its wake. Despite not knowing from which direction it had come, Taylor nonetheless instinctively glanced over his shoulder. His gaze met only swirling gray mist.

He was no expert on animal sounds, but it had sounded vaguely like a cougar, or maybe even a wolf. He wasn't sure. But, in truth, a wolf made no sense at all, since the animal had been nearly extirpated from the State long ago. A cougar was more likely, but even that was dubious; it hadn't sounded exactly like a cougar. Whatever it was, it had sent a shiver up his spine.

He turned back around and closed his eyes for a moment, gathering his wits. The sound had rattled him. He opened his eyes and drew in a deep breath. He blew it out with a shudder and hurried on.

Gradually, Havelock's house appeared through the mist, its outlines taking shape as Taylor neared. It was huge and rambling, two stories high with round turrets and vaulting chimneys. Behind it, the towering redwoods looked like misshapen giants with gnarled arms outstretched as if beckoning him to approach. Walking up the path that led to the front door, he suddenly realized it wouldn't be a good idea to surprise Dorje. Although he had come to know the dog, at least after a fashion, he still didn't quite trust it. And it was obvious the dog was fiercely dedicated to guarding the house.

He stopped in front of the portico and called out, "Dorje! Dorje!"

When there was no answering bark he hopped up onto the porch and knocked on the door. Everything was quiet, and he knocked again, this time louder.

"Havelock!" he called out. "Havelock! Are you in!"

Silence.

He rattled the knob but found that the door was locked. He sidled over to the window, rubbed off condensation, and peered inside, shining the flashlight. The front room was dark but there appeared to be a light coming from the hallway. He swept his flashlight slowly from one side of the room to the other. The beam illuminated first a chair, and then a table, before moving on across a bookshelf to the fireplace at the far end of the room. Everything looked in order; there wasn't any evidence of anything wrong or out of the ordinary, as far as Taylor could tell. The light coming from the hallway, however, intrigued him. No matter how he angled himself at the window, he couldn't see its source.

He wondered whether the house had a back door. Shining his flashlight on the ground in front of him, he walked along the porch as it curved around to the back of the house. The floorboards creaked and groaned under his weight, and he slowed his pace, his footsteps growing tentative and deliberate in the semi-darkness. The wood underneath his feet was rotted and rickety, and occasionally the beam of his flashlight glinted off the metal of a rusty nail that had worked itself loose from the wood. He continued to walk with caution, envisioning himself stepping on a weak spot, crashing through the porch, and stumbling headlong. Although Havelock had paid a great deal of attention to the inside of the house, furnishing it with lavish Tibetan art, artifacts, and tapestries, he had been completely negligent with the outside. Spongy moss clustered on the railing and bushes and weeds sprouted up between the floorboard slats. The woodwork showed signs of neglect and stains and cracks ran roughshod over the walls.

Edging cautiously around the side of the house, Taylor discovered the back door. To his surprise, it was ajar. Stepping back, he illuminated it with his flashlight and saw that the lock was twisted and broken. Anxiety tickled the base of his spine as he stared at the warped metal. He hesitated for a moment and then pushed the door open, allowing it to swing into darkness on creaking hinges. Shining his flashlight, he peered inside. It was the kitchen.

He cleared his throat and called out, "Havelock! Are you there?"

Still there was no answer.

He lingered in the doorway, continuing to shine his flashlight over the room. There was a stove and breakfast table with four chairs. One of the chairs lay on its side, as if it had been knocked over. Against the far wall was a refrigerator. He took a tentative step inside and paused to listen. The house was quiet. The only sound he heard was the monotonous whir of the refrigerator.

He continued to stare around the room, his flashlight illuminating the darkness. He angled the flashlight beam along the walls and ceiling. Except for the chair, nothing was amiss. In fact, like the front room, everything appeared to be in order, though there were some dirty dishes piled in the sink and a carton of orange juice left on the table.

"Havelock!" he called again but received no answer. He looked around the room one last time, searching for clues that might explain the broken door and Havelock's seeming absence. He stepped over to the chair and righted it, placing it up against the table.

He left the kitchen and stepped into an adjoining hallway. Off to his right, light spilled from a room at the end of the hallway. The door to the room was ajar, affording only a narrow glimpse into the room, but not enough to discern any detail. He stood for a moment, staring at the light. Unease swept over him, and he felt the hairs prickle on the back of his neck. He shifted nervously from one foot to the other and gripped his flashlight tighter. But a minute later, he brushed aside the feeling and, taking a deep breath, proceeded down the hallway, his footsteps echoing loudly in the cramped confines.

He pushed the door open the rest of the way and entered. He quickly discovered it was some kind of study. Floor-to-ceiling bookcases lined most of the walls and there was a large oak desk positioned at the far end of the room. The light was coming from a lamp on the table.

The room at first glance seemed empty—but very soon, as Taylor's vision grew accustomed to the dim light, the figure in the chair caught his attention right away. It was Havelock. He was slumped sideways in the desk chair, one arm dangling to the floor.

Every muscle in Taylor's body tensed as he stared at the old man. With his chin resting on his chest, and his eyes half-closed, Havelock looked like he might be dead.

Taylor took a step forward, inclining his head. "Havelock?"

The old man wasn't moving, and, suddenly galvanized, Taylor rushed over. He grabbed Havelock's arm, feeling for a pulse. There was one, though it was weak. Leaning in close, he felt Havelock's breath against his face and could hear the man breathing through his nostrils. It was slow and ragged but audible.

Then Taylor stepped back, fumbled for his cell phone, and dialed 9-1-1.

Chapter 7

"IT WAS A STROKE," Debra Rowland said.

She took a deep breath and slumped down in the waiting room chair. She looked to be in her fifties with dark brown hair streaked with gray. Like her father, her eyes were lively and vibrant. In fact, her eyes were remarkably similar to Havelock's in many respects, especially the color of the irises. Right now, however, deep bags hung under her eyes and her hands kept twisting and untwisting a handkerchief.

"How's he now?" Taylor asked. He was seated across from her, holding a Styrofoam cup with weak, tepid coffee.

It was early morning and they were in the Oceanport Hospital emergency waiting room, an immaculately clean area with plush chairs and bright lights. Music drifted from wall speakers, a soothing melody of pan flutes that Taylor vaguely recognized as a popular New Age tune. It had been playing for the last several hours and, although he knew it was meant to be calming, it was beginning to get on his nerves. Taylor and Debra had been there all night.

"He's in stable condition, but the doctor said the stroke was pretty severe. He told me it was centered deep in his brain."

Taylor winced; it sounded as if Havelock was lucky to be alive. "I'm really sorry," he said, shaking his head.

"He's on a respirator now." She paused, managing to smile weakly. "I really want to thank you for all your help. You were especially kind to come to the hospital with him."

"No problem," Taylor said. "I'm just glad I was able to find him when I did. We've gotten to be friends over the last month."

"I'm so glad," Debra said. "To be honest, he doesn't have a lot of friends. Since he moved up here, he's become a bit of a recluse." She shook her head with obvious frustration. "Half the time, I have no

42

clue what he does up here all by himself." She eyed Taylor with a look of remorse. "I'll admit, I haven't been the most attentive daughter. I probably should have visited him more often. I haven't actually seen him in over a year."

"We all get busy," Taylor said in a consoling tone. He took a sip of coffee and glanced up at the clock positioned on the wall above the check-in counter. It was a little after five o'clock. He yawned, rubbing his eyes. The long night was beginning to take its toll.

Debra resettled herself, daubed at her eyes with the handkerchief, and made an effort to sit up straighter. She paused, staring off into space, but then turned to Taylor. "May I be completely honest with you, Mr. Hamilton?"

He nodded. "But please call me Taylor."

"We haven't always been on the best of terms, my father and I. He's a difficult man." She sighed, as if revealing a confession. "I always thought it had something to do with the fact that I was a girl. I think he secretly always wanted a son. But whatever it was we were never close."

Taylor didn't know what to say so he kept silent.

"Ever since Mom died, he's become even more difficult," she went on, twisting her handkerchief tighter. "I've tried my best with him, but it never did any good. I even proposed moving him to a retirement home closer to where I live." She made a face. "You can imagine how well that went down." She stopped suddenly. "I'm sorry to burden you with all this. I'm sure you don't want to hear about our secret family history."

"No, it's all right," Taylor said.

"Anyway," she said, "you don't have to stay here any longer, Taylor. You've been a huge help, but I'm sure you need to get back home."

He rubbed a bleary eye and nodded. "Yeah, I wouldn't mind getting back." He set his coffee cup down and stood up.

She stood up along with him and reached for his hands, clasping them in hers. "Thanks again."

He smiled and then turned to leave. But a thought suddenly struck him, and he turned back around.

"Actually," he said, "there was something I was kind of worried about. When I got to his house, I couldn't find Dorje anywhere. I'm afraid he might have escaped out the back door."

She looked at him, a puzzled expression on her face. "Dorje?"

"Yeah, his dog."

She continued to stare at him a moment longer, her brow furrowed. Then she shook her head. "He doesn't have a dog."

"She didn't know he had a dog?"

"Apparently not," Taylor said, setting his toolbox on the ground next to several two-by-four slats. He shook his head, still amazed at the idea.

"That's weird," Kate said, scratching her chin. "But didn't you just say she doesn't visit him very often? Maybe she honestly didn't know."

"I guess," he shrugged. He opened the toolbox and began to fumble around for nails and a hammer.

"What are you going to do with that?" Kate asked, pointing at the toolbox.

"Fix the back door of his house. I don't want it left broken. He's got a lot of valuable things in there."

"His Tibetan stuff?"

He nodded.

She looked at him with a wry smile. "When did you become the conscientious neighbor?"

He grinned back at her, slammed the toolbox shut, and gathered up the slats. He jumped to his feet. "See you in a bit."

Taylor left the house, carrying his materials. He wasn't an expert do-it-yourselfer by any stretch, but he did know a thing or two. At the very least, he could hammer the two-by-fours over the door so no one could get inside.

As he walked, he wondered what had happened to Dorje. It seemed odd that the dog had run away. As devoted as he was to Havelock, it was surprising the animal didn't stay at the old man's side throughout the ordeal.

When he got to the house, he examined the back door. The lock was completely busted, and there was a ragged gash in the adjoining wall, as if some tremendous blow had sent the deadbolt crunching through the wood. Indeed, it was almost as if someone had taken a sledgehammer to the door, aiming a solid blow at the lock. But, from what Taylor could tell, the blow had apparently come from the inside. The ragged furrow made by the deadbolt on the adjoining door frame ran from the inside to the outside rather than the other way around. Was someone trying to get out? Why hadn't they just flipped the deadbolt switch and opened the door? Taylor scratched his head. It didn't make any sense.

He checked the door, noting that it didn't sit properly in its frame. It was warped. In fact, he discovered that the door jambs were loose, the wood around them cracked and splintered. A screw from the top door jamb fell and clattered on the floor as he continued to fiddle with the door.

Taylor stepped back, rubbing his chin, pondering the situation. Slowly, as he put all the disparate shreds of evidence together, he came to the following conclusion: A tremendous blow (from what he didn't know) had struck the deadbolt from the inside of the house. The deadbolt, in turn, had torn through the adjoining wall, smashing the door open.

Repairing the damage was beyond his skill set; it required a carpenter. So instead, he opted to use the wooden two-by-fours. As he nailed them in place, he tried to figure out why the door had been broken. Had someone been in the house with Havelock? Had there been some confrontation that had caused Havelock's stroke? And had the person, or persons, escaped out the kitchen? But why had the door been smashed when it could have simply been opened after unlocking the deadbolt? And what on earth had happened to Dorje? He had a myriad of questions, none of which could he supply satisfactory answers.

When the ambulance had arrived to take Havelock to the hospital, sheriff officers had also arrived and investigated the house but, despite the broken back door, had not found any evidence of foul play. Nothing seemed to be missing and there were no signs of any struggle or violent confrontation. They had concluded there were no grounds for further investigation and, as far as Taylor knew, had effectively shelved the case.

The slats in place, Taylor stepped back to survey his work. It wasn't pretty, but he figured it was the best he could do. Gathering his toolbox, he turned and headed for home, glancing back at the door one last time. He may not have any answers, he told himself, but he did have one overriding feeling: The whole thing felt eerily bizarre.

Chapter 8

A FEW MORNINGS LATER, Taylor called Debra Rowland to check up on Havelock. He'd been curious how the old man was coping, if things had gotten any worse, and how he might help.

"I brought him home from the hospital last night," she said.

"So, he's back home now?"

"That's right."

"How's he doing?"

She sighed. "Not too well, I'm afraid. The stroke paralyzed the left side of his body and he has trouble speaking. He's in a wheelchair."

"I'm really sorry."

"I'm going to stay with him."

"Today?"

"No," she said, "I mean, I'm going to move in with him. Be his caretaker."

"Oh, I see."

"I'm moving my stuff in today."

Taylor paused. "Is there anything I can do to help?"

"At the moment, no, but thanks."

"I'd love to see him. Maybe I could swing by?"

"Why don't you come over this afternoon? By then, he'll be settled in a little better."

"Okay, I will. See you then."

Taylor hung up the phone. He walked into the kitchen, where Kate was sitting at the breakfast table drinking a cup of coffee. "Was that Havelock's daughter?" she asked.

He nodded, pouring himself a cup from the pot.

"How's the old guy doing?"

He carried the steaming mug of coffee over to the table and sat down across from her. "Not too well, apparently." He told Kate about the man's paralysis and that Debra had decided to move in with him.

"To be his nurse?"

He blew on the rising tendrils of steam and took a careful sip, nodding.

After a pause, Kate asked, "Is she married?"

"I don't think so. At least she never mentioned a spouse."

They sat in silence for a time, listening to the chatter of birdsong outside the window. The sky was blue and the branches of the big redwood tree outside rustled in a gentle breeze. Eventually, Kate got up, cinched her bathrobe tighter, and went over to the sink where she deposited her soiled coffee cup. Turning back, she said, "Tough job."

He looked up. "What is?"

"Looking after an ailing family member. I don't think I could do it."

Taylor nodded. "It definitely takes a special kind of person."

She gave a mock frown. "Are you saying I'm not special?"

He chuckled. "I'm not either. I don't think I could do it. I'm too selfish."

"Any plans for today?" Kate asked. She went over to the refrigerator and opened the door, examining what was inside. She rummaged around for a few seconds and then took out half a cantaloupe.

"Thought I'd go for a surf, then check on Havelock on the way back."

She gave an annoyed frown and closed the refrigerator door. She carried the cantaloupe over to the counter and placed it on a cutting board. "I was hoping you could keep working on that berry patch today. I noticed you haven't finished it yet."

"Don't worry," he said, "I'll get to it."

———

Later that afternoon, after surfing for two solid hours, Taylor drove to Havelock's house. The weather had deteriorated, and a misty drizzle was falling as he pulled his Jeep up to the front of the house. Debra met him at the door.

"Come in," she said, "he's in the living room."

Taylor followed her into the house. Havelock was sitting in a wheelchair by the fireplace. His shoulders were hunched forward, his eyes glassy and staring straight ahead. He was dressed in pajamas and a bathrobe, with a warm blanket draped over his legs, the sides neatly tucked under his thighs. His complexion was pallid; his face was drawn and haggard. His skin was stretched tight against his face, outlining prominent cheekbones and sunken eyes. His beret had been placed on his head and set at a jaunty angle.

"I just gave him his medicine an hour ago," Debra said. "I also gave him some Prozac so he's kind of out of it at the moment."

Taylor came over and knelt in front of the old man. He reached out and placed his hand on Havelock's wrist and gave a gentle squeeze. "How you doing, Havelock?"

Havelock's face was expressionless, his eyes staring straight ahead without a hint of recognition. His breathing was low and raspy and there was a tiny fleck of spittle on his chin. He looked completely out of it, like a man adrift. But it was the vacant look in the old man's eyes that Taylor found the most disconcerting. It was as if he had lost all vitality, all will to live. Taylor gave a discouraged frown. Although he hadn't known the old man long, Havelock's intellect was the thing Taylor had most admired about the man—his clarity of thought, his piercing intellect. Now it was as if all that had been erased, washed away. He wondered whether Havelock would ever recover his faculties.

Taylor squeezed the man's hand again, this time a little harder, hoping for a response. But Havelock only stirred slightly and blinked his eyes. Taylor continued to crouch in front of Havelock for a moment longer, then, when it was obvious the old man wasn't going to respond, he gave a disappointed sigh and stood up, thrusting his hands into his pockets. He turned to Debra. "I don't think he recognizes me."

"I think it's just the medicine. It tends to zone him out."

"The Prozac, you mean?"

She nodded. "Too bad you weren't here earlier, he was trying to talk to me but I couldn't understand what he was saying. The stroke really affected his speech."

"Will he ever get it back?"

She shrugged. "The doctors tell me it's too early to say."

"How about you?" Taylor asked, fixing his eyes on the deep lines of her face. "How are you holding up? This whole thing's gotta be a huge strain on you."

She shrugged again and turned to gaze out the window. She seemed deep in thought for a moment. The sky was a metallic gray and the drizzle had turned into a hard, steady rain. When she turned back there was an expression of resignation on her face. "It is what it is, I suppose. I only wish I'd reached out to him more than I have."

"You're here now, that's what's important, right?"

She nodded. "But it's been tough. Really tough."

"I can only imagine."

"What I mean is, he's been really difficult to deal with the last few days in the hospital," she said.

"How so?"

"He's had several angry outbursts. The doctors told me that irritability and irrational anger can be common side effects of stroke." She stopped and shook her head. "But this—"

Taylor looked at her, his brow furrowed.

She paused, searching for the right words. "These outbursts aren't normal. Look, I'll be the first to admit Dad is high strung and quick to anger; he always has been. But these weren't just little fits of anger. They were different. They were outbursts of raw, visceral rage and violence. I've never seen anything like it. It's as if—"

"As if what?" Taylor asked.

"I don't know. Like there's something deep inside him that was never resolved. Something from his past, maybe?" She sighed and shrugged her shoulders. "I'm probably talking nonsense. Maybe it's just exactly what the doctors said. They told me that irrational anger has to do with brain damage caused by the trauma of the stroke. That's why he's taking the Prozac."

Taylor remained silent.

"Anyway," she continued, "his doctor said the road from here on out may be pretty rocky, and that I should expect more irrational outbursts. Like I told you before, we've never been particularly close, Dad and me. But I've always respected him." She gestured at him. "And to see him like this just breaks my heart. I've always respected his intelligence and what he's accomplished in life." She paused. "Did he ever tell you what he did in Tibet?"

"A little bit," Taylor said. "Just that he was there several times. On scientific expeditions."

"He was, but he was also involved in helping Tibetan refugees. When the Chinese invaded in the fifties, he was responsible for getting a number Tibetans out of the country. He saved the lives of a lot of people. He was even responsible for evacuating an entire village and bringing them to safety."

"He never mentioned that," Taylor said. "That's amazing." He turned and glanced at Havelock. The old man just stared back, glassy eyed.

"How did he save them?" Taylor asked, turning back to Debra.

"He crossed over into Tibet during the invasion and helped with the evacuation. His life was in danger, but he was determined to save as many people as he could."

"What year was this?"

"I think it was in 1954 or 1955. Something like that. Dad had been to Tibet several times by then so he knew the country, spoke the language, and had a number of Tibetan friends. He used to tell me stories about helping families cross the border into Nepal and India."

Taylor just shook his head, amazed.

Debra went over to Havelock and bent down, arranging the blanket over his knees, carefully tucking the sides under his legs. When she straightened, she asked Taylor, "Would you like a cup of tea or coffee, or something?"

"No thanks," he said. "I should probably get back. Don't hesitate to call me if you need any help." He headed for the front door.

"Oh, by the way," Debra said, "are you sure my dad had a dog?"

Taylor turned back around. "Positive. Why?"

Debra scratched her chin. "It's just that I haven't been able to find any dog things."

"Dog things?"

"I mean like food bowls or bags of kibble. I haven't found anything like that. Not even a bone."

"Really?" He gave a perplexed look. "That's strange."

"How old is it?"

"The dog?" He shrugged. "It's an adult. Maybe three or four, I guess. I'm not real sure."

"Three or four? That can't be right."

"Why not?"

"The last time I visited my dad was a year ago. He certainly didn't have a dog then." She paused. "I guess he could've adopted it."

"He told me he raised it from a puppy."

She thought for a moment. "What did you say the dog's name was again?"

"Dorje," Taylor replied.

50

Havelock let out a muffled cry. Startled, they both turned. The old man's eyes were suddenly filled with emotion.

Debra put her hand on her father's shoulder. "What is it, Dad?" she asked.

But he was unable to say anything; his mouth only quivered mutely, his eyes alive with some emotion the two could only guess at.

It was pouring rain by the time Taylor left the house. He raised the hood of his sweatshirt over his head and dashed to his car. He pulled out of the driveway and turned onto the road leading to his house, his windshield wipers thumping back and forth. He took the road slowly, his mind trying to square what Debra had told him—about the house having no dog gear—and his own observations of the dog. Maybe she had simply been mistaken; maybe she hadn't looked in the right places. Perhaps Havelock kept all the dog food and bowls in the back of some closet.

He was nearly to his house when movement at the side of the road caught his eye. He turned to look and was stunned to see Dorje. The huge dog—as big as life—was standing by the road, rain pelting its thick coat.

Taylor hit the brakes, the tires screeching against the wet pavement. The vehicle lurched to one side before coming to a shuddering stop. He sat for a moment, both his hands on the wheel, staring in stunned amazement at the dog through the windshield. Just moments before he'd been thinking about the animal and now there it was. It was uncanny. Snapping out of his daze, he opened the door and stepped out.

"Dorje!" Taylor called out.

But the dog made no move to come forward.

"Dorje, come here!"

The dog continued to stand in the rain, motionless. Its eyes, two ebon jewels without irises, just stared at him, unblinking. When the dog still hadn't moved, Taylor stepped toward it.

This time, the animal bared its teeth and let out a deep menacing growl that rumbled forth from its chest. The sound stopped Taylor in his tracks. He stood frozen, uncertain about what to do, stunned at the animal's response.

"Dorje!" he called out, "it's me. Don't you recognize me?"

The growl morphed into a snarl and then a vicious bark. Taylor took a step backward, keeping his eyes on the dog. It occurred to him

51

this was not the same big, lazy, indifferent dog he had encountered in the past. This animal was different—angry, aggressive, and capable of anything. He continued to back away but bumped into the open car door. Still keeping his eyes trained on Dorje, he sidled around the door so that it was between him and Dorje, like a shield. Then he backed into the front seat and reached for the door, slamming it shut. The dog continued to bark, its mouth beginning to foam.

Fumbling for his keys, he started the car and drove off, the animal receding in the rain and mist, its bark echoing despite the downpour.

What had happened to Dorje? Had it become rabid? And what the hell should he do about it? There was certainly no way the dog was going to follow him placidly back to the house. He felt he had a responsibility to tell Havelock and Debra that he had found Dorje. But what was he going to tell them? "Hey, I found your dog, but you can't get near him because he might be rabid." Maybe the old man was better off not knowing. He wasn't sure what he should do.

When he got back to the house, he discussed the situation with Kate. She believed the best thing to do, since the animal seemed potentially dangerous, would be to contact animal control.

"What if he attacks someone?" she asked. "If the dog really is rabid, it needs to be caught. Sounds like you were lucky to get out of there in one piece."

Taylor found the number for the Humboldt County Animal Control and placed the call. An hour later, an animal control officer arrived to search for the dog. But he wasn't able to find any trace of Dorje despite Taylor's trying to help. It was as if the dog had simply vanished into thin air.

Chapter 9

KATE DECIDED TO STAY in the city over the next week, rather than come up to Humboldt. She had a particularly difficult case that demanded her full attention, so she opted to work from her office and the apartment. Taylor was plugging away on his new novel, seemingly oblivious to everything except his computer screen and the words he was generating on it.

However, on Wednesday morning, he received a phone call from Kate.

"Have you heard?" she asked. There was a certain breathlessness in her voice that Taylor found surprising.

"Heard what?"

"Remember Mr. Hsing?"

"Who?"

"The guy who sold us the bathroom mirror. Remember?"

Taylor had to think for a moment. "Oh yeah. What about him?"

"Apparently, he was murdered last night."

Taylor was stunned. "What?"

"They found his body in his shop this morning."

"Where'd you hear this?" Taylor asked.

"*The Humboldt Courier* website. I was reading it online this morning before work."

"Do they know who did it?"

"I don't think so. Go to the *Courier* website. The story's there."

Taylor hung up the phone and immediately clicked over to the website. He found the story right away.

Prominent Oceanport Businessman Found Dead

The sheriff's department in Oceanport is investigating the death of 47-year-old businessman Edwin Hsing, the owner of the long-standing Hsing's Second Hand in downtown Oceanport.

His body was discovered by members of the community early Wednesday morning after his wife reported him missing Tuesday night. According to sheriff spokesman Russell Stodges, the body was badly mutilated, which made initial identification difficult.

The store did not appear to have been burgled, despite the back window being broken and store items scattered about.

"It appears Mr. Hsing was mauled by an animal," Mr. Stodges said, "but there are still a lot of questions about the type of animal. We're also not ruling out the possibility of a hate crime, among other possibilities."

No arrests have been made.

Mr. Hsing was a prominent businessman and well-known figure in the local community. A long-time resident, he was an avid supporter of local youth sports.

He is survived by his wife and adult daughter...

Taylor stopped reading. "Jesus," he muttered. He moved his jaw slowly from side to side as he pondered what he'd just read. It was absolutely gruesome—a horrible nightmare come to life. He turned away from the computer monitor and gazed out the window, frowning. The rain that had started earlier that morning was coming down harder now, a steady staccato that drummed against the roof.

If the death of that poor man wasn't terrible enough, there was an additional factor that weighed heavily on Taylor's mind. The other reason he moved up here, to this faraway corner of the state, was to get away from what he called the "rat race," the frantic, stressful, nine-to-five, workaday world, filled with deadlines, hassles, and ill-will. Taylor had spent over ten years living in the city, and the last few years had sorely tested him. The crime, the drugs, the dirt and grime, the traffic, the crush of humanity, and the pollution, all of these had gotten worse. It had gotten so bad, in fact, that the last few years of living there had caused him almost constant stress. He thought he could escape all that by coming up here.

But now that illusion was shattered. Nowhere, apparently, was safe. It didn't matter if you lived in a city or the boondocks. Crime and murder were everywhere; you couldn't escape it.

He turned back and stared glumly at his computer screen. He

reached for the mug of coffee next to him, but finding that it was cold, withdrew his hand. Then, all at once, he stood up. He didn't feel like writing anymore today. He glanced at his watch. It was a few minutes past eleven o'clock. He suddenly felt the need for fresh air.

He grabbed a baseball cap and his raincoat and left the house, locking the door behind him.

———————

It was still raining by the time Taylor pulled his Jeep into a parking space in front of The Bayside Brewery. Rolling to a stop, he shut off the wipers and killed the engine. The Bayside was a small brew pub with a cozy atmosphere of plush leather booths, the pungent odor of hops, and an array of specialty-made ales, stouts, and porters. He and Kate had discovered it several months ago on one of their weekend jaunts to Oceanport.

Exiting the car, he jogged across the parking lot, big, splattering drops striking his back and shoulders. He hopped over several puddles and darted inside out of the rain. The pub was dark but warm. He took off his raincoat and slid onto a stool at the bar.

Taylor glanced around. The pub was only mildly busy. A few patrons were sprinkled about, most of them occupying the booths. The sounds and images of a baseball game, the San Francisco Giants versus the San Diego Padres, came from a wide-screen TV set over the bar.

"What'll it be?" the bartender asked, tearing his eyes away from the game. He was a young man with curly black hair and wearing a Metallica T-shirt. He was drying a pitcher with a towel.

Taylor took a moment to eye the beer menu before looking up. "I'll have the double bock."

"Coming up," the bartender said. He held the pitcher up to the light and scrutinized it before setting it aside.

As the bartender pulled a beer from the tap, Taylor glanced idly over his shoulder, studying the few patrons. At a booth near the window was a young couple, leaning toward each other over their drinks. Nearby were an older man and his wife, sharing some fish and chips. And at the far end of the counter were two patrons, both obvious locals, dressed in checkered flannels and ball caps. Their elbows propped on the table and their beers in front of them, they were discussing something, oblivious to everything else, their voices occasionally rising above the baseball game.

When the bartender came over with his beer, Taylor asked, "Did you hear about Mr. Hsing?"

The bartender frowned and placed the beer in front of Taylor. "Yeah, who hasn't?"

"Did you know him?"

The bartender nodded. "Yeah, I knew him. He coached my little league team when I was a kid. Great guy. Real community minded."

"What do you think happened?" Taylor paused to take a sip of beer.

"I have no idea," the man said, shaking his head. "The whole thing is beyond bizarre. I can't tell if he was killed by an animal or murdered. It's pretty unclear." Then his eyes narrowed. "I just hope they catch whoever or whatever was responsible."

"You think it was a person, maybe?"

He shrugged. "It looks like an animal did it, but who knows?"

Taylor took another sip and sighed with satisfaction, allowing the taste of malt to linger on his tongue. Hunching forward on the bar, he glanced up at the game and watched as a Padres player cracked a single off the Giants pitcher.

The bartender pointed at one of the locals at the end of the bar—a man wearing a Giants baseball cap. "See that guy?"

Taylor followed the man's gaze.

"That's Fred Hipsley. He was one of the guys who found the body this morning."

"No kidding?" Taylor sat up and studied the man for a moment. Slender and short, he had a lean face with deep-set eyes and weathered features. He was still in an animated discussion with his companion. Taylor turned back, started watching the ball game and nursing his beer.

By the time Taylor ordered his second beer, Fred Hipsley got up, hitched up his pants, and headed for the door.

"Heading out, Fred?" the bartender asked.

The man nodded.

"Well, go get some rest, for Chrissake. You deserve it after today."

"I'll be all right," the man said. "Been one helluva day."

The bartender gestured toward Taylor. "I was telling this guy here, I hope the cops figure the whole thing out."

Fred snorted. "So do I, because I've never seen anything like it."

Taylor, who had been listening to this exchange, couldn't help but intervene. He swiveled around on his stool. "I hope you don't mind my asking, but what have you never seen?"

The man stopped, looking Taylor up and down, his eyes narrowed. Then he answered, "I was telling Mike"—he indicated the bartender—"the mutilation was unlike anything I'd ever seen."

Taylor furrowed his brow. "What do you think did it? A pit bull?"

Fred paused, shrugging. "I don't know, maybe. Or some other animal."

"I'm still not entirely sold on the animal theory," the bartender chimed in. "I mean, it still sounds pretty far-fetched. You're telling me an animal broke into the store just to kill poor Ed? That doesn't seem to make a lot of sense. Don't you think—"

"It does sound far-fetched," Fred agreed, "but I don't know how else to explain it." He turned back to Taylor. "I worked for Fish and Game for twenty years, and I once had to clean up the remains of a female jogger after she was killed by a cougar up near Signal Mountain. I hate to say it, but this reminded me of that, except worse."

Taylor furrowed his brow. "So, you think it was a cougar?" he asked.

He nodded. "A cougar, or something like it."

"Something like it?" Taylor shot the man a perplexed look. "What else could it have been?"

The man shrugged and shook his head. "A cougar on steroids."

Chapter 10

"FROM NPR IN WASHINGTON, I'm Lynette Goddard..."

Taylor reached across the desk and turned up the volume on the radio. His writing momentarily forgotten, he sat back and listened to a recap of the day's news. It was late, almost midnight, and he was sitting in front of his computer, the glow from the screen illuminating his face.

He'd been working on his novel for the last few hours, doing edits mostly and idly listening to the radio. As the news transitioned into a lengthy story on Americans building orphanages in war-torn Afghanistan, he decided to shelve his writing for good. He hadn't been particularly productive, anyway. The events of the day had depressed him, and his editing tasks had been half-assed at best.

He listened until the next program came on. Not particularly interested in the subject matter, he leaned over and switched off the radio. The rain had stopped a while back and now, with the radio off, the house was particularly quiet. The only sound he heard was the monotonous *drip drip drip* of water off the eaves outside.

He licked his lips. Although it was late, he wanted a cup of coffee. He knew he probably shouldn't have a cup before going to bed, but he didn't care. He couldn't get a savory cup out of his mind. He'd bought a bag of prized Guatemalan coffee beans at a specialty shop in town a few days ago and was eager to try it.

Glancing at his watch, he noticed the time: fifteen minutes past midnight. He yawned and rubbed his eyes. He shut down the computer and stood up, rolling sore neck muscles. Leaving the study, he padded down the hallway, his bare feet creaking on the hardwood floor.

He turned into the kitchen and switched on the overhead light. Moving over to a cabinet, he took down the bag of Guatemalan roast and his coffee grinder and set about making himself a cup.

While the coffee was brewing, Taylor walked into the living room and peered out the window. A heavy fog had descended so that a billowing gray mist enveloped everything like a thick blanket. He couldn't see very far, maybe ten feet at the most. The only thing he could make out was the faint outline of a nearby tree. Beyond that was nothing.

He returned to the kitchen and poured himself a cup. He had just settled down at the kitchen table when a long, wailing howl rent the air outside. Startled, he clumsily spilled some coffee on the table. The sound reached a crescendo—full of anger and pain—and then died off, lost to the night. The howl sounded like an animal, and it occurred to him it was the very sound he'd heard the night he found Havelock.

He stood up to get a towel to clean the tabletop. Another howl pierced the air, startling him as much as the first. It sounded closer this time, louder. He felt his heart thump in his chest and peered out the kitchen window. But there was nothing—only darkness. The howl gradually faded into the stillness of the night.

He quickly went over to the kitchen door and made sure it was locked. When he'd done that, coffee forgotten, he went to the front room and made sure the front door was securely locked as well.

———————

"You're going to get a what?" Kate spluttered, nearly gagging on her morning coffee.

"A gun."

"I heard you the first time." She frowned, wiping at her chin. "Why on earth do you want to do that?"

"I think it would be good protection."

"From what?"

"C'mon, Kate," Taylor said. "We live in the boondocks now. It's never a bad idea to protect ourselves."

"We live only fifteen minutes from Oceanport," Kate countered. "That's hardly the wild west."

"I just think it would be good protection."

"From what?" she asked again, annoyed he hadn't given her a straight answer the first time.

He shrugged. "From whatever may be lurking around."

"What do you think is going to be lurking around?"

"I don't know exactly, but I'd like to be prepared for anything."

She paused, looking at him keenly. "Is it because of what that guy told you in the pub? About renegade cougars?"

"I just think we'd be a lot safer if we had a gun in the house."

"Safer?" She looked at him as if he'd lost his mind. "I wouldn't feel safer at all. In fact, the whole idea gives me the creeps."

"That's just your inner 'city girl' talking," he said. "There's nothing wrong with a firearm in the house. It'll be properly locked up."

Kate sighed, took a sip of coffee, burned her tongue, and grimaced. "And anyway," she said, giving him a pointed look, "you don't know the first thing about guns."

"I can learn. I'll take a firearms class."

She paused. "What, are you going to join the NRA next?"

He grinned. "Heck, maybe I should."

She gave an exasperated shake of her head and looked away. "I hope you're joking." She turned back, fixing him with a stern look. "If I knew you were going to turn into some gun-toting backwoods redneck, I would've thought twice about relocating up here."

"C'mon, Kate, don't make a mountain out of a mole hill. I'm not joining the dark side." He smiled at her. "I'm still that carefree, bare-footed surfer you fell in love with."

Kate laughed. "You may have been barefoot, but you were hardly carefree," she said. "You were much too driven and intense. Too focused on your writing career."

"Anyway," Taylor said, "I'm simply talking about protection. For both of us."

She fell silent and took another sip of coffee, visibly doing her best to calm herself. Her eyes averted from him. She tapped her fingernails on the table. Finally, she turned her face toward him. "Okay," she said, "but just so you know, I'm not happy about the idea."

He paused, looking at her expectantly. "Is that a yes?"

She nodded.

"That's my girl," he said, reaching across the table and giving her hand a gentle squeeze.

The sporting goods store was located a few blocks up from the wharf, sandwiched between an Italian deli and a laundromat. Taylor parked his Jeep at the curb and got out, closing the door behind him. He went inside and glanced around. The gun rack was located at the back of the building, an entire wall dedicated to handguns, rifles, and hunting gear. Taylor proceeded down an aisle toward it.

The clerk looked up at his approach. He was an overweight older man with gray hair, a full beard, and thick, bottle-like glasses.

"Can I help you, sir?"

"Yes, I'd like to buy a rifle."

"For hunting?"

"For protection," Taylor said. "I'd like one for the house. I live in kind of a remote area."

"I see. So you want something for coyotes and cougars? Critters like that?"

Taylor nodded. "What do you have?"

The man scratched his chin. "Well," he began, "if you run across a cougar a .22 isn't going to be much help, unless you hit it in the head." Adjusting his glasses, he paused to look over his shoulder at the rack. Taylor followed his gaze, running his eyes along all the rifles that stood upright in their racks.

The man turned back around and adjusted his glasses. "I do have a Remington Model 700. It's a classic bolt action rifle. The one I have is a .30 caliber."

"That would bring down a cougar?"

"Yes, indeed," the man said.

"Could I see it?"

The man selected one of the rifles and took it down from the rack. He gingerly laid it on the counter. Its polished wooden stock gleamed in the overhead lights.

Taylor ran his hand along the barrel. The metal was smooth and cold.

"In my opinion, this is the best all-around hunting rifle on the market," the man said. "I also have some shotguns on sale. In fact, I have a Remington 870 pump action that's a great deal."

"Could I see that as well?"

The clerk hoisted it from the rack and laid it alongside the Model 700. The two rifles couldn't have looked more different. The bolt action was sleek and slender and the shotgun blunt and heavy.

Taylor scrutinized both rifles.

"Which do you suggest?" he asked.

The clerk tapped the shotgun. "I'd pick this one. It's a real workhorse. Solid, dependable, and easy to use."

Taylor scratched his chin, considering.

"Where do you live, if you don't mind my asking?" the clerk asked.

Taylor looked up. "At the end of Madrona Lane."

The man nodded. "Ah, that explains it, then."

Taylor studied him with a puzzled expression. "It does? My wife seems to think I'm being overly paranoid."

"Then I guess you haven't heard."

"Heard what?"

"Guy that owns a goat farm up near you had several of his stock slaughtered a few nights ago. Listen to him tell it, you'd think some giant black dog did it." He chuckled, scratching his cheek. "Some werewolf, or something. But it was probably a cougar."

Taylor raised his eyebrows. "Did you say a black dog?"

The man nodded.

"Did he get a good look at it?"

"Not sure. It was around midnight, so he admitted he couldn't see very well." The man paused. "Funny thing is, the goats apparently weren't eaten. They were just ripped apart. He said it was a real bloody mess."

"This farm is near me? Near Madrona Lane?"

"That's right. Just north of you. In Redwood Valley."

Taylor knew the valley; it was a pleasant, secluded area with several farms and ranches surrounded by pasture and thick forest. It was maybe five miles north of his house.

The man continued. "To be honest, the way things have gone recently, I don't blame you for wanting a gun. You tell your wife I said so. First poor Ed Hsing gets murdered, and now this. Things are getting crazy in this town all of a sudden."

Taylor gazed down at both guns again. He paused only for a moment, before looking back up, and locking eyes with the clerk.

"I'll take the shotgun."

"Good choice."

Later, after concluding the transaction and filling out the requisite paperwork, a task that took a good fifteen minutes, Taylor stepped outside and called Kate on his cell.

"Is the deed done?" she asked.

"The deed is done," he confirmed.

"Does that mean you're bringing it home, then?"

"No," he chuckled, "I'm not bringing 'it' home just yet. I won't get 'it' for ten days because they have to do a background check. Make sure I'm not a homicidal maniac."

"Think you'll pass?"

He laughed. "Doubtful."

"You going surfing now?"

"Thought I might." He hesitated. "That okay?"

"No, fine. See you in a couple of hours."

Taylor was about to switch off his cell phone, when Kate suddenly exclaimed, "Oh, I almost forgot. Your friend called the house earlier this morning."

"My friend?"

"Yeah, the old man's daughter, Debra."

"What did she want?"

"She wanted to know if you could look after Havelock on Tuesday night," Debra said.

"This Tuesday?"

"Yes."

He gave a perplexed look. "She wants me to look after him?"

"Yes, but she said she understands if you can't. She knows it's a pretty big responsibility."

"Did she say why?"

"Why what?"

"Why she wants me to look after him."

"She mentioned something about having to go to Arcata for the evening. And anyway, she knows he likes you. And we live close by."

"But what if something happens? I mean, what if he has a seizure or something?"

He heard Kate sigh through the phone. "Then call her and say you can't. If you feel uncomfortable don't do it. She said she understood if you couldn't."

"No," he said. "I'll do it."

"Jeez, make up your mind."

Taylor switched off the phone and returned to his car.

As he drove north along the coast, he tried to put the events of the last two weeks into some kind of logical perspective. To say it had been a bizarre two weeks was undoubtedly an understatement. First, there had been Havelock's stroke and the disappearance of Dorje, followed by Dorje's reappearance—and transformation. Then he found out, in rapid succession, that the guy who had sold him and Kate the bathroom mirror had been found horribly murdered. This was followed, now, by the revelation of some goats hideously mutilated not too far away from his house. And interspersed with these events were the animal howls he'd heard on two separate nights, the first when he went to check on Havelock and the second just last night. His rational mind wanted to chock all these up as mere coincidences, but it seemed obvious that there was something larger at play here, something he simply didn't understand.

Chapter 11

FIFTEEN MINUTES LATER, TAYLOR pulled alongside a battered Ford pickup truck crowned by well-used surf racks. He noted the bumper sticker, I LOVE GERMAN SHEPHERDS, and recognized the vehicle immediately; it belonged to Tim Mahony, who was a deputy in the sheriff's department. They had met out in the water and had surfed together a few times. In fact, Tim was one of the few surfers in the area Taylor had found who was ballsy enough—or perhaps foolhardy enough—to paddle out in the bigger stuff. The few times they'd surfed together, the two men had gotten along quite well.

Taylor stepped out of his vehicle and walked to the edge of the bluff, his shoes crunching against the sand and gravel. Thrusting his hands into his pockets, he scanned the water, squinting against the glare. A lone surfer was out, bobbing up and down on his board just beyond the breaking waves. Taylor put up his hand to shade his eyes for a better look. Although the man was clad from head to toe in thick 5-mm neoprene, Taylor recognized Tim's distinctive board, its blue rails and white deck stark against the gray water.

A set morphed on the horizon and rolled shoreward. Taylor watched as Tim went up and over the first wave but swung his board around in front of the second and paddled hard. The wave lifted him up to the crest and he hopped to his feet, dropping down the face and sweeping into a long, drawn-out bottom turn. He angled up the wave, banked off the top, and then worked his way down the line, rising and dropping. Before the wave died in the shallows, Tim skillfully kicked out, turned his board around, and began paddling out again.

Energized by Tim's ride, Taylor raced back to his vehicle and dragged out his wetsuit. He hadn't surfed in a few days, so the wetsuit was dry. There was nothing worse, Taylor knew, than squeezing into a damp, clammy suit, especially on a cold morning. Luckily, the suit was dry, the day was relatively warm, and there was swell in the water—all the ingredients for a potentially successful and memorable session.

He squeezed into his wetsuit, hood, and booties and extracted his board from the back of the Jeep. Hastily waxing it down, he thrust it under his arm and trotted down to the water's edge. He stood in the shallows and watched as Tim caught another wave, maneuvering his board across the dark green face with practiced skill.

"Lucky bastard," Taylor muttered under his breath. He paddled out, duck-diving under a series of waves before reaching the lineup. He came up next to Tim, straddling his board.

"Look what the cat dragged in," Tim grinned, his face red from the cold water. He put out his arm and made a fist.

Taylor bumped Tim's fist with his own. "I couldn't let you get all the glory," he remarked, grinning back. "Looks pretty fun out here."

"It is." Tim glanced around toward shore. "Surprised there's not a crowd."

"Give it time."

Tim turned back, his gaze resettling on Taylor. "So how you been, pard?" he asked." I haven't seen you around in a while."

"Been busy," Taylor said. "But not as busy as you've been, I'm guessing."

"Holy crap," Tim said, shaking his head wearily. "You don't know the half of it. The department's been pulling its hair out over the Hsing murder."

"Any leads?"

"You know I can't tell you that, bro."

"The paper said it could've been a hate crime," Taylor said, "so that would make it a murder, right?"

Tim nodded. "Maybe some bigot unleashed his pit bulls."

"Is that what you think it was? A pit bull?" Taylor said. He paused, looking at Tim, trying to gauge a reaction.

"I've said too much already," Tim replied. "Anyway, it doesn't matter what I think. We'll just have to wait for the forensics report." The man splashed at the water with his hand, as if in frustration. He took a deep breath, let it out, and said, "Strangest case I ever worked on."

Before Taylor could ask just what Tim meant by "strange," another set rolled in.

"This one's yours!" Tim called out.

Without hesitation, Taylor swung his board around toward shore and, flattening himself on the deck, started paddling. He matched the wave's speed and hopped to his feet, dropping down the concave face. He swept into a long bottom turn, the inside rail of his board gouging a foamy wake. The wave transitioned into a long, tapering shoulder, which allowed Taylor room to maneuver. He exited out the back of the wave as it closed out with a booming crash on the sandbar. He paddled back out, exhilarated.

"Nice one," Tim said.

The two men spent the next hour trading waves back and forth. Each encouraged the other to take off deeper. One would ride a wave and paddle back out as the other was riding in.

During a lull, the two men drifted next to one another.

"Looks like we got company," Tim said, glancing back at shore.

Taylor turned, expecting to see a carload of surfers come racing into the parking lot. But all he saw was a lone figure standing on the bluff, dressed in black, his arms at his sides, looking out at the water.

Taylor squinted. There was something familiar about the guy—about the awkward way he was standing. It suddenly dawned on him the figure was the same young man he'd seen over a month ago. It was the same strange young man he'd told Kate about, the one he'd called Harold Skimpole.

"I know that guy," Tim said.

Taylor spun back around, surprised. "You know him?"

"Well, let me rephrase that," Tim said. "I don't know him, but I've seen him."

"So have I."

This time it was Tim's turn to be surprised, his eyebrows arching upward. "You have, too?"

Taylor nodded. "I saw him about a month ago," he said. "He asked me all these weird questions."

"Yeah," Tim nodded, "the guy's a major weirdo."

"When did you see him?"

"About a week ago. Last time I surfed here. I don't know what his deal is, but I didn't like the way he was loitering around the parking lot. I thought about arresting him, but I couldn't charge him with anything."

"What about loitering? Couldn't you get him for that?"

Tim laughed. "You're kidding, right? No one gets arrested for loitering anymore. Heck, they would arrest me for arresting someone for loitering."

They surfed for another fifteen minutes before Tim announced he was calling it quits for the day. He spun his board around and paddled for a small wave.

"See you around," he called out over his shoulder.

Taylor watched him belly-ride the wave to shore, where, board under his arm, he splashed through the shallows to the sand. Taylor stayed out for another fifteen minutes before he, too, caught a wave to the beach. Crossing the sand, he ascended the bluff and noticed that his Jeep was the only vehicle in the lot; Tim's truck was gone. He also noticed the young man was nowhere to be found. He wondered if Tim had driven him off.

Placing his board on the ground, he stood by his Jeep and proceeded to strip out of his wetsuit.

"It's the man who walks on water!"

The voice startled him. He spun around, noticing the young man standing at the edge of the parking lot. It seemed as if he had materialized out of thin air. He came striding across the dirt, his arms swinging casually at his sides, his dress shoes crunching against the gravel.

Immediately Taylor noticed there was something different about him. There was an arrogant self-assurance in his demeanor, which contrasted with the tentative, overly polite, deferential and even awkward version of the young man he had encountered a month ago. Gone was the goofy, embarrassed grin; in its place was what Taylor could only describe as a self-satisfied smirk.

Taylor didn't want to encourage the guy, so he only nodded, and then deliberately turned away, continuing to strip out of his wetsuit.

But the young man, true to form, was oblivious. He came up to Taylor and stood with his hands on his hips. "I know your secret," he announced.

Taylor stripped his wetsuit down to his waist, and half turned. "My secret? I didn't know I had one."

"It all has to do with the hydrodynamics of planning hulls."

"Really? Well, I'm glad you figured that out," Taylor said, turning away again.

"Newton's laws of motion explain the whole thing," the man

continued. "According to Newton's Third Law, every action has an opposite and equal reaction. This means that when your board presses down on the water, the water presses back, creating—"

"All real fascinating," Taylor intervened, "but I'm afraid I don't have time to stay and chat."

The man stopped talking. Taylor continued to strip out of his wetsuit, very conscious of the man's presence. The silence between them was palpable, the crack of breaking waves out in the water suddenly very loud.

"I believe you're ignoring me," the young man said, his voice carrying an edge. "I don't like when people ignore me." Taylor noticed the man was no longer enunciating every word with exacting preciseness; he was using contractions and there was no awkward pause between words.

"I don't have time to talk," Taylor grunted. He threw on a pair of jeans and grabbed his shirt from the back of his car, trying his best to forget the young man was there. He hoped he would just go away.

"I don't like when people ignore me," the young man repeated. There was a cold menace in his voice.

Taylor glanced around sharply. He saw that an angry scowl had darkened the young man's face.

"I heard you the first time," Taylor said. He put on his shirt, zipped up his fleece jacket, and stepped into his sandals. Then he stowed his board in the back of his car and slammed shut the gate.

"You'll regret ignoring me," the man said.

Taylor was walking around the car to the driver's side door when the man said it. He stopped and spun around, returning the man's glare. "What's your problem?" he said, angry now. "I told you I don't have time for this. Is there something you don't understand?"

The young man just stared at him, his eyes narrowed, his lips compressed tightly. He seemed to be quaking with barely controlled rage. When he didn't say anything, Taylor turned back, squared his shoulders, and got into his car. He started the engine and drove off.

As he pulled away from the parking lot, Taylor glanced in his rearview mirror. The young man was continuing to stand in the parking lot. His arms were at his sides, but his fists were clenched so that the knuckles showed white.

Chapter 12

"YOU MEAN IT WAS the same guy?" Kate asked, surprised.

"Yeah, same guy." Taylor was standing at the door of his house, talking on his cell phone. He had just exited his car and was now fumbling in his pocket for his keys.

"What was that name you called him?"

"Harold Skimpole," Taylor said. "But this time it was like his evil twin had taken over."

"What do you mean?"

"Remember I told you that he was kind of clueless."

"Yes."

"This time he wasn't. He was belligerent and angry."

"What did you do?"

"I basically told him to take a hike," Taylor said, pulling his keys from his pocket. "I thought he was going to take a swing at me."

"That's weird. What is the guy's problem?"

"I have no idea." He inserted the key and unlocked the door.

She paused. "Maybe you shouldn't surf there anymore."

"No, I'll be okay." He stepped inside and closed the door behind him. "I can handle myself. The guy is just a nut."

"That's exactly what I mean. In this day and age, nuts can be dangerous. Who knows what the guy is capable of?"

"Don't worry," he said, switching on the hall light. "I'll be all right."

"Okay." Kate paused. "Don't forget you agreed to stay with Havelock tonight."

"Yeah," Taylor said, "I'm going to take a shower, and then head over."

Havelock's house was quiet. Except for the monotonous ticking of an

70

old grandfather clock positioned along one wall of the living room, stillness and calm pervaded. Taylor had turned off the TV an hour ago and was now sitting in a chair reading a novel. Occasionally his eyes would drift up to check on Havelock, who was sitting in his wheelchair across the room. But he needn't have worried. The old man's eyes were closed, and he was snoring softly, his chin on his chest.

Taylor stopped reading. He put the book face down on the table beside him and glanced at his watch. It was a little past eleven o'clock. He rubbed his eyes and stood up. Then he crossed the room and stood beside the old man for a moment.

He wondered what Havelock was thinking; indeed, if the old man was thinking at all. He seemed more like a vegetable than a sentient human. When Taylor had first entered the house, Havelock had tried to speak, but Taylor hadn't understood a word. He'd listened closely, trying to make out the words, but it had been futile. Havelock had slurred his words so badly Taylor simply couldn't make out what the man was trying to convey. This went on for a minute or so before Havelock gave up in frustration and promptly fell asleep.

Taylor crossed the room and slumped back down in the chair with a sigh. Picking up his novel, he scratched the side of his nose and started reading where he'd left off. But he soon discovered, after he'd read the same paragraph three times, that his attention was beginning to fade. He closed the book for good and set it aside.

Restless, Taylor stood up and began to wander the living room, gazing at all the art and artifacts. He had, of course, seen much of the Tibetan artifacts twice already—when Havelock had invited him those nights—but a few he apparently missed now caught his eye. One was a small statue of what he could only surmise was a Tibetan deity. It was a grotesque little figurine with an oversized head, large round eyes, and a huge mouth from which a row of jagged teeth and scimitar-like canines protruded. The head was set atop a body that was part man, part what might have been an eagle. Its hands were long and fingernails curved talons.

He picked up the figurine and studied it in the dim light of the living room. It was hard to believe this fearsome little creature had anything to do with a religion that was concerned—at least as Taylor understood it—with contemplation, quiet of mind, and inner peace and tranquility. Then he suddenly remembered what Havelock

71

had told him about the nature of Tibetan Buddhism. The old man had explained that Tibetan Buddhism was really a curious hybrid of Mahayana Buddhism and the old aboriginal Bon religion of the Himalayan region, which itself was composed of strong shamanistic and animistic elements. It was a religion that propitiated a host of deities, some benign, some malevolent.

He set the figurine back down and picked up another. This one was about three inches high and depicted a seated Buddha. Its legs were crossed in the lotus fashion and its hands rested on its lap. With its eyes closed and a gaze of calm serenity on its face, it looked deep in the throes of blissful meditation. This figurine was much more in keeping with how Taylor had always envisioned Buddhism—a religion preoccupied with transcendent and rarefied states of mind. He scrutinized it for a moment longer and then set it back down next to the first figurine. He stood looking at them both, side by side. They were a study in contrasts. One could almost view them as symbolic of the human condition, of our Janus-like nature. The demon figurine, grotesque, squat, and malevolent, seemed to exemplify all the worst traits of the human animal—anger, lust, violence—while the Buddha, calm, serene, and content, encapsulated all those idealized virtues to which we aspired.

Eventually, Taylor wandered down the hallway and into the study. He switched on the light and stood looking around the room. As before, he noted the floor to ceiling bookshelves, each one crammed to overflowing with books of all sorts. He stood before the nearest bookshelf and ran his eyes across a sea of upright spines. Some books looked very old, while others appeared to be much newer. Many of the older volumes had gold filigree soldered onto their spines. Most of the books seemed to be dedicated to academic subjects, like history, astronomy, physics, botany, zoology, or anthropology. Many others were more difficult to classify, a hodge-podge of numerous subjects, from travel narratives and historical studies to nature essays and memoirs. He paused to read a few titles. *The Wild Plants of Inner Mongolia. Guide to the Wildflowers of the Italian Alps. A Record of Travel through Manchuria, Nepal, and Tibet. A Star Gazers Guide to the Night Sky of the Southern Hemisphere.*

Taylor stepped forward, stretched up on his tiptoes and, at random, slipped a book from one of the upper shelves. He turned the book over and gazed at the cover. *Astral Traveling and the Near-Death Experience*. He furrowed his brow. He was still having trouble accepting that Havelock believed all these weird paranormal phenomena, given the man's scientific background and training.

Reaching up, he slipped the book back into the shelf, and then turned and walked over to the large oak desk. He switched on the reading lamp. The light illuminated a haphazard scattering of papers and books. In fact, he guessed the man's desk probably hadn't been organized in years. In addition to several monographs was a small leather-bound notebook and a stack of old black-and-white photographs. Taylor lifted the notebook and opened to the first page, which read: *Journal of the 1951 Nepal-Tibet Expedition*. Interested, he began thumbing through it. The text was handwritten in a precise, neat scrawl. Taylor stopped randomly at an entry dated June 5, 1951. He smoothed the spine and started reading.

> *I'm told it's a three-day journey to the Lödrang Monastery from here. The route is supposedly very steep and treacherous, but I'm eager to attempt it. So is Fletcher. Like me, he's heard stories about the high lama that defy logic. Apparently, the man is held in especially high esteem by the peoples of the region—from lofty bureaucrats to lowly villagers. They also believe, amazingly, that he has the ability to perform miracles. Of course, my rational, scientific mind rebels at the very notion of "miracles." And yet at the same time, I can't help but be intrigued. Could the stories possibly be true? Does he really have the ability to levitate or make objects appear out of thin air, as many claim? Is the man a saint or a charlatan? Or a mixture of both. Either way, I'd like to find out.*
>
> *My task this evening is to convince our guide to take us to Lödrang. But he is a lazy and stubborn man who is constantly complaining about every little thing; no doubt it will be an uphill battle to garner his agreement. He is a Khamba tribesman from the western frontier of Tibet and seems governed by one thing, and one thing alone: His belly. Perhaps if I sweeten the pot with promises of extra tsampa rations...?*

Taylor flipped forward several pages. Another entry was dated Tuesday, June 10, 1951. He started reading.

*The head lama of Lödrang is a man named Tsering Gyalt-
so Rinpoche. In physical appearance, he is unprepossessing; he
is short and slightly built with a shaved head and a wrinkled,
weather-beaten face. His eyes, however, are alert and intelligent
and seem to radiate an inner calmness of spirit. He seems a pro-
foundly serious fellow, but occasionally, and surprisingly, likes to
break into a laugh that is quite infectious. Like the other monks
he wears a red and saffron robe but goes about without shoes—or
at least in the short time I have been able to observe him he doesn't
wear shoes. The soles of his feet must be as tough as old leather!*

*I was surprised to learn the lama spoke exceptionally good En-
glish with a precise British accent. When I inquired as to how he
had learned it, he proceeded to tell me a remarkable story. He grew
up as an orphan near the southern border with India. At age four,
he was adopted by English missionaries, a man and his wife who
raised him and taught him English. He lived with them for many
years as they conducted their missionary activities throughout Tibet. One day, when Tsering was fourteen, he was accompanying
his adoptive parents over a high mountain pass to visit a remote
village when there was a terrible avalanche. His parents were
killed but Tsering survived, though he was severely injured. Some
monks from the nearby Lödrang Monastery heard the avalanche
and went out to investigate. They found Tsering half buried in the
snow, frostbitten, and with a horribly broken leg. They took him
back to the monastery and tended to his injuries.*

*According to Tsering, the monks effected a miraculous healing.
Being by his own admission young and impressionable, Tsering
was astounded at being healed, so, right then and there, decided to join the monastery as a monk. He trained for several years,
rising to a position of authority and then, eventually, through dil-
igence and his considerable abilities becoming the head lama.*

Taylor stopped reading, closed the journal, and shook his head in
amazement. A miraculous healing? What had Havelock meant by that?

He put the notebook back on the desk and turned his attention to
the stack of photographs, picking one up at random. It was a shot of
a high-altitude camp with towering, snow-capped peaks in the background and several canvas tents in the foreground. He placed it back

on the table and picked up another one. This one showed a Tibetan stupa, a dome-shaped Buddhist shrine, perched impossibly on the edge of a cliff. He dug into the stack and pulled out another. This one was a group shot—undoubtedly taken during one of Havelock's expeditions. It depicted several men standing shoulder-to-shoulder, some in beards, others with wild, unkempt hair, all dressed in an assortment of warm clothing, big parkas or heavy sweaters. The men looked jovial but exhausted. There was a sense of deep camaraderie between the men, as if they had together achieved something for which each man could be eminently proud. Taylor guessed that perhaps it was taken after a successful day of fieldwork, or at the conclusion of the expedition. The man in the middle Taylor recognized as Havelock. He was younger, to be sure, but it was unmistakably the NASA scientist.

Taylor was about to put the photograph back when he stopped. He noticed that one of the men, a younger man with wavy blond hair and glasses, looked strangely familiar. He was standing next to Havelock wearing a threadbare sweater and a knit balaclava. He was smiling a goofy, lopsided grin. Taylor lifted the photo for a closer look, and squinted, staring at it in disbelief. He blinked, shook his head, and blinked again. There was no doubt about it; the man in the photo was a dead ringer for the strange young man he'd seen twice now at the State Beach parking lot. He studied the photo for a full minute, brow furrowed, turning the photo this way and that, looking at it from different angles. It had to be coincidence, and yet the two men—the strange young man and the man in the photo—looked exactly the same.

A muffled cry came from the living room. Taylor immediately dropped the photo, which fluttered to the table, and raced down the hallway. When he got to the living room, he saw that Havelock was awake and agitated. The old man's right arm was up and clutching at the air, as if he were fighting some unseen enemy.

Taylor rushed over and grabbed the old man by the shoulders. "Havelock! You okay?"

The old man stopped clutching the air and dropped his arm. It thumped against the wheelchair's armrest like a weighty branch. He looked directly at Taylor, his eyes wide, the pupils large and dilated.

"Are you all right?" Taylor asked again.

Havelock tried to speak, the muscles of his throat moving, but no sound except a wheeze issued from his mouth. Then, as if the effort to speak was too much, he drew a ragged breath and his shoulders sagged. He relaxed under Taylor's grip. His eyes glistened and began to brim with tears. Soon he was sobbing, tears streaming down his cheeks, his shoulders shaking uncontrollably.

Taylor wasn't sure what he should do. But before he could devise a plan, the old man fell asleep, his hands resting on his lap, palms up and fingers curled.

Chapter 13

TAYLOR AWOKE LATER THAN usual the next morning. It had been a late night and he hadn't gotten back to the house until well past midnight. Nor had he slept particularly well, his sleep punctuated by strange dreams.

Yawning and scratching his head, he padded into the kitchen and started brewing a pot of coffee. He glanced outside, watching the morning mist swirl among the redwoods. Then he sat down at his computer and booted it up. The first thing he did, almost instinctively, was check the surf report, but finding that conditions were poor—it was one to two feet and blown out with strong northwesterly winds—decided to spend the rest of the morning writing. But he soon discovered that the words were not flowing easily. His mind was preoccupied with other thoughts, especially with the photograph he'd seen last night. He still couldn't get over the resemblance of the young man in the photo with the young man he'd seen twice now in the beach parking lot. It was uncanny. The two might have been twins.

His cell phone rang, startling him out of his thoughts. He picked it up and glanced at the caller ID. He saw that it was Debra. He answered it. "Hi, Debra."

"Good morning, Taylor. Hey, I never got to thank you last night for looking after my dad. I really appreciated it. Sorry I got back so late."

"No problem."

"Did Dad try to talk at all?"

"When I first got there he did, but I couldn't understand what he was saying, I'm afraid."

"His doctor thinks there's a good chance he might recover his voice eventually. He's been responding well to the medicine." She sighed. "But I'm still having trouble coping with his mood swings. Did you have any problems last night?"

"He was fine. He slept like a baby most of the time I was there. There was only one time around midnight when he woke up pretty agitated. I think he had a bad dream or something. But I was able to calm him down."

"I'm glad to hear it," she said. "Anyway, thanks again."

"No problem," he said. "Take care."

"You, too."

Taylor hesitated briefly. "Oh, hey, before I go there's one last thing."

"Yes?"

Taylor cleared his throat, unsure about how to proceed. His gaze lingered on the far wall. Finally, he blurted out, "This question is kind of out of left field, but did you happen to know any of the scientists on your dad's Nepal expeditions?"

"The scientists?" She paused. "Gosh, not really. I mean, I was pretty young when Dad was doing all that." She paused again. "Why do you ask?"

"I told you it was out of left field."

She laughed. "So you did."

"I was reading your dad's Nepal expedition journal last night," Taylor said. "It's pretty interesting stuff. I hope you don't mind."

"Oh, that old thing? Yes, I'm sure it is. Anyway, thanks again for looking after him."

Taylor switched off the phone and set it down next to the computer. He walked into the kitchen and poured himself a cup of coffee. He returned to the study and had just settled himself in front of his computer when the phone rang again.

This time it was Kate.

"Hey, babe, what's up?"

"You're not going to believe what I just read," Kate said.

"What?"

"Are you logged on now?"

"Yes," he answered warily.

"Check out the *Courier* website."

Taylor tensed. "Jesus, what now?"

"The wife of that storeowner who was killed reported that a giant dog tried to break into her house last night."

"What?" Taylor was dumbfounded.

"Maybe your theory about killer cougars isn't so far-fetched after all."

When he'd switched off the phone, he immediately brought up *The Humboldt Courier* webpage. He found the story after scrolling down a list of local news items.

Wife of Deceased Storeowner Menaced by Animal

In a bizarre twist to an already bizarre story, Harriet Hsing, 44, the grieving wife of the deceased owner of Hsing's Second Hand, Edwin Hsing, reported a wild animal attempting to break into her Humboldt County home last night. The attempted break-in occurred a few minutes after midnight.

Mrs. Hsing reported that the animal, which she claimed was an exceptionally large black dog, repeatedly banged its paws against the front door.

"It was barking and foaming at the mouth," Mrs. Hsing said. "I thought it was going to kill me."

The animal succeeded in breaking the door but was prevented from entering by a neighbor who had received a frantic call from Mrs. Hsing. The neighbor, Gerald Tucker, 35, took several shots at the animal with his rifle.

"I hit it, but I don't think I did it any damage," he said. Like Mrs. Hsing, Mr. Tucker claimed the animal was an immense black dog.

According to Mr. Tucker the animal suddenly seemed to lose all interest, turned, and walked off into the night.

"There was nothing I could do," Mr. Tucker added, "it just lumbered off and was gone. It was as if someone just flipped a switch in its brain, or something. One instant it acted rabid and the next it was completely calm."

Mrs. Hsing plans to vacate her house and move in with relatives in Arcata...

Taylor was stunned. For a moment he just stared at the monitor, unblinking. Then he shook his head in amazement, trying to come to grips with what he had just read. It seemed incredible but he had no doubt the animal was Dorje. It had to be; it fit the description. But the incident was almost too bizarre to contemplate from any rational perspective. Why was the animal trying to get into the house of Edwin

Hsing's widow? Why did it seem like it was deliberately targeting Edwin Hsing and his family? Was it mere coincidence? Taylor shook his head. No, it was too weird—too fantastic—to be coincidence. There was some connection, but he had no idea what it might be.

He sat back, rubbing his chin. He tried to remember what it was Edwin Hsing had said about Dorje the day he and Kate had bought the bathroom mirror. He'd pretty much dismissed the comment at the time, but now it didn't seem so outlandish. He squeezed his eyes shut and furrowed his brow, trying to remember. What words had the man used?

His eyes shot open as he suddenly remembered. He'd said there was something "not right" about the dog, something "unnatural" about it.

His own interactions with the dog, such as they were, hadn't inclined him to think that Dorje was "unnatural." The term had seemed a needless overreaction when the man had uttered it. By the same token, he'd be the first to admit the dog was odd. In many ways it didn't seem like a typical dog. There was something definitely strange about it—the incident with the horse was enough to confirm that—but he wouldn't go as far as to call it "unnatural." And yet, perhaps Ed Hsing, before his death, knew something that he didn't...

———————

"Do you really think it was his dog?" Tim Mahony asked.

Taylor nodded. "I know it sounds crazy, but yeah, I do."

The two men were seated in Tim's office in the sheriff's department in Oceanport. It was late morning and the sun slanted in through vertical blinds, throwing narrow columns of light on the floor. The smell of freshly brewed coffee drifted about. Beyond Tim's office, Taylor heard a flurry of activity. Department headquarters was in the throes of another busy morning. The sound of voices, telephones ringing, computers humming, and faxes churning away filled the air.

Tim was silent for a long moment, scratching his chin. His gaze was directed at the far wall. Finally, he turned back to Taylor.

"What kind of dog did you say it was again?"

"A Tibetan mastiff."

He blinked. "Tibetan? That's a breed?"

Taylor nodded.

Tim took up a ballpoint pen and flipped open a small notebook.

He scribbled a few notes, and then looked up. "Did the dog ever show signs of aggression?"

"Not at first. At first it was just this big, lazy dog. All it did was lie around. But when I saw it after Havelock's stroke it had changed. It was aggressive. I'm pretty sure it had become rabid." He proceeded to tell Tim about his last encounter with the dog.

"So what did you do?"

"I called Animal Control. But they couldn't locate it." He added he thought he had heard its howling on at least two separate occasions.

"Do you know anything about the dog's history?" Tim asked.

"What do you mean?"

"Was it ever sick? Mistreated?"

"No, totally the opposite. He loved that dog. He doted on it. It was his constant companion."

Tim was quiet as Taylor spoke, occasionally jotting a note or continuing to ask a clarifying question. The man's face was an inscrutable mask. All the same, Taylor had the feeling Tim was only humoring him. There was something in the officer's demeanor that suggested complete incredulity.

After an interval, Tim stopped writing. He tapped the pen against the top of the notebook for a moment. Then he put the pen down and scanned what he'd written, rubbing the side of his face. As if to confirm Taylor's suspicions, Tim said, "I gotta tell you, this case is so bizarre I don't know what to make of it, but frankly, I'm not convinced Mrs. Hsing and her neighbor saw some huge black dog. I think it's more likely they were dealing with a black bear."

"But they both swear it was a dog not a bear."

"It was also very dark that night, with only a sliver of a moon showing. They could easily have been mistaken."

"I suppose, but..." Taylor was silent for a spell. He let out an irritated sigh. "Has the forensic team finished its investigation of Hsing's death?"

Tim shook his head. "Not yet."

"Well, I've told you all I know."

"I appreciate it," Tim said. He gazed at his notes one last time and then flipped the notebook closed.

An awkward silence fell between the two men, and they just stared at each other for a moment. Then Taylor turned away and shook his head. He got to his feet.

"You been out in the water recently?" Tim asked, as if wanting to fill the silence.

"No, not since we surfed that time together."

"Supposed to be some swell coming. Gonna be big, I hear. Should be good as long as the weather holds."

Taylor nodded distractedly.

Tim stared at him for a moment, then sighed. "Look," he said, "it's not that I don't believe you, but there are so many unknowns in this case, I just don't want to jump to any wild conclusions."

"No, I get it," Taylor said. He left the office feeling frustrated. He had the distinct impression Tim thought his theory—about Havelock's dog carrying out the attacks—was complete bullshit.

Shoving his hands into his pockets he descended the short flight of steps to the curb where his vehicle was parked. He opened the door and slid into the driver's seat, slamming the door behind him with a resounding ring. He sat in silence, staring across the street at a small breakfast café, his hands resting on the steering wheel, his eyebrows knitted together. He let out a long sigh. Then, shaking his head, he clicked his seatbelt and started the car. Pulling away from the curb, he drove off.

He cruised slowly down Oceanport's main drag. Maybe Tim was right, Taylor mused, maybe the dog theory was complete bunk. Maybe Taylor was only kidding himself. Rationally, he didn't blame the officer; it did sound far-fetched—crazy even. Still, he couldn't escape the conclusion that there was something truly strange going on here, and that Dorje—that "unnatural" dog—was somehow in the center of it. Compounding all this, of course, or at least adding a completely confusing layer, was his discovery of how the young man in the photograph was the physical match with the young man he'd seen in person.

Taylor wished he had Havelock's expedition journal to read. Maybe it held some clues to all this. Maybe it would be able to explain just what the hell might be going on. And he wanted to scrutinize that photograph again—just to prove to himself he wasn't crazy.

When he turned onto the tree-lined road that led to his house, he noticed something lying along the side of the road. He slowed the Jeep for a better look. Pulling parallel and rolling to a stop, he stuck his head out the window and looked down. The "something" was in fact a deer—or what was left of it. It lay sprawled in a grotesque position, half on the asphalt and half on the dirt. He opened the door and got out. The creature had been ripped apart, its stomach disemboweled so that guts, viscera, and intestines spilled out. Flies buzzed about the carcass. He stood over it for a moment, looking down at all the blood and gore. The animal's large, vacant eyes stared back at him.

It was then and there that he wished the county would hurry up and clear him for a gun.

"You want my honest opinion?" Kate said.

"Yes," Taylor replied, speaking into his cell phone. He was seated at the breakfast table, a mug of freshly brewed coffee before him.

"I think it sounds crazy. I mean, I can understand a rabid dog going after livestock, but you seem to be implying the dog is deliberately going after that poor man's family. Deliberately targeting them."

"It sure seems like it. Either that, or it's one of the oddest coincidences ever."

"C'mon, Taylor," Kate said, "you can't seriously believe that? That would mean the dog is somehow cognizant of what it's doing."

Taylor was silent. He scratched the back of his neck.

Kate's voice sounded mystified. "Don't tell me you believe something like that?"

Taylor was a moment in answering. He stared down at his coffee mug. A myriad of thoughts raced through his mind and he tried to sort through them all. Finally, he raised his head. "There are so many weird coincidences here that I'm not ruling anything out." He leaned forward. "Don't you find it odd that the same man who not a week before his death was telling us he feared Dorje and thought the dog was unnatural? And then after his death, his wife and family are menaced by a big black dog?"

"But the police haven't concluded it was a dog that killed him, let alone a big black one," Kate said. "We don't know what killed him. You're jumping to some wild, completely unfounded conclusions." She paused for a moment. "I see this in my work all the time."

"Thank you, counselor, but I'm not one of your clients," Taylor said a bit too testily.

"I'm sorry, I didn't mean it like that." She sighed. "I'm just saying you need to take a breath and look at this rationally. Look, I'll grant you this whole thing has been bizarre, but I really don't think there's any need to invoke the supernatural."

"I'm not 'invoking the supernatural,' as you put it. I'm merely pointing out some really weird coincidences that so far defy any rational explanation."

"There's always a rational explanation for everything," Kate said.

Taylor sat back and let out a sigh. He fingered the rim of his coffee mug and glanced out the kitchen window, frowning. He hadn't yet told her about the additional bit of information he'd managed to dredge up: about the young man in the photograph. This was because he knew she probably wouldn't believe it and because he wasn't sure he believed it either.

Chapter 14

"COME IN," DEBRA SAID, opening the door.

"Thanks," Taylor replied, stepping inside.

Earlier he'd called Debra to ask if he might borrow Havelock's journal.

"That really intrigued you, didn't it?" Debra said.

"It was pretty fascinating," Taylor said. "Have you read it?"

"No, I never did. I know Dad was pretty proud of it. I recall one time he thought he might want to try to publish it." She handed him the journal.

"How come he didn't?"

"Publish it?" She shook her head. "I'm not sure."

Before he left, he asked Debra if he could look at the photographs on Havelock's desk.

"Sure," she said.

He went into the study and began rummaging through the photos. Most were shots of Tibet, of the flora and fauna of the region, or shots of a Tibetan village or religious shrine. Others were shots of mountain peaks, lakes, or glaciers. Then he found what he was looking for. It was the same photograph he'd looked at before—the group shot of the expedition members he'd scrutinized two nights ago. He studied the young man standing next to Havelock. There was no doubt about it. He looked exactly like the State Park denizen—Harold Skimpole.

Taylor continued to rifle through the photographs and found several other group expedition shots. One in particular caught his attention. It was a shot of Havelock and the young man standing with their arms over each other's shoulders, like two good friends. In the background was a picturesque glacial lake. This time the young man wasn't wearing a balaclava so that Taylor was able to get a good look at his face. But this only confirmed his suspicions. It was indeed "Harold Skimpole." The tell-tale lop-sided grin, blue eyes behind little round glasses, unruly blond hair—all of these were unmistakable.

He turned the picture over and was surprised to see a caption at the bottom corner. It was written in pen and was somewhat faded but read "...with Fletcher at Jamyang Lake, June 1951."

So, this was Fletcher, Taylor thought, the young man mentioned in Havelock's journal. He flipped through the remainder of the photographs but couldn't find any more photos of Fletcher. He picked up the journal again and spent several minutes flipping through its pages. Near the beginning of the book, in an entry dated April 14, 1951, Taylor saw a list of the expedition members. Listed was one Fletcher Hendrickson of Charlottesville, Virginia.

He walked back into the living room with the journal. "Thanks for letting me borrow this," he said.

"No problem," Debra answered. "Thinking of using it for one of your mysteries?"

"Not a bad idea," Taylor said.

He noticed that Havelock was sitting in his wheelchair by the fireplace. As usual, the old man was sleeping, his eyes closed and head bent forward. His shoulders rose and fell, and his breath came out in wheezing gasps.

"How's he doing?" Taylor asked.

Debra sighed. "His awareness seems to come and go. Sometimes he seems coherent, and other times he just mumbles as if lost in dreams."

"Can you understand what he's saying yet?"

"No," Debra said.

He brought the journal back to the house and, making a big pot of coffee, closed the door to his study. He sat down at his desk and switched on the reading light.

He opened the journal and flipped forward several pages, frowning in concentration, trying to find where he had left off.

June 11, 1951

> *Lama Tsering was gracious enough to receive us for another interview. I was intrigued by the story he'd told me about the monks healing his leg when he was a boy, so I asked him about it. He told me that to understand it one must understand the Tibetan*

concept of thoughts. He told me Tibetans believe thoughts aren't simply abstract mental phenomena but are in fact real, tangible entities. They believe that through sheer mental discipline, and with enough mental energy, an adept can turn a thought into a three-dimensional, corporeal "thing"—a physical object. He told me the story of how as a young monk he once sat in meditation for an entire day and visualized a rose. His concentration was so great—so intense and focused—that when he opened his eyes a rose lay on the ground before him just as he had visualized it. He explained that this was how the monks were able to heal his leg when he was a boy. They simply visualized the image of his healed leg until it became a reality.

Of course, being trained in the Western, scientific, rational paradigm, I told him it was difficult for me to accept the validity of what he was telling me. I frankly did not believe thoughts could be made manifest. I told him I believed it to be against the laws of physics. He simply smiled and told me personal experience should be my guide to whether I accept something as true or valid. This did not satisfy me in the least; I replied that the human mind is notoriously subject to self-deception. He countered that, for the man who has "control," self-deception is not possible...

June 12, 1951

A remarkable event occurred today, one so remarkable that had I not witnessed it with my own eyes, I simply would not have believed it. Even now, as I write these words, I am at a complete loss to explain exactly what happened. The event has challenged my most cherished beliefs and created something of a crisis in how I view reality. I will nonetheless do my best to relate the event as accurately as possible, leaving nothing out and embellishing nothing.

This morning, myself, Fletcher, and Lama Tsering were gathered in his chambers, having one of our discussions. I brought up the fact I was still finding it difficult to accept one of his major philosophical tenets: that thought—mental activity—is tangible and can be made manifest. I told him that my view of reality, the Western perspective, was quite different from the Tibetan perspective. He agreed that indeed they were but expressed every confidence that the Western view would eventually catch up with the Tibetan. I laughed at this, figuring he was being mildly face-tious. I then told him that one of the hallmarks of Western science was empiricism—that knowledge is gained through experience and observation. I told him, in short, that assertions demand-ed proof. He agreed this was a commendable and most valuable viewpoint. It was then that, perhaps indelicately, I asked for proof that thoughts could become reality.

He was quiet for several minutes, as if mulling over my request. Then he nodded and closed his eyes. He took several deep breaths and then seemed to fall into deep concentration or trance, I don't know which. We were seated on the floor of his chambers, facing each other, with a space of maybe three feet separating us.

He sat in that position for a long time. Although his eyes were closed, and his face was calm I could tell he was concentrating as there was a deep furrow to his brow.

Fletcher and I sat silently, almost as if holding our breaths, waiting for something to happen. But the minutes dragged on, seemingly ad infinitum.

I must've drifted off because the next thing I knew Fletcher was nudging me with his elbow. "My God, look!" he whispered. I snapped awake and looked to where he was pointing—at the space on the floor between the lama and myself. Slowly but with increasing clarity, the outline of what appeared to be a small dark ball began to appear. I hesitate to use the cliché "out of thin air" but that is exactly what was happening. As the object took form and solidity, Fletcher and I noticed it wasn't a ball at all but a small piece of fruit, round and dark red like a plum. I glanced up at Lama Tsering. He hadn't moved, changed position, or opened his eyes throughout all this.

In moments, the fruit took final form and a ripe plum appeared on the ground before us—solid and tangible. I was speechless, amazed that I was looking at something that had literally ap-peared out of nowhere. My first thought was that there had to have been some chicanery on the Lama's part, that he had some-how duped us. But I had concluded over the last few days from our numerous conversations that the lama is utterly guileless and could simply not conceive of engaging in such subterfuge. Conse-quently, I was forced to confront the possibility that what I had just witnessed was, in fact, some sort of physical manifestation, the source of which was hitherto unknown to the scientific world.

To my surprise, Fletcher reached out and impulsively picked it up. At that moment Lama Tsering opened his eyes. I expressed my amazement at what he had done but he only nodded.

Fletcher examined the plum for several minutes and then handed it to me. I held it in my palm and studied it; it felt exactly like a ripe plum should feel: plump and slightly weighty. I gave it a pinch and felt the flesh give. Then I tore off part of the skin and examined the pulpy flesh. It was moist and juicy...

Chapter 15

FULLY ENGROSSED AND UNABLE to put the journal down, Taylor continued reading late into the night.

June 13, 1951

> *Yesterday's demonstration has been weighing heavily on my mind. I still don't really know what to make of it. On the surface, my eyes witnessed what many might classify as a "miracle." I witnessed the creation of a three-dimensional object seemingly out of nothing. The only thing to which I can compare it —the only thing that immediately springs to mind—is the story of Jesus's conjuring of the loaves and fishes as depicted in the New Testament. But, of course, I've never believed the story to be literally true. In my mind it has always been a fable, or at most, a metaphor.*
>
> *At the same time, a part of me cannot accept what my eyes witnessed. It goes against everything in which I've long believed. It is simply not possible to create something out of nothing. This is a physical law. There is no place in science for miracles. So my dilemma revolves around the question: How to square what my eyes witnessed with what I know inherently to be true?*
>
> *I don't believe in miracles. I don't believe that consciousness, or the mind, interacts and can affect matter. But for the moment let me set aside that idea and try to effect some type of explanation using concepts from my scientific, Western upbringing. A good scientist should be skeptical but open-minded. I reject any notion of artifice on the Lama's part, so I will assume prima facie that Lama Tsering manifested a fruit—a plum—seemingly out of "thin air." Of course, as I've said, our understanding of reality suggests one can't get something out of nothing. Yet that is what appeared to*

have been done here. I use the word "appeared" deliberately; perhaps if we apply certain concepts from physics, we might be able to come up with an explanation, as outlandish as it may seem.

According to our current understanding of space and time, matter and energy are equivalent; that is, one is simply a different form of the other (Einstein likes to call matter "frozen" energy). For example, when we collide an electron with a proton, the mass of both particles is annihilated, and they convert to energy in the form of photons. Thus, the only difference between mass and energy is the amount of external energy applied. We know, for example, and multiple experiments have shown, that we can take a seemingly empty region of space and "create" an elementary particle. We know this to be true because an "empty" region of space really isn't empty at all. It is in fact, on the quantum scale, a teeming, roiling frenzy of particles continually erupting into existence and annihilating each other. Thus, if an energy fluctuation is big enough, it can momentarily cause an electron (and its opposite, the positron) to erupt into existence, even as I have said, this region is initially "empty."

Is it possible that Lama Tsering somehow can harness and manipulate energies with his mind in such a way to create a solid object? Does he have the ability to create an energy fluctuation with his mind? Of course, this scenario is patently absurd—since consciousness cannot affect matter. It is utterly and totally impossible.

I have requested another audience with Lama Tsering tomorrow...

June 14, 1951

I had another audience with the lama today. As always, we met in his chambers and he poured two glasses of yak butter tea for us to enjoy. We discussed the plum he had conjured, and I asked him, yet again, how he'd done it. To my surprise, he said that ultimately it is of little consequence. It was done merely to make a point about the efficacy of human thought. He told me not to dwell on such things, for they are distractions and impediments to achieving enlightenment, the ultimate goal of all Buddhists. I nonetheless pressed him for an explicit answer, knowing my forwardness would be considered rude by most Tibetans. But I didn't care; I had to have an answer. He patiently explained, as he had before, that my failure to comprehend what my eyes had witnessed was due to my inability to accept the idea that thoughts are real. He did not mean to say, as many might suppose, that one can turn a thought into reality, such as, for example, an engineer might design a bridge first on paper and then construct it in material reality. What he meant is that thoughts ARE real. Every mental action creates a wave of energy.

He told me to consider the Tibetan concept of vibrations. While we Westerners believe that physical reality—at its most basic level—is composed of elementary particles, such as quarks and bosons, which cannot be reduced to anything smaller, the Tibetan concept of reality is decidedly different. Tibetans believe everything is composed of a dynamic manifestation of vibrations, which are distinguished from each other by the amount of energy they contain. Everything is a temporary and changing configuration of vibrations.

Thoughts, he told me, just as physical objects, sounds, or colors, are vibrations. He said the energy of a thought is called "tsal" in Tibetan. When a thought is conjured, it travels outward as a vibration. Each of these things, whether a physical object, sound, or a thought, has a different vibratory rate. A thought has an extremely low vibratory rate as compared to, for example, an orange.

For a thought to become tangible all it requires is a stronger vibratory rate. This can be accomplished, Lama Tsering said, by a concentrated mental effort in which mental energy can be transferred to that thought to make it tangible. Of course, he admitted that most people do not possess the required mental concentration to bring such a thing about. But one can train one's mind. Control of one's mind is the key, he said.

I asked him exactly what he meant by "control." He explained that the untrained mind is plagued by uncontrolled thoughts and emotions. These thoughts and emotions run rampant through our minds on a regular basis, certainly through our waking hours and even into our dreams. In a very real sense, these thoughts and emotions control us rather than the other way around. If one cannot control one's thoughts, he explained, then the mind is only capable of so much. However, with the proper control of the mind, the ability of the mind is nearly limitless.

*He went on to explain that controlling the mind requires ded-
ication and practice. The first step involves learning to quiet the
thoughts that continually plague us, to separate ourselves from our
thoughts, especially the ones that are emotionally disruptive. This
is achieved by not paying attention to, or becoming emotionally involved with, these thoughts. As we gradually learn how to
do this, he said, we are able to access deeper parts of the mind to
which we typically don't have access.*

*With a sudden, impulsive action to which I thought myself not
capable, I asked Lama Tsering if he would be willing to teach me
these practices.*

The next several entries, Taylor noted, were devoted to Havelock
and Fletcher's entry into the world of Tibetan monasticism. Havelock described a rigorous routine, which began at three o'clock in the
morning when the two men were bade to wake and assemble in the
communal hall for a three-hour period of stillness meditation. This
was followed by breakfast of tea and *tsampa*. Each new initiate was
then required to have an audience with the lama, which usually lasted
half an hour. This audience took the form of a Socratic dialogue, where
the initiate could ask questions and the lama would supply answers.
The session usually concluded with the lama posing a philosophical
question which the initiate was to ponder for the remainder of the day.

After lunch, which again consisted of modest fare, the initiate
would spend another three hours in concentration and visualization
exercises, called *sadhanas*. This consisted of studying a physical object,
a small icon or a knot of rope, for example, and then replicating the
image in one's mind. When this concluded, the initiate was allowed
free time to read, relax, and reflect, or spend his time in some physical activity—anything from calisthenics to woodworking. Havelock
noted that he spent much of this free time writing in his journal. The
initiate was then served supper sharply at sunset and expected to retire to his room for the night, whereupon the following morning the
entire regimen was repeated.

July 12, 1951

*Trying to silence my mind is proving much more difficult
than I had imagined. Each time I try not to think of anything,*

93

a stray thought will invariably drift into my consciousness and I will find myself dwelling on it. Tsering has instructed me to allow the thought to drift by without my paying it any attention, like watching a "cloud carried away on the breeze." As I've said, this is extremely difficult. Visualization has proven equally difficult. I find it immensely demanding to hold a detailed image in my mind—let alone even a simple image—for any length of time. When I tell Tsering of my difficulties, he just smiles and tells me to "practice, practice." That has been his mantra over the past several days: "practice, practice."

By the same token, I've come to an interesting realization over the last several days. Although the routine has not varied, and the schedule is demanding, I'm beginning to feel a sense of deep satisfaction in the unvarying sameness. This has surprised me greatly. As the days have blended, I have noticed a calmness and peace descend on me. I've never felt anything like it; it's as if a whole new world—a world I never knew existed—has opened up before me. My mind is less agitated, more content, more at ease with the world around me. I notice that colors seem more vibrant, smells sharper, and my focus more concentrated. Those things to which I would've normally paid little attention now seem to grab me in a way that's difficult to explain. I'm beginning to see beauty all around me, in everyday, common things.

Just yesterday, for example, I spent a long time staring at a beetle crawling on a flower. I was spellbound by it. All my senses were so focused on the beetle inching along the flower petals that everything else, the world and everything in it, just seemed to melt away. I know this sounds foolish. And as I read back these words, I am somewhat embarrassed. But the bliss of that experience is impossible to translate into words. The long meditations are beginning to open something inside of me I didn't know existed; I can't really say what that is except that the change is noticeable—and freeing.

When Fletcher and I talked about our respective experiences, he related something equally remarkable. He told me that during one of his long meditations, he was suddenly overtaken by a feeling of indescribable joy. He said it literally "exploded" upon him, and that he was so overwhelmed, tears streamed down his cheeks. All thoughts of fear and discontent vanished, and he was filled with the utter joy and beauty of life. But the feeling didn't last, he said. It vanished as fast as it had come upon him, and yet from that moment he felt as if he had touched something so profound that it was all he could think about.

July 13, 1951

Today's discussion with Lama Tsering centered upon the topic of thought control. It is a topic we have discussed on numerous occasions, but one that nonetheless never ceases to interest me. I asked the Lama about his assertion that with control of the mind "nearly anything is possible." He reiterated that this was indeed true, telling me that, with the proper control, the mind's ability is unfathomable, that the universe is truly "at one's fingertips." Proper thought control allows one to cultivate the "siddhis," which he explained are mental powers. He was quick to warn me, however, that control of the mind did not necessarily mean one had achieved an elevating wisdom. The two did not go hand-in-glove. The acquisition of wisdom, he said, was achieved through hard work and practice—just as much as control of the mind. One had to work just as hard at it as at controlling one's thoughts. In fact, he pointed out, control of one's thoughts must be tempered with wisdom; otherwise, what was the point of such miraculous abilities? Just because one can create things with one's mind does not mean that they should be created. Lama Tsering seemed particularly adamant on this point, adding, "One must know how to protect oneself from the tigers to which one has given birth."

July 14, 1951

I am disappointed I can only spend so long here. Fletcher and I must get back to Nepal by the end of the summer. Nonetheless, I plan to continue practicing Tsering's mental regimen, and I hope to get back to the monastery someday. This may prove difficult, however, because of the Chinese. They are increasing their hostilities against the Tibetans seemingly day by day. Reports have been filtering in of attacks on villages and people slaughtered. There is even information floating about that several monasteries have been ransacked and monks killed.

I fear the Chinese are planning an all-out offensive against the Tibetans with the goal of annexing the country. I sincerely hope I am wrong, but I am not optimistic.

Taylor marked the page and closed the journal. He'd been reading for a while now and his eyes were beginning to tire. He rubbed them and looked at his watch and was amazed to see that it was nearly midnight. Putting the book aside, he stood up and glanced out the window. A half-moon hung over the trees, casting its silvery light downward.

The content of Havelock's journal was amazing, almost unbelievable. He wasn't sure what to make of it. Had Havelock actually witnessed these miraculous events? He peered deeper into the darkness and wondered.

Chapter 16

A FEW DAYS LATER, Taylor received word that he could pick up his shotgun. He drove into town and parked on the street outside the sporting goods store. He went inside and made his way down an aisle to the back of the store. At the gun counter, he noticed the same older man who had initially sold him the shotgun.

"Good morning," Taylor said. "You called about my rifle."

The man squinted through his thick glasses. "The name was Hamilton, right?"

Taylor nodded.

The man rummaged under the counter and came up with the gun, which was encased in heavy plastic. He carefully set it down on the counter. "Here it is," he said. "All bright and shiny."

Taylor looked it over.

"You gonna want some ammo with that?" the man asked, plunking down two small boxes of cartridges on the counter.

"Yeah, I guess I do." As Taylor signed the final paperwork, the man said, "So, your wife good with it now?"

Taylor looked up. "My wife?"

"Yeah, weren't you the guy said his wife thought you were crazy for wanting a firearm?"

Taylor cracked a smile. "Yes, that was me, and no, she's still not good with it, but that's too bad. She'll just have to get used to it."

"Well, you tell her 'Bernie the gun guy' says her husband's just being smart."

"Thanks," Taylor chuckled. "I will."

"With all this craziness going on lately you're good to protect yourself." He regarded Taylor for a moment. "You hear about Ed Hsing's widow?"

"Yeah, I read about it in the paper," Taylor said.

"Pretty crazy, huh?" Bernie the gun guy leaned in close and his voice dropped to a whisper. "You ask me, the whole thing's a conspiracy."

"A conspiracy? What do you mean?"

"I think someone's been gunning for Ed and his family."

"Who?"

The man shrugged. "I don't know, but this ain't a coincidence."

"It does seem pretty strange," Taylor said. "Any more happenings up in Redwood Valley?"

"Yeah, as a matter of fact. A couple of items that never got into the papers. Apparently that big black dog—or whatever the hell it is—was spotted on at least two occasions. One guy even took a shot at it."

"Did he hit it?"

"Says he did, but it apparently didn't have any effect. Said the thing just shook its head and walked away."

"That's weird," Taylor said. "And this guy said for sure it was a big black dog?"

The man nodded. "I gotta admit," he said, "when I first heard about all this, I thought for sure they were dealing with a cougar. Because of all the livestock killing. But now—" He paused to scratch his chin.

"What do you think now?" Taylor chimed in.

"I don't know," he shrugged. "But I guess you gotta believe 'em when they say it's a dog. But a big ass, aggressive one. And one that apparently bullets have no effect on."

Taylor exited the store and stowed the shotgun in the back of his Jeep. Then he slid into the driver's seat but didn't start the ignition right away. The man's words about the creature's imperviousness to bullets were no doubt hyperbole, he thought. Dorje, no matter how big he was or thick his hide, could be brought down with a well-placed bullet. Taylor was convinced of that. Or at least he told himself. At the same time, Ed Hsing's word "unnatural" used to describe Dorje kept resounding in Taylor's mind like a gong.

He shook off the thought and called Kate on his cell.

"Hey, hon," he said. "Wanted to let you know I just picked 'it' up."

"Great," Kate said, the single word response oozing with sarcasm.

But Taylor didn't miss a beat. "And in celebration, I propose we have dinner tonight at Bayside. What do you say? I'll buy you some artery-hardening fish and chips and a 12-ounce microbrew. How does that sound?"

"I'll settle for a crab salad and white wine."

"Done."

———————

Taylor watched as Kate picked mechanically at her salad, her expression glum, her eyes directed down at her plate. She seemed slightly more interested in her wine but even that seemed to arouse little enthusiasm. He watched as she lifted her wine glass, sighed, took a perfunctory sip, and then set the glass back on the table.

Finally, he couldn't stand it any longer. He put his fork down and looked across the table at her, frowning. "What's wrong, babe?"

She looked up distractedly. "Oh, sorry. My mind's on other things."

"Yeah, no kidding," Taylor said. He paused, studying her. "It's not the gun, is it?"

"No." She managed to crack a smile. "I've made my peace with that." She sighed and shook her head. "It's work. I'm sorry, I should have told you earlier."

Concern etched his features. "What's going on?"

"There's this client who is a complete asshole. But he's Bob's golf buddy so we're supposed to kiss his ass at every turn. Anyway, Bob wants us—really meaning me—to do some pro bono work for the client, which amounts to more ass kissing."

Taylor reclined in his chair. "Is that all? I thought you were going to tell me Bob wanted you to do something unethical."

"No, nothing like that, although this guy is pretty sleazy."

"You gonna do it? The pro bono work, I mean?"

"Of course." She threw up her hands. "What choice do I have? I'd better do it if I want to make full partner eventually. But it means I'm going to be tied up in the city all next week and maybe even the week after that."

"Don't worry, we'll make it work."

"I know, but it just means we won't be able to see each other for a while, with you being up here and me being down there with my nose in probate records."

Taylor reached across the table and placed his hand on top of Kate's wrist. "Well, we have tonight, at least." He grinned at her mischievously. "Let's make the most of it, shall we?"

She shot him back a grin that was just as mischievous. "What did you have in mind?"

He sat back, folded his arms across his chest and raised an eyebrow, continuing to grin. "Oh, I don't know, a little subdued lighting, a little champagne, a little Berry White on the iPod."

"Clichéd," she smiled, "but I like it."

It was dark by the time they reached the fork in the road that led to their house. Taylor was about to turn right when Kate suddenly put her hand on his arm.

"Look at that," she said, pointing down the road toward Havelock's place.

Taylor stopped the Jeep and turned to look, squinting through the windshield. He saw several sheriff's vehicles parked in front of the house, the lights atop their cars blinking.

"I wonder what's going on?" Kate said.

Taylor continued to stare for a moment, and then he spun the wheel around, turning the car. "Let's go find out."

As they neared, Taylor saw three sheriff vehicles parked on the gravel in front of the house, the doors hanging open. Several officers were milling about the grounds with flashlights, the beams skittering over trees and shrubs. Taylor drove up and parked a distance from the front of the house. At the car's arrival, one of the officers broke away from his companions and came striding over, flashlight in hand, boots crunching against the gravel. He wore the tan uniform and green tie of the department.

"Everything all right, officer?" Taylor asked, sticking his head out the window.

"Who are you?" the officer demanded, training his flashlight on Taylor.

"I'm Havelock's neighbor," Taylor said, putting up a hand to shade his face from the bright light. "Taylor Hamilton."

The officer, a young man with close-cropped hair, slowly lowered his flashlight. "You live at 1585 Madrona Lane?"

"That's right," Taylor said, nodding. "Just down the road. My wife and I were returning from dinner and saw all the commotion. We wanted to see what was going on. Havelock and Debra are friends of ours."

"There was an attempted break-in," the officer said, his voice precise and to-the-point.

"Did you catch who was responsible?"

"No."

Taylor saw Debra standing in the doorway, talking to one of the officers. She was dressed in a bathrobe and her face was flushed and hair messy. She was cradling her left elbow in the palm of her right hand, as if she had injured it. The officer had his notebook open and was jotting notes as she spoke. She glanced over and her eyes widened when she saw Taylor.

"Taylor," she called out, "thank God you're here."

He got out of the car and walked toward her. "What on earth happened?" he said.

"Someone tried to break in." She pointed at the cracked window next to the door. Shards of plate glass lay scattered about, splintered and broken, reflecting the lights of the sheriff vehicles.

Taylor stared at the jagged pieces of glass, and then looked back at Debra. "Are you all right?"

"Yes," she nodded. "Just shaken up."

"What about your arm?"

"It's all right. I think it's just bruised. I landed on it funny. It'll be all right with some ice."

"And Havelock?"

"He's fine."

Debra said something to the investigating officer and then came down the short flight of steps. Taylor gave her a hug, felt her body shaking.

"Are you sure you're okay?" Taylor asked, stepping back and holding both her shoulders at arm's length. He gazed at her gravely. Her face was drawn and haggard. It looked like she had gone through quite an ordeal.

She shuddered but nodded. "I'm okay now, but I thought I was going to die."

"Why don't we get you and Havelock to our place," Taylor suggested.

"So," Taylor said, sliding a cup of hot herbal tea across the table, "tell us what happened."

Debra wrapped her fingers around the offered mug as if to steady herself and closed her eyes. The surface of the tea trembled slightly. She took a deep, steadying breath, fighting to keep her emotions in check. Then she opened her eyes and looked at them. Taylor noticed that color was beginning to return to her cheeks.

The three of them, Taylor, Kate, and Debra, were seated around the kitchen table. Havelock was in the other room in his wheelchair, seemingly oblivious to the whole event.

"It was a little after eight o'clock," Debra began, "when I heard someone pounding at the front door. I had just given Dad his medicine and a tranquilizer."

"Why a tranquilizer?" Taylor asked.

"He'd had a bad episode earlier that evening. Was really angry and upset about something. Yelling one moment and crying the next. It was terrible. I just wanted to calm him down, let him sleep." She shuddered. "Anyway, once I'd finally gotten him calmed down and put to bed, I was startled to hear a knock at the door. I wasn't expecting anyone, so I was kind of surprised." She looked at Taylor. "In fact, at first I thought it might be you. When I opened the door, I saw this young man I'd never seen before. Had blond hair and glasses."

Taylor felt a shiver run up his spine.

"He wanted to know where Havelock was. I asked him who he was, but he wouldn't give me his name. In fact, he was really arrogant. Wouldn't tell me anything. He kept calling Dad 'his person.' I had no idea what he was talking about. He started to get belligerent, so I tried to close the door. That's when he knocked me down and stepped inside. I was terrified. But he seemed kind of confused once he entered so I took the chance when his back was turned and pushed him out the door. Then I locked it. I immediately called 9-1-1. But he kept pounding on the door, yelling to see 'his person.'" She took a sip of tea and shivered; the images were still fresh in her mind.

"Havelock was asleep through all this?" Kate asked.

Debra nodded. "The sedative I gave him was pretty strong. I don't think he heard a thing."

"What happened next?" Taylor asked.

"This guy continued to pound at the door and scream to be let in. I'm not sure how long this went on. It was a blur. Finally, he put his hand through the glass by the door. Completely shattered it. Dad's cane was next to the door, so I grabbed it and began to hit his hand. I guess it worked because he finally left. That was when the sheriff arrived."

There was silence between the three of them.

"And you have no idea what he wanted with your father?" Kate said.

"None whatsoever."

Taylor was silent for a moment, then he sprang to his feet and began to pace the room. "What was he dressed like?"

"Dressed?" Debra looked up at him with a perplexed expression. "You mean the intruder?"

Taylor nodded.

"In black. He was dressed in black. In a black turtleneck and black slacks."

"And shoes? Was he wearing black shoes?"

"I don't remember. I think so." She paused and gave him a hard stare. "Do you know this person?"

"I think so, yes," he said, sitting back down.

"Who is he?" she asked.

"Wait a minute," Kate said, reaching over to grab Taylor's arm, "he sounds like that strange guy—that Skimpole guy—you saw out at State Beach."

Taylor nodded. "Yes, he does."

Debra's eyes narrowed, and she looked quickly from one to the other, her expression confused but expectant.

Taylor explained the incident at the beach, how the first time the young man had been completely oblivious and credulous about nearly everything. But that the second time he was completely different—irascible, arrogant, and belligerent. He was, however, careful not to mention the man's resemblance to Fletcher because it seemed so far out he wasn't sure she'd believe him.

After hearing Taylor's story, Debra regarded him for a long moment in silence. "You think this is the same guy?"

"Sounds like it."

"What did he want with my dad, do you think?"

That was a question he couldn't answer. He just shook his head. "I don't know," he said.

"I think you and Havelock need to stay with us for the time being," Kate said. She turned to look at Taylor, as if for confirmation.

"Yes," he nodded in agreement. "You and Havelock can stay in the guest room."

"We couldn't impose on you."

Kate gave a dismissive wave of her hand. "It's done. You're staying here."

103

Chapter 17

MUCH LATER THAT NIGHT, after Debra and Havelock had settled into the guest room, Taylor and Kate sat down in the living room. The house was quiet and still; the only sound was the ticking of the clock on the wall. After the dramatic events of the evening, the silence was a welcome change.

"What do you make of all this?" Kate asked, her eyes searching his face. "Do you think this guy is a serious threat? Who is he? What on earth does he want with Havelock?"

"I honestly don't know," Taylor said.

They were both silent.

"You don't think we're in any danger, do you?" Kate asked.

Taylor's last encounter with Fletcher flashed in his mind. He moved uneasily in his seat. "I don't know. But—"

Her brows knitted in thought. "But what?"

Taylor tried to make sense of everything he'd learned in the last couple days, but none of it made any sense. Finally, he just shrugged his shoulders. "It's nothing," he said, lapsing into silence.

Kate sighed and glanced up at the wall clock. It was well past midnight. She stood up, lifted her eyeglasses, and rubbed a bleary eye. "It's been a long night," she said, yawning. She leaned down to kiss him on the cheek. "I'm going to bed."

She walked down the hallway but stopped when Taylor called out her name.

"I'm sorry tonight didn't turn out as we planned," he said.

She shrugged. "Things happen."

As she walked off, he asked, "What time are you leaving for the city tomorrow?"

"Early," she said over her shoulder. "I'll probably be gone by the time you get up."

Once Kate had shuffled off to bed, Taylor went out to the garage where he had stowed the shotgun in one of the cabinets. He took down the weapon, placed it under his arm, and grabbed a box of cartridges. He returned to the house and sat down on the big leather chair in the living room. He laid the weapon horizontally across the tops of his knees. The gun was solid and heavy, and he studied it for a moment. Then he drew back the bolt release with a clang and scrutinized the dark, cavernous breech. He opened the box of cartridges and selected one at random. He carefully levered it into the breech, heard a click as it fell into place. There was room for another one, so he inserted a second one. Heard that click as well. Then he slammed the bolt shut. Sitting with the loaded shotgun on his knees, Taylor didn't know if 'Bernie the gun guy' was right about Dorje—that bullets had no effect on him—but he felt a lot better with a weapon in the house. He stood up and placed the gun and cartridges on the mantel over the fireplace.

He walked into the study. Slumping down in the desk chair, he clicked on a reading light and picked up Havelock's journal. He flipped forward several pages, trying to find where he'd left off.

July 15, 1951

Yesterday, during our daily meeting, Lama Tsering left me with a thought that gave me pause. Although he never uttered the word morality, that was exactly what we had been discussing: the morality of doing miraculous things with one's mind. On the face of it, it seems absurd; of course one should do miraculous things because, well, they're miraculous. They turn the laws of physics on their head; they prove that the human mind is capable of so much more. They prove that human potential is not limited, that humans can achieve fantastic heights. Think of what we can do! Think of the good that can be done with such abilities! Think of how one might change the world! We can feed the hungry! Heal the sick! Fix the environment! Alleviate the world's suffering! Perhaps even prevent war.

Lama Tsering then asked me how one person can possibly know what is good for the world and all its inhabitants. Perhaps, he told me, the world is proceeding along as it should.

This perplexed me greatly, and I asked him how he could possibly say such a thing with all the sickness, misery, strife, and bloodshed in the world.

He told me strife and misery are frequently great teachers, and that sometimes they are the only vehicles whereby individuals learn profound lessons. He said everyone is on a different life path. Some have chosen to confront particular difficulties or illnesses in their lives in order to progress as individuals. They may consciously not know any of this, but their larger selves do. Consequently, he said, we must be very careful when we intervene in someone's life, even when we think it is for their "own good."

To me, this seemed callous and a recipe for turning a blind eye to the world's problems. To this, he simply shrugged and remained silent.

When he finally spoke again, he told me that if I want to awaken all of humanity, I should awaken all of myself; if I want to eliminate the suffering of the world, then I should eliminate all that is dark and negative in myself. Truly, he said, the greatest gift I have to give the world is my own self-transformation.

Lama Tsering said one must be mindful in the use of one's acquired powers. The Buddha himself, he told me, viewed them as distractions to one's true spiritual path, and only engaged in them infrequently. He told me that, yes, with the proper training and concentration, the mind can manifest many wonderful and miraculous things. But he said one must be incredibly careful, for these can potentially be dangerous.

As if to emphasize his point, he related a story about a particular monk many years ago who created a tulpa. It was the monk's intention to use his tulpa as a servant—to assign mundane tasks to it so that the monk would be able to focus solely on his spiritual training.

Taylor stopped reading. He lowered the journal and furrowed his brow, a look of puzzlement on his face. What was a tulpa? He'd never heard the word. Havelock was writing as if the reader already knew. He flipped back several pages, scanning the text, searching for the term, assuming he had missed mention of it. But he couldn't find it anywhere. Frustrated, he flipped back to where he'd left off and continued reading.

At first, the tulpa was friendly, attentive, and obedient—the perfect companion for the monk. It was with him constantly, even learning to make the monk's tea. Unfortunately, the monk was not as adept as perhaps he should have been. His ability to control his mind was only partially developed. Consequently, not long after creating his tulpa, which took the form of a kinnara, a part human, part bird creature, the monk found himself prone to mindless daydreaming. One thought that persisted was that the tulpa was plotting against him. Although he knew it was absurd, he nonetheless persisted in this thought. Gradually the tulpa began to exhibit behaviors at odds with its initial friendliness and courtesy. It soon became mischievous and then downright naughty. This, of course, only fueled the monk's belief that the tulpa was out to get him, which, in turn, led to more bad behavior. The tulpa would deliberately pour hot tea on the monk's hand or hide his belongings. When the monk would get angry, the tulpa would get angry. Finally, this mischievousness turned into malevolence. The monk soon became convinced the tulpa was out to kill him. One night the monk woke up to discover the tulpa's hands around his neck, trying to strangle him. He fought with the creature and managed to fend it off. The tulpa ran off into the night, escaping the monastery.

The monk told the high lama the whole story and was thereby thoroughly admonished for playing around with something he should not have been playing around with. The high lama organized a search party to find and dissipate the tulpa, because the monk, through his undisciplined thoughts, had created a creature that was now harmful to the surrounding population—an evil-minded entity bent on creating misery and mayhem. And, sure enough, as the party ventured forth from the monastery, they began to hear tales of the creature's wickedness. They encountered peasants who had suffered the ravages of the tulpa. One man's livestock had been slaughtered, another man's wife had been molested, and a third man's winter food cache had been ransacked.

After several days of searching, the party finally cornered the creature in a canyon. The creature did not want to be dissipated so threw rocks at the lama, intending to do him great bodily harm. But the high lama was not a man to be easily dissuaded, and after much drama was able to dissipate the tulpa before it could do any more harm.

Taylor closed the journal and put it aside. He sat quietly for a moment, leaning back in his chair, mulling the story over in his mind.

Then, leaning forward, he reached across the desk and fired up the computer. Navigating onto the Internet, he typed the word "tulpa" into the Google search engine. Several entries popped up, and he clicked on the first link, which took him to a website called Worldreligions.com. Under the heading "Tibetan mysticism," Taylor found a brief mention of the term tulpa, which stated: "A term used in Tibetan Buddhism to describe a sentient being created through the power of thought. Also known as a 'thoughtform.'"

Taylor scratched his chin and read the entry again. It wasn't overly informative, so Taylor followed another link. This took him to Wikipedia, which contained an entire page on the concept of the tulpa. Like the previous webpage, it described the word's origin as Tibetan, though in Sanskrit the term "nirmita" was used, and went on to define it as "a magical emanation, or conjured thing, which is created by sheer mental discipline, or by a powerful concentration of thought. It is a thought that has materialized and taken physical form..."

Continuing his research, he soon discovered that the concept wasn't limited to Tibet but also featured in various sects of Buddhism and Hinduism, and even in Western occultist literature, where the term "familiar" was commonly used.

Taylor stood up and stepped away from the computer, his mind a flurry of thoughts. He paced the room, and then went over to the window and stood looking out into the night. The sky was surprisingly clear with a brilliant full moon shining above the trees. Wisps of ragged cloud drifted by, floating on a slight breeze. He furrowed his brow. Tulpas? Familiars? Was it possible such things existed? That one could create such beings with one's own mind? He shook his head. No, it was crazy, he told himself. He might as well have been contemplating the reality of ghosts and demons, of incubi and succubae. Such things didn't really exist. They were fodder for fantasy and horror writers and moviemakers. They weren't reality. Kate was right: There was a rational explanation for everything.

And yet...

He sat back down at his computer, staring blankly at the monitor. His mind spun with the implications. It was incredible—seemingly impossible—but he couldn't escape the possibility that perhaps what he was dealing with, in the form of Dorje and Fletcher/Harold Skimpole, were tulpas. Corporeal creatures created from pure thought.

Chapter 18

"I WANT TO THANK you so much for taking us in," Debra said. "I really didn't know what to do last night. Where to turn."

"I was just glad we could help," Taylor said. He dished her a plate of scrambled eggs he'd just made, and then poured two cups of coffee. He piled some eggs on his own plate and sat down at the kitchen table across from her. Pale morning light filtered through the window, and the aroma of breakfast lingered in the room.

"Is Havelock still sleeping?" Taylor asked.

She nodded. "Just so you know, I'm going to call to have the window repaired today. Once it is, we can move back, I promise."

"Stay as long as you like," he said. "It's not a big deal. We have room."

"Thanks." She was silent for a moment as she ate her eggs. "I'm also going to have deadbolts installed on all the doors." She paused, and sighing, put down her fork. "God, I've been racking my brains trying to figure out what that guy wanted with Dad. The fact that the police didn't catch him just makes me wonder if he's going to be back."

Her statement lingered in the air as they ate their eggs. Taylor was silent for a time, looking down at his plate. He finally looked up, hesitated briefly before asking, "Did you know Fletcher Hendrickson?"

Startled, Debra raised her head and lifted her eyebrows in astonishment. Mention of the name seemed momentarily to catch her off guard. "Fletcher Hendrickson! Of course." She paused. "Wait, let me rephrase that. What I mean is, I never actually met him because he was dead before I was born, but I certainly remember Dad talking about him. Dad used to talk about him a lot."

"Who was he?" Taylor asked.

"He was Dad's first grad student at the University of Virginia."

Taylor furrowed his brow. "I thought he taught at Berkeley."

"He did, but he had a short stint at Virginia before he went to NASA and then Berkeley. Anyway, Fletcher accompanied Dad on his first Nepal-Tibet expedition. He was tragically killed in Tibet."

"How'd he die?"

She took a sip of coffee. "That's a whole story unto itself. He was killed by the Chinese during the invasion."

"Really?"

Debra nodded. "He saved Dad's life. You obviously noticed Dad's limp, right?"

Taylor nodded.

"He hurt it when he and Fletcher were escaping from the Chinese. Fletcher basically carried Dad to safety before the Chinese killed him."

Taylor was astonished. "Sounds like quite a story," he said.

"It is."

Taylor took a sip of coffee. "I'd love to hear it.'

"Like I said, it happened during Dad's first expedition to Nepal. He was there to photograph the planet Venus."

Taylor nodded, remembering Havelock had told him the same thing.

"Anyway," Debra continued, "Dad and Fletcher had a chance to stay in one of the remote Tibetan monasteries right after the expedition ended. That's where Dad got his start with meditation and all that weird Tibetan mystical stuff."

"Weird, Tibetan mystical stuff?" Taylor raised an eyebrow, listening.

"Dad still talks about his time at that monastery," Debra said. "I don't know all the details, but the head lama had an enormous influence on his life. They stayed for several months but eventually left. Somewhere near the Nepalese border, they ran into a Chinese patrol. They narrowly escaped but Dad fell and broke his leg. Fractured it in several places. Fletcher got him across the border but was shot by the Chinese. Dad has always credited Fletcher with saving his life."

"Amazing story," Taylor said.

"Dad said it was the most difficult thing he ever did. They had to cross several high mountain passes in the driving snow. He said he was delirious most of the time, hobbling on a broken leg with no pain killers and half freezing to death. He said he thought he was going to die."

She stopped and studied Taylor for a moment. "Why are you asking about Fletcher? How on earth did you come across his name? Did Dad mention him to you?" She paused, shaking her head. "Fletcher

Hendrickson! God, I haven't thought about that name in years."

"I read about him in Havelock's journal."

"Of course," she said, frowning, her voice suddenly oozing with sarcasm. "He would've been in there, wouldn't he?"

Taylor noticed the tone in her voice. She had said it with a raw vehemence that surprised him.

Almost immediately, Debra gave an embarrassed smile, as if caught in some duplicity. "Sorry," she said. "I didn't exactly mean it like that. It's just—" She paused and shifted in her chair.

"I'm sorry," Taylor said. "I didn't mean to—"

"No," she said, waving a dismissive hand and shrugging. "It's all right. You already know some of our family's secrets. What's one more?" She sighed and paused to stare down at her coffee mug. When she looked back up there was an expression of resignation on her face. "Fletcher was more than just Dad's first grad student. According to my mother, he was also Dad's lover. It nearly broke up the marriage. Dad was traumatized from Fletcher's death and everything else he'd seen in Tibet. When he returned, he fell into a deep depression. It was a depression that nearly broke him. Of course, I didn't know about any of this until I became an adult. Mother finally told me the whole story just before she died."

Taylor nodded. "I see."

"Mom said Fletcher was the love of Dad's life. That he was the only person Dad truly ever loved."

"Must have been hard on your mother," Taylor said.

"It was, but they persevered in the marriage. Made it work somehow. Of course, Dad never forgot Fletcher. Never forgot what the Chinese Communists did to him. And he's harbored an intense hatred toward the Chinese ever since. He used to get into shouting matches with his left-wing colleagues at Berkeley when Mao was all the rage among the intellectuals. At one point, in fact, he nearly lost his job when he wrote an unflattering op-ed about Chinese foreign policy that was published in the campus paper. Apparently, his colleagues wouldn't speak to him for months."

Taylor was silent for a time, digesting all this information. "Did you ever see a photo of Fletcher?" he asked.

"A photo?" She shook her head. "No, I never did. As you might imagine, Mother wasn't too fond of the subject. She made Dad promise never to speak of him in her presence, nor mine. You might say they reached an agreement. That's why I never knew much about him growing up. But Dad being Dad, he broke the agreement every once in a while and talked about him, at least when Mother wasn't around. I just don't think he could help it."

"So, you never knew what he looked like?"

"No, why? I mean, Dad briefly described him as a skinny young man with blond hair. But that's about it."

Taylor nodded and took a sip of coffee. Outside he heard the wind soughing in the big redwood tree.

Debra finished her coffee and eggs and stood up. There was something in her demeanor that suggested what she had told Taylor had taken a lot of effort. That things had been bottled up inside her for far too long. She looked drained. But, after a moment, the color returned to her cheeks. "Speaking of, I should check up on Dad and make those phone calls. Thanks for breakfast." She pushed in her chair and sauntered off down the hallway.

Taylor remained sitting for a while, thinking about all that Debra had told him, taking occasional sips of his coffee, and staring out the window.

Later that morning, Taylor drove down Oceanport's main drag, the back of his Jeep loaded with grocery bags. He'd stopped at the market and picked up some extra food for the house, figuring he'd have a few more mouths to feed for at least the next couple of days.

His cell phone rang. He glanced at it and was surprised to see it was from Tim Mahony. He swung over to the side of the road and answered it.

"Tim, what's up?"

"Taylor, glad to get a hold of you. Got a minute?"

"Sure."

"The results have come back from the autopsy."

Taylor paused, his anticipation growing. "And?"

"I shouldn't be telling you this," Tim said, "so I'm relying on your discretion, but your dog theory may have some validity. Bite marks on the victim were consistent with a large dog or a wolf. Not a cougar. So, I wanted to ask you some more questions about your neighbor's dog."

"Of course," Taylor said. "I'd be glad to help."

They proceeded to discuss Dorje for the next fifteen minutes. Taylor reiterated what he had already told Tim the last time they talked and added the additional bits of information he'd learned since—especially what 'Bernie the gun guy' had told him.

"How big was this dog again?" Tim asked.

"Well over two hundred pounds. Probably close to three hundred."

"Christ," Tim said, "that is big. Like a Saint Bernard?"

"Bigger."

Taylor heard Tim whistle through his teeth. "Sounds like a monster."

Taylor didn't answer but thought Tim might be closer to the truth than he knew.

"Anyway," Tim said, "here's the really weird part. We collected some animal fur from the crime scene and sent it out to be tested for DNA fingerprinting. Try to figure out what this thing is, you know? The results that came back were—" he paused.

Taylor just listened. He could hear the sound of his own heart as his curiosity mounted.

"Well," Tim said, "they were odd."

"How so?"

"Like I said, I shouldn't be telling you this so for Chrissake don't breathe a word of it." He heard Tim pause again. "The hairs were protein, but of a type that is apparently unrecognizable. The amino acid sequence was all over the place."

"What do you mean? I don't understand."

"Neither do I, really," Tim said, "but apparently the animal fur was not recognized as keratin. Remember your high school biology? Hair is a protein called keratin. Well, this wasn't recognized as keratin."

"What was it then?"

"That's just the point. The examiners don't know."

"But it was protein?"

"Sort of."

"That makes no sense." Taylor paused. "So, I assume the DNA fingerprinting went nowhere."

"That's right."

Taylor furrowed his brow. "Run that by me one more time. The hair was some type of protein but not keratin. But it doesn't look like any protein they've ever seen?"

"Yes."

"But the teeth marks are indicative of a dog or wolf?"

"Yes."

"Well," Taylor said, "maybe the lab just screwed up. Or maybe the hairs got contaminated."

"That's possible, I guess. But they were collected according to every procedure in the book. I was there. And the lab is really reliable. We've used them numerous times in the past and never had a problem."

"Strange."

"I'll say. Anyway, we're going on the premise this thing is a rabid dog since there aren't any wolves in the state."

"As far as we know."

"Yeah, as far as we know. All right, I gotta go, bro. Let me know if anything weird happens in your neck of the woods."

Before Tim could hang up, Taylor said, "Speaking of weird, you already heard about the attempted break in at my neighbor's house last night, right?"

"He's the one owned the dog, right?"

"The same."

"Weird coincidence."

Taylor was silent.

"Okay," Tim said. "I gotta go. Talk to you later."

Taylor clicked off the phone. He sat for a moment. This was just getting weirder and weirder. And, no, he didn't think this was a coincidence. Not by a long shot.

Taylor left town and drove north along Highway 101. The road, which ran right along the coast, was slick from the heavy marine layer and the sky was overcast, threatening rain. A strong onshore wind was blowing from the northwest, buffeting the car. He drove a ways, and then impulsively, pulled off into a turnout that overlooked the water. He exited the car and strode up to the edge of the cliff. The smell of salt was heavy in the air and below him, the rocks lay exposed with the low tide, slimy with sea grass and seaweed.

The wind struck him in the face, and he shivered. He zipped up his fleece jacket against the chill and thrust both hands into the pockets of his jeans. He gazed out at the water, his brow furrowed in thought, watching the wind whip at the surface, raising whitecaps.

How on earth was he going to convince anyone of the validity of his theory about tulpas and familiars? That they might be dealing with forces here that were beyond all rational understanding? Who in their right mind would ever believe him? Debra hadn't bothered to read her father's journal, so she was completely ignorant of any such notions. And Kate had already expressed the opinion she thought a supernatural explanation was a product of a feeble, easily duped mind. Tim, of course, was just being a good cop, following leads wherever they led, though Taylor doubted he'd have any patience for a supernatural explanation, either.

He took a deep breath, collecting himself. What Taylor did know was this: Things were getting dangerous. Hell, they already were dangerous. A man had been killed and two women, Ed Hsing's widow and Debra, had been harassed. What was next?

He squinted out at the horizon, thinking back over events. When he had first encountered Dorje and the young man, both had seemed harmless, odd maybe, but harmless. Dorje had been a big, lazy dog and Fletcher a naïve young man. But they had changed. Both had become...what was the word? He furrowed his brow, thinking. Malevolent. That was it. Malevolent. It seemed a strong word to use but Taylor couldn't think of a better one. The dog had become downright vicious and murderous, and the young man irascible, combative, and, considering the attempted break in, even violent. Why? What had caused them to turn? To change? Taylor believed it corresponded with Havelock's stroke, though he couldn't say exactly how or why.

If these things really were supernatural beings, then what could be done? Dorje had been shot on a few occasions but had apparently come away unscathed. And though Debra had fended Fletcher off, she really hadn't done him any harm.

The story of the monk he'd read about in Havelock's journal—the one who had created the kinnara tulpa—suddenly flashed in his mind. How had they gotten rid of it? Havelock had written that they had "dissipated" it. What did that mean? Was such a thing possible? He shook his head. None of these were questions he could answer. The bottom line was: He needed help. But where to find it? To whom could he turn?

The clouds thickened overhead and soon the first drops of rain began to fall.

Throwing up his collar, he got back in his car and drove off. The rain began to intensify as he drove east, forcing him to turn on the wipers. They thumped back and forth like a metronome, slapping away the rain.

Chapter 19

THE DOOR TO THE kitchen banged open as Taylor stumbled in, clutching a bag of groceries in each arm. A gust of wind followed him, blowing against his legs and spattering rain drops on the floor. He caught the door with his heel and slammed it shut.

Debra was sitting at the kitchen table, tapping away on her laptop. A hot cup of tea was at her elbow. She looked up.

"Wet out there?"

Taylor nodded and dumped the bags down on the counter. He took off his raincoat and hung it on the rack by the door.

He gazed around the room, noticed that the kitchen was immaculate. The dishes had been washed and neatly stacked on the counter. And the floors had been mopped to a deep shine.

"Looks great in here."

"Thought I'd earn my keep. It's the least I can do."

Havelock was sitting in his now familiar wheelchair, staring vacantly out the window. His eyes were open, but his eyelids were heavy and drooping. He was wearing a bathrobe, which was partially open, revealing the few strands of wispy white hair on his chest. As always, he looked completely in his own world—like a soul adrift at sea.

Taylor turned back to Debra. "How's everything going?" he asked.

She nodded. "Fine. Just trying to get some work done. Oh, by the way, I was able to get hold of a window repair guy. He's coming this afternoon, so we'll have the windows repaired and be able to move back tomorrow morning."

"What about the locks?"

"I arranged that as well. A locksmith is coming tomorrow." She glanced at the grocery bags. "I hope you didn't go to any extra expense on our account."

"No, not at all." He proceeded to put away the groceries and then sat down across from her. He glanced at Havelock and nodded towards the old man. "How's he doing today?"

"About the same."

Taylor cleared his throat. "I wanted to ask you about your dad's meditation practices. Earlier you mentioned he was into all that 'weird Tibetan mysticism.'"

"Yes, he was." She closed her laptop. "He used to meditate for hours." She paused, frowning. "Actually, it began to place a strain on the family."

"How so?"

"His interest in Tibetan mysticism increasingly took him away from his familial duties. He'd disappear and sit in the dark for hours. It made him into a much more distant and absent father than he already was."

Taylor furrowed his brow. "What was he trying to accomplish, do you think?"

"With all his meditation?"

He nodded.

"I never really knew," she shrugged. "But he was dedicated to it, whatever it was he was trying to do. He was certainly more dedicated to it than being a father. Anyway, when I went off to college, I never really looked back. After graduation, I went off to nursing school. Did that for a while, then started my own business. Got married and then divorced—basically got on with my life. But Dad just got increasingly more reclusive and secretive. When Mom died, I thought he might want to reconnect."

"When was that?"

"Oh, gosh, about twenty years ago. He moved up here about that time. I tried to visit him, but he made it abundantly clear he didn't want my company. So, I just ended up calling him on occasion. First weekly, then monthly, then every few months. Then eventually once or twice a year."

"And you never knew what he was doing all this time? What he was up to."

"No, I didn't have a clue. I still don't." She shook her head. "I didn't even know he had a dog. How pathetic is that?" She turned, fixing her gaze on Havelock. "I guess the best I can do now is look after him until—" She hesitated, and shook her head slowly, as if she didn't want to finish the sentence.

Taylor turned to look at Havelock. The old man was sitting quietly, seemingly oblivious.

She turned back and started to take a sip of tea, but abruptly put the mug back down. "You know what," she said, "all this reminiscing about my past just jogged my memory. Like I said, I never knew what exactly Dad was up to when he went to meditate, but I do remember this one time when we were living in Berkeley. Dad had been meditating all afternoon in his study. Being a typical little kid, I was curious to know what he was doing in there so when he went out, I crept inside. I saw all these anatomy books."

"Anatomy books?"

She nodded. "Yeah, you know, the ones with pictures and diagrams of body parts. I noticed all the books were open to diagrams of human arms. I remember that distinctly. When Dad came back, he yelled at me and told me to leave. I asked him about all those books. The only thing he said was, 'I want to get it right.'"

Taylor sat for a long moment, not speaking, just mulling over everything Debra had told him. He rubbed his chin reflectively. The sound of the rain was loud against the roof.

"What do you think he meant?" Debra asked.

He looked at her. "You've never read your Dad's expedition journal?"

She shook her head. "No, why?"

"It might help you understand."

———

Taylor couldn't sleep. He lay awake in bed, tossing and turning, reacting to the house's every little creak and groan as if each sound was evidence of someone trying to break in. But he was relatively certain he'd done his best to secure the house; he'd bolted all doors, shut and locked all windows, and loaded the shotgun. He wasn't sure there was anything else he could do. And it wasn't as if he was expecting a break-in, but he certainly wasn't ruling one out either.

The rain had stopped earlier in the night and now a curious silence filled the house. Unfortunately, the silence only exacerbated his anxious feelings, and he couldn't seem to dismiss the intense sense of foreboding that gripped him. He turned on his side, then his stomach, and then his side again. Finally, he lay on his back and stared up at the ceiling, into the darkness, trying his best to shut down his thoughts. But he was too agitated.

When it was obvious he wasn't going back to sleep any time soon, he sat up and flung off the covers. Swinging his legs over the side of the bed and planting bare feet on the hardwood floor, he glanced at the digital clock. It was a little past three in the morning. He ran a hand through his hair and switched on the reading lamp.

He shivered in the cold and rubbed his hands together. Standing up, he padded across the floor and grabbed a bathrobe from the closet. He slipped into his sandals and left the bedroom, walking down the hallway. He was about to go downstairs when he stopped. He turned and proceeded to the end of the hallway. The door to the guest room was locked. He put his ear to the door, listening. He could hear Havelock snoring. Nodding in satisfaction, he retraced his steps and quietly descended the staircase.

In the living room, he started a fire to take the chill off. Once he had it going, he sat down in the big leather chair. He rubbed his chin and stared at the fire, watching the flames engulf the wood, the logs crackle and pop.

Everything seemed to be all right at the moment. The house was quiet, and Debra and Havelock seemed safe and secure. But Taylor nonetheless felt on edge. He couldn't shake the feeling that somehow the house was under siege. He felt that something—or someone—was watching from the shadows just waiting to strike. He was suddenly glad Kate had left for the city; he didn't want her to be in any danger.

His mind drifted to what had been occupying his thoughts all day, namely, the possibility that Dorje and Fletcher were tulpas. That Havelock had created them out of pure thought energy. If that was the case, what could possibly be done? How could one stop a thought?

He needed help, needed to consult with someone. Someone who understood such things. Someone who might be able to tell him what the hell was going on, and, importantly, how these things could be stopped.

He wondered if anyone at Humboldt State—some professor—was knowledgeable about Tibetan esoterica. Maybe there was someone in the anthropology or religious studies departments who might be able to supply him with information.

He went into the study and sat down in front of his computer. On the Internet, he quickly found the Humboldt State website and navigated to the anthropology department. He clicked on the icon labeled "faculty" and scrolled down the list of professors, reading their bios and particular areas of study, but didn't see anyone who had an expertise in Tibetan Buddhism. Most were North American specialists, though there was one professor who specialized in the cultures of Southeast Asia, though her specialty seemed to be on economics rather than religion. Frustrated, he sat back and sighed. He switched over to the religious studies department and scrutinized the faculty. It was apparently a small department with only three professors—one of whom was an emeritus. One, however, caught his attention. He noticed that a Dr. Stephen Rohrbacher was a specialist in Buddhism. He taught courses in world religions, Buddhism, Zen, Hinduism, and apparently was a specialist in Sanskrit texts. He perused the man's course list and found that one of his classes was called "Buddhism in India and Tibet." He read the course description:

> *"This course familiarizes the student with the historical origins and development of Buddhism in India and its transformation in Tibet. It includes exploration of Theravada, Mahayana, and Tantric Buddhism, with attention to the diverse spiritual practices of mystics, devotees, and philosophers."*

Taylor clicked on the man's email address and composed an email explaining he was a writer, which was true, who was doing research for a novel that included tulpas—which wasn't true. Would Dr. Rohrbacher be willing to sit down for an interview? He sent it off with a click of his mouse, and then sat back, staring at the screen. As much as he would've liked to be straight with the professor, he figured doing so would only make him sound like a complete nutcase.

Chapter 20

THREE DAYS LATER, TAYLOR pulled his Jeep into one of the multi-story parking structures on the Humboldt State campus. Maneuvering into a space, he killed the engine and dug into his pocket for the scrap of paper on which he'd written Dr. Rohrbacher's address: 243 Hardt Hall. He glanced at it and then checked his watch. He was ten minutes early for his four o'clock appointment. He quickly consulted the campus map he'd acquired at the entrance kiosk and grabbed his notebook and pen. Exiting the car, he walked across the lot and out onto campus.

It was a cold, blustery day, and Taylor was wearing his fleece jacket zipped up to his neck. The wind rushed through the pines and redwoods that were scattered throughout the campus in dense clusters, kicking up leaves and debris.

The scent of pine drifted in the air as he followed a path that cut through the main quad. Tall brick buildings lined either side of him, most of them with architecture reminiscent of the 1960s or 1970s, though a few looked wholly modern. He passed the occasional student hurrying along, backpack loaded with books. A few others stood on the grass of the quad, talking or laughing. Overall, though, there didn't seem to be a lot of activity and the campus seemed relatively quiet.

He followed the map to the northern part of the campus where Hardt Hall, a three-story brick structure, was set behind a grove of redwoods. He went through the wide glass doors and consulted the registry, where he saw Dr. Rohrbacher's name listed. He ascended the stairs to the second floor and walked down a long hallway, noting the office numbers on the doors as he passed.

He wasn't happy about feeling he had to lie to Dr. Rohrbacher about the nature of his visit but felt there was no other choice. He'd thought about it all last night and had decided that, in this particular case, deliberate subterfuge was the best course of action.

He finally came to room number 243 and knocked.

"Come in!" came a booming voice from inside the room.

Taylor opened the door and poked his head inside. "Dr. Rohrbacher?"

At the far end of the room, a man was sitting at his desk, his face blocked by the back of a computer monitor. When he stood up, Taylor was surprised to see a very large man with broad shoulders and a barrel-like torso but with an alert, friendly expression. He had white hair and a well-trimmed beard and was wearing glasses. For some reason, Taylor had expected to see a smaller man, though he couldn't have said why he thought that. By contrast, Dr. Rohrbacher, with his shock of white hair and broad shoulders, reminded Taylor of a polar bear, albeit one that had a Ph.D. and a string of published papers to his credit.

"Come in, come in," the man said, gesturing at Taylor to come forward, his face breaking into a wide, genial grin. "You must be the writer."

Taylor stepped into the office. "Thanks for taking the time to see me."

"Not at all," the man said, "glad I could accommodate you." He extended his hand over his desk. "I'm Steve Rohrbacher."

"Taylor Hamilton."

The two men shook hands. Dr. Rohrbacher gestured at the empty chair in front of his desk. "Please, sit down."

Taylor took a seat and placed his notebook and pen on his lap. He glanced around him, noticing that the office was cramped and cluttered. Nearly all available wall space was occupied by bookshelves. On the desk was a computer with a wide-screen monitor, the rim of which was encircled with yellow Post-it notes. The desk was littered with books and papers.

Dr. Rohrbacher sidled around the end of his desk to a small side table on which sat a coffee maker. He lifted a full pot and turned to Taylor. "I just made a fresh pot. Want a cup?"

"Thank you," Taylor said.

"I have to confess," Dr. Rohrbacher said, pouring two mugs of coffee, "I was surprised to get your email. I usually don't get requests like yours. I once got a request from a journalist. But I don't think I've ever gotten a request from a novelist. This is a first. Cream and sugar?"

"Just black."

Dr. Rohrbacher handed one of the mugs to Taylor and then settled his large frame into his chair. He glanced out the window. "Windy outside, isn't it?" Turning back, he said, "So tell me, what's the novel about? Besides tulpas, I mean."

Taylor had already anticipated such a question and so had concocted a brief premise. "It takes place in the 1950s in Tibet," he said. "During a scientific expedition. An avalanche strands some of the expedition members in a remote monastery where they're menaced by a tulpa."

"Sounds exciting." He paused. "I tried to write a novel once when I was younger. I wasn't very good at it. All that pacing and character development. I've stuck with what I know best: academic papers." He leaned forward. "Anyway, I know you didn't come here to learn about my failed attempts at novel writing. You want to know about tulpas."

"That's right. I want the depiction of them in the novel to be as authentic as possible." Taylor flipped open his notebook.

"Well," Dr. Rohrbacher said, rubbing his hands together, "it's a fascinating subject. In a nutshell, there are practitioners of some very esoteric sects within Tibetan Buddhism who believe that with enough mental energy and concentration, a three-dimensional entity can be created."

"You mean an actual person?"

"That's right," Dr. Rohrbacher said. "Or an animal. Or a monster, for that matter. That's what they believe, at least."

"Can these things think independently? Are they sentient?"

"There's some debate about that."

"What do you mean?"

"Well, some people think they can only respond to the thoughts of their creators, while others believe that, over time, they gradually develop the capacity for independent thought."

"What do you think?"

He chuckled. "To be perfectly honest, I have no idea."

"I still don't fully understand how tulpas are created," Taylor said. "You mentioned mental energy and concentration."

"What I suppose I really wanted to say was visualization. Intense visualization. The process involves imagining something to the extent that you can picture it in three-dimensions, and importantly be able to hold that image without distraction. It's actually a very difficult thing to do."

Taylor was silent for a second. Then he shook his head. "It just sounds so unbelievable."

"For us Westerners, yes, it does. But you've got to remember that for Tibetans, visualization practices are taught in childhood. It's something that is taught at a very early age."

"I can understand visualization as an aid to concentration exercises, but literally bringing an image—a thought—to life sounds like science fiction."

"I agree. It sounds utterly fantastic, but I think that has to do with our particular cultural worldview. How we were brought up to view reality."

"What do you mean?" Taylor asked.

"In this case, we're dealing with two entirely different ways of looking at the world. The Tibetan and the Western. One says that thoughts can be made into actual things and the other that the idea is impossible, preposterous even."

Taylor paused. "But there must be a way to objectively evaluate these two worldviews. How can something as intangible as a thought be made tangible? It seems to me that the laws of physics are immutable. They supersede any cultural beliefs."

"But how much do we really know about these so-called 'laws?' Take quantum mechanics, for instance. We used to think nothing could exceed the speed of light, but we now know that 'instantaneous action at a distance' characterizes most quantum particles. Does this mean that the speed of light idea has to be reevaluated or that something else is going on? Frankly, we don't know."

Taylor knew from his readings in physics that the professor was referring to "quantum entanglement"—a concept in physics whereby two objects, such as electrons, while separated in space, nonetheless can influence one another. When one is acted upon, the other experiences the same action at exactly the same moment, seemingly violating the "law" of the speed of light.

Dr. Rohrbacher continued. "My point is, it's becoming increasingly clear that the more we discover—the more we learn about the nature of reality—the more puzzling everything appears to be. As we learn more about the physical world, many of our supposed laws have to be dropped, revised or changed."

"But that's how science works, isn't it? It's constantly changing and revising itself."

"That's exactly my point," Dr. Rohrbacher said. "Frequently what we consider 'laws' can change as we gather more information, making the concept of immutable laws irrelevant, or at the very least questionable. What if immutable laws are simply relics of a particular age and its level of technology? Who's to say the Tibetan view of thoughts is wrong? What if on some level—like the quantum level—they are tangible. And, one day, through scientific experimentation we discover that they are. Quantum mechanics has already been hinting at the prospect that consciousness can affect matter on a sub-atomic level. Take the placebo effect, for example. No one's ever been able to explain it in rational terms. And yet its efficacy is proven in test after test. Or the famous double-slit experiment. That's the classic example, of course."

Taylor sat quietly, thinking about what the professor had told him.

"We always get so caught up in who's right," Dr. Rohrbacher went on. "Is it the Tibetans, or us? Maybe we're both right. Hell, maybe we're both wrong. Is such a judgment even useful?" He paused. "Maybe the better question to ask is which worldview better helps the individual achieve his or her goals, become a more productive, happier, more well-adjusted, useful individual. Maybe the world can be explained in multiple ways, each valid."

Taylor considered that.

"Have you ever heard of the writer Alexandra David-Néel?" Dr. Rohrbacher asked.

Taylor was surprised at the seemingly abrupt change in subject. He shook his head.

"She was a French travel writer and Buddhist scholar who traveled to Tibet in the 1920s and 1930s. She wrote several books, which were popular at the time. Her most famous book was called *Magic and Mystery in Tibet*. Offhand, I can't remember the names of the other ones. But you can look them up online. She studied with several prominent lamas during her travels, and actually became a practicing Buddhist. In *Magic and Mystery*, she claimed to have created a tulpa during a journey through the mountains. Apparently, it was a jolly little monk. She described it as a sort of Friar Tuck-like character."

"How did she create it?"

"Through intense concentration and visualization. At first, it was only in her imagination, kind of like an imaginary friend. But gradually, as she continued to feed it energy, it took on objective form. Soon her companions began to see it as well. It would appear from time to time around camp. They started asking who the stranger was. At first, the monk was friendly and jolly."

Taylor could see where this was going. "But it began to change?"

Dr. Rohrbacher nodded. "It began to take on a sinister aspect and developed its own personality, which apparently was quite different from what David-Néel had intended. So she was forced to dissolve it."

"How did she dissolve it?" Taylor asked.

"Unfortunately, she's pretty vague about that, as I recall." He stood up and walked over to the nearest bookshelf. Adjusting his glasses, he scanned the volumes. "I have her book somewhere." After a moment, he slipped out a small hardbound book with a tattered and yellowed dust jacket. "Here it is."

Taylor watched as the professor opened the book and thumbed through its pages, a frown of concentration on his face.

"Let's see if I can find that passage," he said. He continued thumbing through the book. "Okay, here it is." He began reading.

"I ought to have let the phenomenon follow its course, but the presence of that unwanted companion began to prove trying to my nerves; it turned into a 'day-nightmare.' Moreover, I was beginning to plan my journey to Lhasa and needed a quiet brain devoid of other preoccupations, so I decided to dissolve the phantom. I succeeded, but only after six months of hard struggle."

Dr. Rohrbacher looked up. "See what I mean? She's pretty vague, except to say that it took a six-month struggle. Her creature was pretty tenacious of life. It obviously didn't want to be dissolved."

Taylor thought back on the story of the kinnara tulpa he'd read about in Havelock's journal. Its dissolution had also proven a very difficult struggle.

Dr. Rohrbacher flipped forward a few pages, then backward, running his index finger down the text. "Here's another interesting tidbit," he said. "She goes on to say that tulpas have the ability to free themselves from their maker's control. Kind of like an unruly teenager, and that titanic struggles have taken place between these creatures and their creators, sometimes resulting in the death of the creator."

Taylor pondered this for a moment.

Dr. Rohrbacher slapped the book closed and replaced it in the bookshelf. He sat down at his desk, took a drink of coffee, and then chuckled, shaking his head. "All in all, probably not a good idea to create one of these things."

"Do you possibly think that story has any validity?"

Dr. Rohrbacher looked at him. "Are you asking if I think these creatures are real?"

Taylor nodded.

"Well, having never seen one, I must plead agnostic on the subject." He paused, his face thoughtful. He leaned forward, as if to add gravity to his words, and put his elbows on the table. "But I don't necessarily dismiss them out of hand. I think it's far too easy and ethnocentric to say that it's all just superstition. Like I said earlier, the Tibetans have an altogether different way of looking at the world from us Westerners. Not necessarily wrong, simply different. How they view reality is just as valid for them as how we view it. Perception often is reality."

After a moment, Taylor said, "I've read that tulpas, or things like them, are mentioned in Western folklore, too."

"That's an excellent point. Yes, our own folklore, especially European folklore, talks about similar creatures."

"You mean 'familiars,' right?"

Dr. Rohrbacher grinned. "You've done your research, I see. Yes, familiar spirits have a long and rich history in Europe. They were long seen as the consorts and helpers of witches and warlocks and greatly feared. The Golem of medieval Prague was one such creature. The famous Rabbi Loew created him to guard the Jewish ghetto from anti-Semitic attack. There was also the war dog of Prince Rupert."

Taylor perked up at the mention of a dog. "Who was Prince Rupert?"

"He was a German nobleman who fought on the side of the Royalists in the English Civil War of the seventeenth century," Dr. Rohrbacher replied. "The dog would charge into battle at the side of the Prince and cause havoc. The Parliamentarian troops he fought against were reportedly terrified of it."

"And he supposedly created the dog?"

Dr. Rohrbacher nodded. "Yes. According to the Parliamentarian propaganda of the time, Rupert had magical powers and was aligned with the devil. He supposedly sold his soul to the devil in order to create the dog. Or something like that."

"Is there a description of the dog?"

"Wood carvings of the time depict a very large, white dog with a vicious temperament." He grinned. "A real Cujo."

Taylor sat perfectly still, just listening as Dr. Rohrbacher went on to describe the legend of the dog in greater detail. The dog, named Boy, was supposedly invulnerable to attack, completely tireless, and singularly loyal to Rupert.

"You also mentioned the Golem," Taylor said. "What was that?"

"A huge, quasi-human creature that Rabbi Loew created and told to guard the Jewish ghetto in Prague. Kill anyone who tried to attack."

"What time period was this?"

"The sixteenth century. The Golem legend forms a whole series of stories and folktales. There was even a silent movie made about it in the 1920s."

Taylor paused, tapping his pen against his notebook. "Any modern cases of tulpas?" he asked.

Dr. Rohrbacher sat back in his chair and brought both hands together, steepling his fingers. "Well," he said, "I once ran across a very odd account in, of all things, a medical journal."

Taylor raised his eyebrows, his curiosity piqued.

"It happened at the San Diego Naval Hospital in the late 1940s during the last days of World War II. A young navy seaman was brought to the hospital after suffering terrible burns during a kamikaze attack in the Pacific. He kept telling the doctors and nurses over and over that they needed to be careful when they worked on him or otherwise his polar bear would 'get them.'"

"Sounds like he was delirious."

"The strange thing is," Dr. Rohrbacher continued, "a number of medical personnel claimed to have caught glimpses of a giant, angry polar bear when the young man was in pain. The top of its head and its shoulders would appear, but it couldn't quite manifest completely. It was like it was trying to come alive in the hospital room."

"And this was in a medical journal, you said?"

Dr. Rohrbacher nodded. "I know it sounds crazy."

"How many people witnessed this?"

"A handful, apparently. Doctors and nurses."

Taylor gave an amazed shake of his head. "What finally happened to the young man?"

"He died of his wounds. He'd been so severely burned, he didn't recover."

"Incredible story."

"By the way," Dr. Rohrbacher said, "if you're interested in doing further research on tulpas, there's a Tibetan center down in Big Sur that you might want to check out. It's the real deal, I can assure you. Not some American hippie hybrid. Actually, it's a working Tibetan monastery, but they allow visitors. I've sent several of my students down there on research assignments. It's called the Maitreya Center."

Chapter 21

ON THE DRIVE BACK, Taylor mulled over his conversation with the professor. As crazy as it sounded, he was becoming increasingly convinced that Fletcher and Dorje were tulpas—creatures created by Havelock's mind. He thought it might be a good idea to talk with someone at the Tibetan organization in Big Sur. They might understand how to dissolve the creatures or at least provide help.

When he got back to the house, he was surprised to see Kate's Prius parked in the driveway. He pulled next to it and parked. Climbing out, he locked the door and walked to the front of the house. Still absorbed in his thoughts, his chin buried in the collar of his fleece, he almost didn't hear Kate's voice.

"Where have you been?"

The voice startled him, and he drew to a halt, looking up. Kate was standing on the front porch, holding a wine glass. To his surprise, she was wearing a single-piece, figure-hugging dress with a scooped neck that displayed the pleasing curves of her cleavage. He remembered the dress, though he hadn't seen her in it in a long while. He'd bought it for her during one of their romantic weekend getaways.

"What are you doing here?" Taylor asked, staring at her.

"Is that any way to greet the love of your life?" Kate said with a mock pout.

"I just didn't expect you to be home. I thought you'd be tied up at work all week."

"I got a brief reprieve. I got two nights off, but I have to go back on Sunday."

He walked up to the front steps. "How come you didn't call and let me know?"

She grinned. "I wanted to surprise you." She motioned for him to come inside. "C'mon in out of the wind and have a drink."

Taylor hopped up the steps and gave her a kiss on the cheek. "It's good to see you." His eyes ran up and down her figure. "You look fantastic."

"That's better," she said.

He followed her inside and was immediately surprised by the savory aroma of sautéing garlic. He looked around. The lights were subdued and the fireplace blazing. There were two long-stemmed wine glasses and an open bottle of wine on the coffee table in the living room.

"Pour yourself a glass," she said, noticing his gaze. "I'm making dinner."

He did a double take. "*You're* making dinner?"

She glared at him. "Don't be sarcastic."

"What are you making?"

"Pasta carbonara."

He walked over to the table and picked up the wine bottle by the neck, scrutinizing the label. It was a Beaujolais they had bought during a wine tasting trip to the Napa Valley several years ago. He poured himself a glass as Kate hustled off to the kitchen. He stood drinking the wine and staring into the fire, his thoughts still occupied with the events of the day. A whole host of sounds emanated from the kitchen, clanking pots, the opening and closing of the refrigerator door, and boiling water.

"You need any help?" he called out.

"No, I'm fine. Just make yourself comfortable."

He took a sip of the wine, noticing the hint of cranberry. He swallowed and then took a deep breath, felt himself relaxing. Taking off his coat, he tossed it over a chair and walked to the fireplace. He warmed his hands against the flames. Outside a strong gust of wind roared through the trees, and the walls of the house creaked in response.

Twenty minutes later, Kate poked her head out of the kitchen. "Dinner's ready."

They adjourned to the dining room where Taylor found another surprise. Kate had placed two candles on the table, their lights flickering in the semi-darkness. She had also arranged the table with a white linen tablecloth and put out their best silverware.

As Taylor seated himself, he asked, "So what's the occasion?"

Kate served him a plate of pasta and topped off his wine glass. "Do I need a reason to indulge my man?"

"Not at all," he grinned. "In fact, I encourage it."

"I just thought it'd be nice. We haven't really had a chance to spend a decent night together in a while."

He nodded sincerely. "It is, babe. Thank you." He twisted his fork around in the pasta and lifted it up to his mouth, taking a bite. He chewed slowly, savoring all the delicate array of flavors.

She sat down and looked across the table at him. "How is it?"

He swallowed and took a sip of wine to wash it down. "Really good. Excellent."

A sly smile crossed her face and she adjusted her glasses. "I know last week we planned something similar, but events intervened. So, I thought why not tonight?"

Taylor perked up. "I like where this is headed," he said. He took a sip of wine and winked at her.

"Just hold your horses," she said. "You have to eat first."

They spent the next hour eating, sipping wine, talking and laughing. It reminded Taylor of the first several months of their courtship when they didn't care about anything, except each other. He was the proverbial struggling writer working for an alternative city newspaper and trying to publish his first novel, and she had just gotten out of law school and was nosing around for work. Despite their shared poverty, it had been a wonderful and magical time—a time, perhaps ironically, made more magical by the fact that they didn't have much money, that they only had each other and their respective dreams. Now, as Taylor stuffed pasta into his mouth and sipped wine, he realized how good it felt to eat a home-cooked meal, enjoy Kate's company, and, at least for a little while, bask in the moment, allowing things to flow naturally without thinking too deeply about anything.

Finally, when the candles had burned low, Kate stood up and sidled around the table. She approached him slowly, her hips swaying. Without a word, she placed her hand lightly on his shoulder. The sensation sent waves of desire coursing through him. He looked up at her, saw her face in the subdued lighting, the mouth partially open, the slight elevation of her breathing, the wide dark eyes expectant. He stood up and enveloped her in his arms. They kissed. A flood of arousal coursed through him as their lips pressed together hungrily. She broke away from him and leaned down to blow out the candle. Then, spinning back around, she grabbed his hand and hastily led him to the bedroom.

Taylor gradually became aware of Kate's slow, rhythmic breathing. He opened his eyes and rolled over. Kate was sleeping on her side, her back to him, her shoulders rising and falling with each breath.

He gazed at her, noting the pleasing way her hair spilled onto her shoulder in complete disarray. He rolled over onto his back and rubbed his eyes. For a moment he relived the evening—the delicious pasta dinner, far too many glasses of wine, and the love-making that had rapidly devolved into something resembling the frenzied rutting of two sex-starved teenagers. The whole thing had been wonderful, like a giant release of tensions that had been pent up for much too long. Taylor had certainly needed it, and he suspected Kate, with all the recent stress in her life, had needed it as well.

He propped himself up on an elbow and reached over, gently stroking her shoulder. She stirred slightly, muttered something, and then promptly fell back asleep. He sighed in disappointment. There wasn't going to be a second round. He glanced over her shoulder at the digital clock on the side table. It was a little after four in the morning.

Taylor sat up, careful not to wake Kate, and slipped out of bed. His boxer shorts lay on the ground, and he pulled them on. Then he grabbed a shirt from the drawer and crept silently out of the bedroom and down the hallway to the study. He fired up the computer and typed the web address of the Maitreya Center Dr. Rohrbacher had given him. Soon he was reading about the Tibetan retreat in Big Sur. It was located in a secluded valley just east of Highway 1 in Big Sur, among the rugged Santa Lucia Mountains. A community of monks lived there full time, though there was also an outreach center and guest accommodations.

"What are you doing?"

Kate's voice startled him, and he looked over his shoulder. She was standing in the doorway, yawning, clad in a bathrobe. Her hair fell about her shoulders and her eyes were cloudy from sleep; nonetheless, they watched him curiously. "What are you looking at?"

"There's this Tibetan monastery in Big Sur. I'm checking the website."

She gave a perplexed look. "At four in the morning?"

He shrugged. "I couldn't sleep."

"Everything all right?"

"Yes, everything's fine."

She continued to linger in the doorway, as if she didn't believe him.

He swiveled around in the desk chair to face her. He audibly cleared his throat. "There's something I need to tell you."

Her face grew anxious, and she came up and sat down on the edge of the sofa. She gathered her bathrobe tight around her throat. "What's wrong?"

"You know I've been reading Havelock's expedition journal, right?" he said.

She nodded.

"Well," he said, "I think they're helping me understand what's going on around here."

"Going on?"

He nodded. "With the break-in at Havelock's. And the dog attacks. They're all connected."

She was completely silent, just listening to him, but her eyes were wary.

He paused for the briefest of moments to gather his thoughts, and then told her everything—about what Havelock had written about tulpas, about his conversations with Debra, about his meeting with Dr. Rohrbacher, all of it. When he'd finished, Kate was silent for a long time, her expression blank, her face an inscrutable mask. Taylor knew from experience it was her "lawyer face"—a face that gave nothing away, a face that betrayed no hint of what the mind was thinking.

Finally, as if snapping out of a spell, she said, "My God, Taylor, are you serious? Mind creatures? Have you completely lost it?"

"Look, I know it sounds crazy, but—"

"Sounds crazy?" she interjected. "It is crazy!"

"Kate," he said, "you've got to believe me. I thought it was crazy at first, too."

She put up her hand, as if to silence him. "I never thought I'd say anything like this but ever since we moved up here you've become this weird recluse, this weird, gun-toting conspiracy nut. And now you're talking about mind creatures? What did you call them?"

"Tulpas."

She shook her head and stared at him as if she'd never seen him before.

"C'mon, Kate. It's not like that at all."

She was angry now. "And you told me you'd lock the gun up. But it's sitting on the mantel above the fireplace. I'm not stupid, Taylor, I notice these things!"

"I'm sorry, I meant to lock it up, but when Debra and Havelock were staying here, I thought it needed to be handy."

Aghast, she said, "You mean it's loaded?"

He nodded.

"Good God, Taylor. You're paranoid!"

"You should read Havelock's journal, then you'd understand."

"You're kidding, right?" Her eyes were wide with disbelief. "You want me to read some old journal as if it's the Gospel truth? Some journal that was written, what, sixty years ago?"

"Look, I'm just saying there's a lot in there that—"

"I don't want to read his journal!" Her eyes flashed with anger. "Here's a newsflash, Taylor: Just because someone writes something down doesn't make it true. People lie in their journals, too."

Taylor was silent. He didn't know what to say. There was simply no convincing her, and he didn't want to prolong the argument.

"I just don't understand what's gotten into you," Kate said. She continued to stare at him as if he was another person.

"Nothing's gotten into me."

"Oh, this is pointless!" Kate spun on her heel and stormed out of the room.

Chapter 22

SOUTH OF CARMEL, HIGHWAY 1 began its serpentine route through Big Sur, following the coastline's myriad curves and indentations. It was a beautiful day with crystal blue sky and puffy white clouds. To the west, the ocean sparkled in the sunlight. The surrounding hillsides were carpeted with densely bunched chaparral and coastal sage, broken here and there by clusters of madrone and oak. Stands of white-tufted jubata grass, an invasive species that had originally come from South America, snaked up the cliffs. Overhead, a turkey vulture soared in the updrafts, casting a slow-moving shadow on the terrain below.

But Taylor's mind was far from any floral or faunal considerations. He was looking for the turnoff that led to the Maitreya Center. Apparently, it was an unmarked road that was fronted by a locked gate. But he'd been given the combination when he'd made his reservation, so at least he could breach that barrier. Finding the road, however, was another matter.

However, by mid-afternoon, he found the gate. It was an unobtrusive wood and metal structure with a large padlock. Dialing the combination, he unlocked the gate and drove through, heading east. The paved road gradually faded, and a rutted dirt road took its place. The Jeep rocked and jolted along the uneven surface, kicking up dust and gravel in its wake. For a while, the road paralleled a boulder-clogged stream, until finally veering off and ascending into higher country.

The road grew increasingly rugged as he gained elevation, pockmarked with potholes and rocks. But Taylor drove carefully, avoiding the obstacles. The smell of salt gave way to that of pine and conifer. The forest grew thicker and denser, the trees closer together, and overhead the canopy heavier until the blue sky could only be seen in brief glimpses.

Eventually, the road ended at a turnaround, where a dusty white minivan and a Subaru Forester were parked. Just beyond, set under large redwoods, was a cluster of rustic cabins, each festooned with multi-colored Tibetan prayer flags. The nearest cabin was weathered and made of thick, hand-hewn logs. The roof was covered with moss and a stone chimney jutted up on one side.

Taylor parked near the Forester. Shouldering his duffel bag, he exited the vehicle. The smell of pine and loamy soil struck his nostrils. He looked around. The air was still and quiet and columns of sunlight filtered down through the canopy, illuminating patches of suspended dust particles.

The door of the nearest cabin creaked open and out stepped a short Tibetan man. His head was shaven in the Tibetan style of a monk but instead of the ubiquitous scarlet and saffron-colored robe that Taylor had been expecting, the man was dressed in Western-style clothes. He was wearing jeans, sandals, and an Oxford-style dress shirt with the sleeves rolled up. He came forward, his sandals crunching against the pine needles that littered the ground. He was carrying a white scarf, which Taylor later learned was called a *khata*, or Tibetan prayer scarf, in both hands.

"Welcome!" he called out.

Taylor put up his own hand in greeting. The man approached, stopping a few paces away to bow. He held out the scarf, indicating that Taylor should allow him to place it around his neck. Taylor bent forward, permitting the man to drape it around him. Then the man stepped back and clasped his hands together in the traditional Tibetan-style of greeting. He bowed again. "*Namaste.*"

"Thank you," Taylor said, not exactly sure what type of response was appropriate.

"You are Taylor Hamilton?" the man asked, looking back up.

Taylor nodded.

The man put out his hand. "I am Norbu."

They shook. Taylor was surprised by the man's grip. Despite his small stature, his grip was strong and firm.

"You are a friend of Stephen Rohrbacher?" Norbu asked.

"Not exactly. I mean, I just met him once, but he was very accommodating."

Norbu nodded vigorously. "Dr. Rohrbacher is a good friend of the

Center. His friend is our friend."

Norbu insisted on taking Taylor's duffel bag, and led him into the interior of the nearest cabin. It was cozy and well-lighted inside but sparsely furnished with the overall look of a makeshift office. There was a multi-colored rug on the floor and a desk with a computer at one end of the room. At the other end was a refrigerator, a sink, and a small stove with multiple burners.

"You would like some tea?" Norbu asked, placing Taylor's duffel bag on the rug and walking over to the stove.

"Thank you, yes." Taylor walked up to a map that was tacked to the wall. It was old and weathered with frayed edges; it looked as if it had hung on that spot for years. It depicted the monastery grounds. He studied it for a moment, noting the large central building, which was identified in the legend as the main temple. Around it were a number of other buildings, most of which he assumed were monks' quarters or storehouses. He turned back around.

"So, I take it you're not a monk?"

"No," Norbu said, filling a kettle with tap water. "I am the manager."

"So, this is a working monastery?" Taylor asked.

"Yes, but it is also a cultural center. We have twenty-four monks in residence and seven staff." Norbu put the kettle on one of the burners and turned on the gas. He turned back and began to explain the history of the Maitreya Center, how it began in the 1970s when several Tibetan refugees were looking for an isolated place to build a monastery and cultural center. "Our purpose is to keep Tibetan culture alive. You know of the Chinese invasion, yes?"

Taylor nodded, remembering what he'd recently read about the invasion of the 1950s.

"We are dedicated to keeping our traditions alive so that people will not forget, and that we may pass on our knowledge to the younger generation." Norbu paused. "Dr. Rohrbacher tells me you are interested in Tibetan culture."

"That's right," Taylor said.

"He said you are a writer. This must be for research, yes?"

Taylor nodded. "I'm especially interested in some of the more esoteric Tibetan practices."

Norbu smiled. "I see." He paused. "Would you be interested in speaking to one of the monks?"

"Yes, very much so. I hope that won't be any trouble."

"I do not think so. Of course, some monks are more talkative than others. Of what subject are you most interested?"

"I'm primarily interested—"

At that moment, the kettle whistled. Norbu lifted it off the burner and proceeded to fill two mugs with hot water. He dropped a tea bag in each. "I hope you do not mind Darjeeling?"

Taylor chuckled. He had been expecting something more exotic—like yak butter tea. "No, not at all."

Norbu handed Taylor a mug and then sat down in his desk chair. He dipped his tea bag in and out of his mug to saturate the water. "You were about to tell me what subject interests you the most."

"I'd like to learn about the concept of the tulpa."

Norbu grew quiet and fixed his dark eyes on Taylor. "I see." He hesitated, continuing to dip his tea bag methodically. "Then you will need to speak to one of the older monks."

"Why's that?"

"Because it is a concept associated with the older generation. Not many younger monks believe in it. They do not think such a thing is possible." He paused. "The Tibetan religion is—how do you say?—rife with many superstitions. Many younger monks believe that tulpas are just a superstition, like ghosts or fairies."

"I take it you don't believe in them either?"

Norbu looked at Taylor evenly. "No, in all honesty, Mr. Hamilton, I do not. But there are some who do."

"I'm sorry, I just assumed all Tibetan Buddhists believed in the concept."

"It is really no different from your own Christian religion," Norbu said. "Like the transubstantiation, for example. Some Christians believe such an event occurs and others do not. Or angels."

Taylor nodded. "I see what you mean."

"My uncle, Lobsang, however, is a believer in the old ways. He is a monk here. He believes in tulpas, and many other things."

"Would it be possible to speak with him?" Taylor asked.

Norbu smiled, took a sip of tea, and nodded. "Yes, I believe so."

Taylor savored the evening air. The resinous scent of pine drifted about, mixed with the smell of salt that wafted in from the coast. He took a deep breath, allowed the crispness to fill his lungs, held it a moment, and then let it out.

He was standing in front of one of the guest cabins, where Norbu had settled him an hour ago. The room was small and sparsely furnished with a military-style cot and a small desk and chair. It was comfortable but Spartan—pretty much what he had expected monastic accommodations to resemble.

He had never quite understood the fascination some people had for wanting to spend time in a monastery. He'd read articles about celebrities, CEOs, politicians, and other high-powered executives who spent time in monasteries to re-charge their batteries and had always thought it sounded hokey and contrived. But now, as he gazed about at the beautiful setting and heard the lilting cadence of monks chanting from the main temple, he began to have an inkling. It began to make sense. There was something in the air—an intangible quality—that created a deep sense of tranquility that was undeniable.

He set out walking along one of the gravel paths that led through the main monastery grounds. The buildings looked to be constructed from a combination of wood, stucco, stone, and modern materials. Each structure was painted white with a red overhanging roof. Several were topped with the characteristic multi-tiered Tibetan pagoda, which was painted yellow.

Taylor stopped outside the main temple and stood motionless, listening. The monks had begun their evening chants half an hour ago; he had been told it was a prelude to a group meditation session that would last several hours.

The monks' voices were deep and resonant, and carried through the air, rising to an austere crescendo and then falling, echoing off the walls until they blended together to form a single voice that sounded unearthly and far removed from the realities of life.

Taylor gazed up at the structure. The oratory was the central building of the monastery, a rectangular stone structure. He wondered whether the architecture was responsible for the unusual acoustics. Whatever the reason the results were remarkable.

He continued on the trail, which led away from the monastery. Overhead was a thick canopy of trees. Eventually, the path ascended the side of a hill, rising in a series of switchbacks that led to the flat-topped summit, which was crowned by a maze of trees. Pine needles crunched under his feet. A stream ran alongside, water trickling and splashing over rocks as it cascaded downward. Except for the chants of the monks, which grew increasingly muted, the sounds that surrounded him were natural in origin: the faint whisper of the breeze in the branches of the trees, the croak of frogs, and the chirp of insects.

He climbed to the top and came to a small stone bench set beneath a large redwood tree. Its top was covered with needles and leaves, which he brushed off. He sat down. Below him stretched the monastery, placid and substantial. Beyond it, to the west, the hills glowed with sunset. He sat for several minutes and watched as the sun sank into the horizon. When it had disappeared, its afterglow was soft and warm but fading fast.

Below him, the monastery lights began to flicker on as the evening deepened. The stillness in the air was almost tangible, and he sat completely still, just taking in the ambience.

Tilting his head back, he gazed up at the sky. Small pinpricks of light began to appear, first one, then another. Before long, the vast expanse of the night sky spread out above him. It was a dazzling profusion of stars and planets; they seemed so close it was almost as if he could reach up and pluck them one by one. Force of habit made him locate those constellations that were familiar. Soon he'd identified Orion, Scorpio, Cassiopeia, and Cetus the whale.

A million questions swirled around in his head as he pondered the night sky. The events of the past several weeks had challenged his perception of reality and existence, had made him question some basic tenets of Western cosmology. Did we really know as much as we thought we did? Did the standard explanation of the cosmos, one that was taught to every school kid, really suffice anymore? If thoughts could be made manifest, what did this say about our understanding of reality? In fact, there was so much about reality we didn't know, didn't have a clue about. He was beginning to realize this, beginning to understand our tenuous grasp on reality, on the nature of the universe. Despite all our theories and our wildly sophisticated technologies, we still had no good answers to many of the fundamental questions—those existential questions of nature, reality, being, and consciousness—that have plagued humankind for centuries.

He wondered whether some of these questions could, in fact, ever be answered intellectually. Might some, he thought, require something other than the intellect, such as intuition, or emotion? Was reality entangled with what was in our own mind? Perhaps reality was ultimately the product of our own consciousness rather than the other way around. What had the famous scientist Max Planck said? "Science cannot solve the ultimate mystery of nature because, in the last analysis, we ourselves are a part of the mystery we are trying to solve."

He lowered his gaze and let out a deep sigh. He stared in the direction of the main temple, but now it was only a vague outline in the dark of the night.

Chapter 23

THE OLD MONK WAS silent for several minutes, his eyes downcast, his brow furrowed. He was silent for so long, in fact, that Taylor was suddenly worried his questions had somehow offended the man. He cast an uneasy glance at Norbu, who was seated beside Lobsang. But the younger Tibetan was equally silent.

Finally, Lobsang raised his eyes and looked directly at Taylor. The man's irises were dark and small but contained a penetrating quality. It was a quality that seemed to pierce deeply into Taylor's soul.

"Not good," the monk said, abruptly shaking his head. "Not good." The second statement was accompanied by a definitive swipe of his hand.

Taylor gazed at Norbu for an explanation, but before the young Tibetan could answer, Lobsang spoke up again.

"Here," he said. He lifted a gnarled finger and tapped the side of his temple for emphasis. "Created here." He was about to say something else but turned to Norbu instead and spoke in Tibetan. Norbu listened expectantly and then nodded. He turned to Taylor.

"Lobsang means to say that such creatures are created by the mind. He says that only a high lama should create a tulpa. It should not be—how do you say?—the 'plaything' of an amateur. He says that one must have perfect control of the mind. He says that the human mind is too prone to uncontrolled emotions."

"Could he elaborate on that?" Taylor asked.

The two Tibetans conversed for several minutes. As they did so, Taylor observed the old monk. Lobsang's face was lean and his skin weathered and wrinkled, with dark eyes set above a prominent, hawk-like nose. Unlike the typical Tibetan face, Lobsang's countenance seemed longer and curiously more European. His robes hung from a boney and skeletal frame. It was obvious he was of an advanced age, yet Taylor couldn't say for sure just how old he might be. He could've been as young as seventy or as old as ninety. His hands trembled slightly from what Taylor deduced might be a mild case of Parkinson's disease or some similar neurological condition. Nonetheless, the ailment didn't seem to cause him any undue trouble, and when he spoke the words were uttered with a clear and forceful emphasis.

They continued conversing so Taylor took the opportunity to examine Lobsang's chamber more closely. He let his gaze drift about, noticing that the room, not unlike his own guest room, was sparsely furnished. It was small and cell-like with walls of stone and illuminated by two candles. A military-style cot was positioned against one wall and, opposite that, sat a dresser made of wood and a table and chair. Everything was plain and devoid of decoration. Next to the table and chair was a bookcase filled with ancient looking volumes and scrolls. Taylor wondered what arcane wisdom they possessed.

Finally, Norbu turned to Taylor. "Lobsang says that the creation of a tulpa requires intense concentration and discipline. It is an endeavor that must be embarked upon with a pure mind free of prejudice, ill-will, delusion, or other mental impediments. Tulpas have no thoughts except what they are given by their creators. If the creator's thoughts are angry, the tulpa is angry. If the creator is sad, the tulpa is sad. That is why the creator of the tulpa must always be in perfect control of his own mind. An undisciplined mind creates an undisciplined creature, which can lead to many problems."

Taylor considered this for a moment. "But tulpas can develop independent thought, right? They can break away from their creators?"

Norbu conveyed Taylor's question to Lobsang. Understanding, the old monk shook his head and spoke in Tibetan. Norbu translated, saying, "No, he says that is not true. These are creatures that do not think for themselves. They only know the thoughts of their creators."

Taylor rubbed his chin and directed his gaze at the far wall for a moment. This information was different from what he had been led to believe. Lobsang made it sound as if the tulpa was simply a mindless automaton, a being that could only respond to, and mimic, the thoughts, moods, and emotions of its creator.

"I don't understand," he said, focusing his gaze back on the two men. "I was led to believe that tulpas learn to think for themselves.

145

That they have the ability to learn and digest information."

When this was translated to Lobsang, the old monk spoke, and Norbu translated. "Lobsang says that, yes, a tulpa can learn many things, but, no, they do not have independent thought. They are not autonomous. They are always influenced in everything they do by their creators."

Again, Taylor directed his gaze at the wall as he pondered what the old monk had told him. When he shifted his gaze back at Lobsang he was surprised to see that the old man was staring back at him intently, his eyes fixed and unblinking. Taylor was slightly unsettled by the man's gaze. It was if the old monk was contemplating something that had suddenly disturbed him. He turned to Norbu and spoke in Tibetan. Norbu listened for a long time, then, when the monk had finished, he turned his attention to Taylor. He spoke cautiously, measuring his words, as if he didn't want to offend.

"Lobsang says there is something else."

Taylor blinked. "Something else?"

"With all due respect, he says that you are leaving something out. There is something you are not telling us because of fear."

Stunned, Taylor didn't know what to say. He sat silently, looking at Lobsang, suddenly wondering whether the old monk had the ability to read minds. A moment elapsed. Finally, flustered, he said, "I'm not sure I understand."

"Lobsang says that your questions are prompted not by a writing project but by concerns that are troubling you. He please asks that you be completely truthful."

Taylor was amazed not only by the bluntness of the remark, but by the man's ability to perceive the reality of the situation. After a moment, which allowed him time to regain his composure, he replied, "Yes, Lobsang is correct. And I apologize for being less than truthful." He paused and briefly closed his eyes, gathering his thoughts. When he opened them, he looked straight at Lobsang. "I'm not sure how best to put this but I'll do the best I can." With that, Taylor launched into his now familiar tale, Norbu translating as he spoke. He told the old monk about Havelock, about Fletcher and Dorje, about the damage and murder that had already been committed, and about his fears that more damage—and murder—were distinct possibilities.

Lobsang was silent as Taylor spoke, his face thoughtful, nodding occasionally as Norbu translated, but on the whole, he seemed strangely unmoved by the story.

When he finished, Lobsang sat quietly, as if studying Taylor, his dark eyes unreadable. Then he closed his eyes. Again, he was silent for several minutes. Taylor was equally silent, watching and waiting for the old man's reaction. Anxiously, Taylor glanced at Norbu but the young man, too, was silent.

The old monk's eyes opened, and he turned to Norbu. The two men spoke briefly in Tibetan. Then, without a further word, Lobsang slowly got to his feet, a task that seemed to cause him some discomfort, and Taylor guessed he might be suffering from arthritis. Standing, he turned to Taylor and bowed in the Tibetan fashion, and then shuffled from the room, his sandal-shod feet scuffing against the floor.

Surprised, Taylor cast a questioning glance at Norbu, but the young man was watching Lobsang. When the old monk had left, disappearing down some dimly lit corridor, Norbu turned to Taylor.

"What did he say?" Taylor blurted out, unable to contain himself. He was fairly bristling with anticipation and curiosity.

"He will contact you in two weeks' time."

Taylor furrowed his brow, expecting more. "What else did he say?"

"That is all he said. He will contact you in two weeks' time."

"Did he say how?"

Norbu shook his head. "I'm afraid not."

"But how will he find me? And what is he planning to do? I mean, will he be able to help me?"

"That I cannot answer," Norbu said, shrugging. "But he says the situation is grave."

Taylor got cell phone reception just south of Carmel. As his Jeep rattled over the famed Bixby Bridge, his cell phone beeped. He glanced at it and saw on the screen that he had a voice message from Kate. He continued across the bridge and then pulled off on the shoulder, rolling to a stop. He picked up the phone and looked at the message. It was a day old. He punched "play."

"Hi, it's me," the message began, Kate's voice calm and measured, "I'm sorry we fought. I don't want to stay mad and I hope you don't either. I know you're down in Big Sur, but I was thinking when you drive back you could stop in the city and we could have dinner or something. I love you. Call me."

Taylor didn't want to continue arguing either. He hated fighting with Kate; he always ended up saying stupid things that made him feel bad afterward.

He turned and stared out the window, watching a line of pelicans flying over the water, their flight perfectly synchronized. They swooped low and raced in front of an oncoming wave, wings flapping in unison, gliding on the air currents. Swells were rolling in and he suddenly wished he had his surfboard. It had always been a great way to forget his problems. He'd simply paddle out and, focusing on the waves, his land-based problems would always vanish like wisps of cloud on the breeze.

He turned back and stared down at the phone in his hand. He missed Kate; of that he was certain. He lifted the phone and pressed her number.

Chapter 24

THAT EVENING, TAYLOR AND Kate dined at the Cliff House, a restaurant they had frequented during the early years of their courtship. From their table by the big bay window, they could view the long sweep of Ocean Beach, stretching south and disappearing into salty mist and twilight. To the north, the Marin Headlands were visible, stark and imposing. And to the west, out over the Pacific, the sun began its gradual descent, casting the sky in brilliant shades of orange and purple.

"I'm sorry for the way I acted," Kate said from across the table. "I'm sorry I blew up at you."

Taylor took a sip of wine and waved her off. "Forget it," he said. "Let's just forget the whole thing."

Kate paused for a moment as she buttered a warm sourdough roll. The clink of utensils and the soft murmur of voices filled the dining room.

"I still think the whole thing's pretty weird," she said, but quickly added, "but let's not discuss it right now. Let's just enjoy the evening." She nodded toward the sunset, smiling, her face illuminated by the golden glow of the setting sun. "It's beautiful, isn't it?"

Taylor glanced out the window. The sun was beginning its descent. It hung just above the horizon, round and red, then gradually it began to flatten at the bottom until it looked like a red half-orange. Finally, only a sliver remained; eventually that dissipated, and evening settled in. Far out to sea, a long cargo ship cruised northward, its running lights just now switching to life.

"Reminds me of when we were first dating," Kate said, turning back, a smile still plastered on her face. "We used to watch the sunset all the time, remember?"

Taylor grinned. "Of course I remember."

He picked up the wine bottle that sat between them.
"More wine?
She nodded.
He poured her a glass.
"I also remember you couldn't keep your hands off me," she added, her eyelids fluttering coyly.

He nodded, remembering. Their first year had been utter bliss, and for a moment, he found his mind drifting backward in time. It had been a year filled not only with sunsets, but also with long, lingering dinners in North Beach, the theater, the symphony, movies, scenic drives across the Golden Gate Bridge to Sausalito and Marin, evening strolls along the Embarcadero—and lovemaking, lots and lots of lovemaking.

Their dinner soon arrived, and they continued chatting as they ate. The night unfolded and the city's lights began to blaze to life. The distant bark of the sea lions on the rocks below ceased. With the strong wine working on his head and the face of his beautiful wife in front of him, Taylor began to relax. He took a deep breath and let it out, feeling his tension release, all the tension that had built up over the past several days. Whatever the next several days brought—no matter how "grave" the situation—Taylor was at least going to enjoy the moment.

"So, what did you learn at that monastery?" Kate asked. "Anything interesting?"

Taylor had just taken a bite of food as she asked the question. He swallowed it hastily. He looked at her, not knowing what to say. Where on earth to begin?

The following morning, Kate and Taylor had breakfast at a small café in the Haight, and then Taylor made the long drive back to Humboldt. He got to the house in the early afternoon, just as a light drizzle was falling. He lugged his duffel bag up to the front door, fished in his pocket for his keys, and let himself inside.

Tossing his duffel bag aside, he went around the house switching on lights, his footsteps echoing as he made his way from room to room. The inside of the house was cold, and he contemplated making a fire. But he was too tired and worn out from the drive. Instead, he plopped down on the couch in the living room, grabbed the TV remote, and mindlessly began to flip through the channels. When he realized there was nothing of interest, he turned off the TV and sat quietly, listening to the rain. It had increased now to a steady downpour so that it drummed against the ceiling.

All told, his conversation with Kate had gone surprisingly well. Although he certainly hadn't convinced her of the supernatural nature of events, at least this time she hadn't accused him of being a complete nutjob. He had been able to explain the concept of a tulpa to her. Whether she had bitten her tongue, or she had actually been interested, he didn't know. She had listened with what could best be described as patient disapproval, but she hadn't said anything.

Half an hour later he was sitting in front of his computer. He really needed to get some work done on his new novel but, with all the things that had been happening recently, he simply couldn't focus on his writing. So, instead, he went online and checked the *Courier* website. To his surprise, he came across the following article:

Rabid Dog Sightings in County

In something that might have come from the pen of Sir Arthur Conan Doyle, the famed creator of Sherlock Holmes, several residents have reported seeing a large black dog roaming the county. These sightings have occurred over the past several weeks, with a number of residents claiming that the animal is rabid and dangerous. It has been described as having thick black fur and resembling a Rottweiler or Bernese Mountain Dog, though the breed has not been positively identified.

Several residents, especially those living in the rural communities east of Oceanport, have reported attacks on livestock. One resident has claimed firing at the animal with a shotgun, but it is not clear whether the creature was hit.

The Sheriff's department and Humboldt County Animal Control have searched for the dog but been unable to find it.

Perhaps it's time they enlisted the aid of Conan Doyle's famous detective?

Taylor stopped reading and frowned. He didn't like the overall tone of the article. There was a flippancy to it that bothered him. It was as if the writer—with his less-than-artful allusions to Doyle's *The Hound of the Baskervilles*—thought the whole thing was a giant lark, a great big humorous spectacle the reporting of which occasioned nothing more serious than a well-placed literary reference. There was no mention of Ed Hsing's death or even the attack on Ed Hsing's widow.

Taylor gave a disgusted shake of his head and pushed away from the desk. He rose to his feet, and restlessly walked over to the window and stood looking out at the rain. It was falling in a heavy torrent now. His thoughts drifted back to what Lobsang had told him about tulpas: They are creatures that carry the thoughts of their creators. If this was so, then the behavior of Dorje and Fletcher could only be understood in reference to Havelock's own thoughts and moods. Taylor recalled the time he encountered Dorje in the rain a few days after Havelock's stroke. The animal had turned into a vicious beast and he had feared for his life. At the time, he had simply assumed the animal had turned rabid; but as he now reflected on the situation, he remembered Debra telling him that Havelock had had several angry outbursts after coming home from the hospital. Was Dorje's behavior, then, a reflection of Havelock's own anger? Had Havelock's descent into a combination of dementia, anger, pain, and self-pity created these dangerous, volatile creatures?

Following this line of reasoning, he explored several other incidents. Perhaps the broken back door of Havelock's house was the result—not of someone trying to break in—but a reaction to the pain, confusion, and fear of Havelock's stroke. Taylor could imagine the animal, driven by these same emotions, running helter-skelter through the house, knocking over furniture, as it sought relief from the pain.

Then there was the death of Ed Hsing. He was speculating here, but assuming it was, in fact, Dorje that killed the man—and it certainly seemed that way—perhaps the death was really the result of Havelock's animosity toward the Chinese in general, rather than anything Ed Hsing had actually done. Or maybe at one time the two men had had words and Havelock's dementia had twisted the argument out of all proportion. The stroke had caused significant brain damage; Taylor remembered Debra telling him that the stroke had affected Havelock's emotions. If his mind was slipping into dementia and as a consequence he was unable to control his emotions, it was possible that old animosities and prejudices would have a chance to well up without any rational safeguards.

The key to all this, then, was Havelock; specifically, the old man's mental state. If it could be controlled, then the tulpas could be controlled.

He turned from the window and began to pace the room. But how? Massive sedation? How would he be able to convince Debra of this? Was something like this even feasible? More importantly, was it ethical?

He sat back down and shook his head in confusion.

———————

Taylor awoke with a start, his heart pounding. The nightmare was still vivid in his mind and for a moment he looked around in the darkness, not exactly sure where he was. But as he came out of the fog of sleep, he realized he was in his own bedroom, warm and secure in his blankets. Taking a deep breath, he tried his best to calm himself, telling himself everything had been a dream. All this obsessing over tulpas had rattled him.

Despite this, the images lingered in his consciousness, intense and frightening. In the dream, he had been running from some unseen enemy, some creature he could never see but that was intent on his destruction. He'd fallen and the creature had pounced. He'd felt the creature's claws rip into him and tear his flesh into ragged strips. That was when he had jerked awake.

He rubbed his eyes and sat up. The room was quiet and still, a strange juxtaposition to the frenzied and violent atmosphere of his dream. He crawled out of bed and tossed on a robe against the chill, tying it at the waist. The digital clock by his bedside read a little after five in the morning. Outside the sky was just beginning to brighten.

He made his way down the stairs, the floorboards creaking under his footsteps. He went to the kitchen and made himself a cup of coffee. Sitting down at the kitchen table, and sipping his brew slowly, he thought about the contents of Havelock's journal. Had he read something like that just a month ago, he would've dismissed it out of hand as pure nonsense, as pure fantasy. Now he wasn't so sure. Indeed, more and more, as strange event after strange event accumulated, he was beginning not to take anything for granted.

Chapter 25

THE NEXT WEEK PASSED without incident. Taylor kept close tabs on the *Courier*, checking the website daily to see if there were any news reports of black dogs roaming the countryside and causing havoc. He also checked to see whether anyone had reported any incidents involving a belligerent young man randomly assaulting passersby. He even found the Sheriff Department's digital blotter site, which reported all police incidents and arrests. But there was nothing that raised his suspicions.

He called Debra during the week to check on Havelock's status. She told him the doctor had prescribed a second, lithium-like drug that was designed to deal with his mercurial mood swings. But she wasn't entirely optimistic about its efficacy. One of the side-effects, however, was drowsiness. Consequently, Havelock had spent much of the week in bed asleep.

Early Saturday morning, Taylor received a call from Debra. He had just gotten out of the shower and was drying himself when his cell phone rang. He rushed to answer it because he didn't want to wake Kate, who was still sleeping. The tone of Debra's voice made it abundantly clear she needed to talk to him urgently.

"Everything all right?" he asked.

"Yes, everything's fine."

"Havelock's okay?"

"He's the same. But I really need to talk to you. I found something I think you'll be interested in seeing."

Without hesitation, Taylor said, "I'll be right over."

Taylor threw on clothes, careful not to wake Kate. She was sound asleep, wrapped up in the blanket, her hair splayed on the pillow in brilliant disarray. She'd gotten home late last night, sometime around midnight, and had crawled into bed, exhausted. Since then she hadn't moved a muscle.

He closed the door quietly behind him and stepped out into the hallway. He thumped down the stairs, grabbed a jacket against the chill, and went out the front door.

As he trudged up the road to Havelock's house, his mind raced over the possibilities of what she'd found. Debra had sounded serious on the phone but not desperate or hysterical. What could it possibly be?

When he got to Havelock's house five minutes later, Debra was there to meet him at the door. Taylor could tell from the expression on her face that she was agitated. The bags under her eyes indicated she hadn't gotten much sleep, either.

Debra took Taylor's arm and hastily led him into the living room where they sat down.

"What's wrong?" Taylor asked.

"I finally took your advice and read Dad's Tibetan journal." She rubbed a bleary eye. "I spent all last night reading it."

Taylor nodded, but didn't say anything, just allowed her to continue.

"I had no idea about any of this," she said. "I mean, I knew he was into all this Tibetan mysticism, but I had no idea he was absolutely obsessed. And all the stuff he said he experienced. It's absolutely incredible. It's like science fiction. I'm not sure I believe it."

"You don't think he was lying to his journal, do you?"

"No," she said, shaking her head quickly, "but, my God, it's all so fantastic." She paused. "By the same token, it helps explain a lot of his behavior, especially when I was growing up."

She stopped talking and turned to the small table next to her, on which sat a notebook Taylor hadn't seen before. It was very different from the leather-bound journal that contained Havelock's Tibetan expedition entries. Unlike that, it looked like a scholastic notebook, something one would see in a campus bookstore. She picked it up and fingered the spine for a moment.

"I went looking around for his books and papers and found this." She handed it to Taylor.

He glanced at the cover, but it was blank. Opening it, he began flipping through the pages, recognizing Havelock's small, precise handwriting. It appeared to be another journal with entries arranged by date; some were several paragraphs in length, others a single paragraph or simply a few lines. He looked up, his brow furrowed.

"Another journal?"

She nodded. "It's his meditation journal. It contains all his daily meditation notes for the past several years. It explains what he's been doing up here all this time."

"Which is?"

She looked at him. "I have a feeling you already know. Or at least suspected."

Taylor was quiet for a moment, staring off into space. Then he nodded. "Yes."

Debra sprang to her feet and began to pace the room in nervous agitation. "This is a nightmare. All this time he's been here, he's been trying to create these...these..." She stopped in apparent confusion. "I don't even know what to call them."

"Tulpas."

She pointed to the notebook in Taylor's hand. "Open to the first page I marked and read the entry."

Taylor noticed she had turned down the corners of several pages. He opened to the first marked page and started reading.

Feb. 25, 2019

Success! All my hours of concentration are beginning to pay off. He's not fully corporeal yet but I know he's there. I can sense him, even feel him in the air. When I close my eyes, I can almost see him; he's a vague outline at this point, kind of like when someone shines a bright light behind a person's shoulders so that you can only see the person's outline in silhouette.

Feb. 26, 2019

His presence has become so powerful that even when I'm not doing any concentration, when I'm just sitting quietly and I think of him, I immediately feel as if someone is standing next to me. There's a thickness in the air that is undeniable. It's as if he's just waiting to spring to life, just waiting for me to apply the finishing touches.

Feb. 27, 2019

I awoke last night and he was standing at the foot of my bed, staring at me. As my eyes adjusted to the dark, I saw that the expression on his face was one of curiosity. At the same time, he seemed confused, like someone who has just walked into a room but suddenly didn't know why they had entered. There was an awkwardness and naiveté about him.

Once I came fully awake and turned on the light, I told him to sit down. He did so immediately, like a dog eager to please its master. He sat quietly, his hands folded in his lap, an awkward half-smile on his lips. I noticed he had the habit of not blinking. It was very disconcerting.

As I looked at him, I realized I still had work to do. I hadn't quite captured Fletcher's face to my complete satisfaction. The creature's face was slightly narrower than Fletcher's, his teeth larger...

Taylor finished reading and looked up. Debra was still on her feet, her arms crossed. She paced the floor a few more times and then, sighing, sat down. She stared at him, her face uncertain.

"What do we do?" she asked.

Taylor rubbed his chin. The journal confirmed everything he had suspected. He wished he had a definitive answer for her. But he didn't.

"He created the dog the same way," Debra added. She pointed at the journal. "It's all there. He created the dog first and then Fletcher." She wrung her hands and shook her head. "Why? Why did he do this? What was the purpose? Why did he create these...these monsters?"

"For companionship, I think." Taylor paused. "And to relive old memories."

She scrutinized him, perplexed, as if the answer couldn't possibly be that simple. "Do you really think that?"

Taylor nodded. "Yes, he was a lonely man. He had very few friends. Lived all alone in this big house."

"I tried to reach out to him."

"It's not your fault. It was the way he wanted it."

She was silent. "But why are these things so dangerous? So angry? I can't believe Dad would deliberately create something that would hurt people. He certainly had his issues and he had a temper, but he was never a violent person. He abhorred violence."

Taylor said, "I don't think he created them to hurt anyone."

She gave him another perplexed look.

"My theory is that when he created these things, they were

essentially harmless. They were just his companions, his friends. But after his stroke, they changed. As his mind deteriorated, he became increasingly unable to control his emotions or his deep-seated prejudices. What he was feeling—all the anger, fear, and pain of his past—was transferred to Dorje and Fletcher. His mind created monsters."

Debra sat in silence for several minutes, apparently mulling over his answer. She crossed her arms over her chest and sighed.

Taylor told her about his visit to the monastery, how they would contact him in two weeks' time.

"Do you think they'll be able to help?" she said.

"I hope so. It's the only chance we have."

"What do we do in the meantime?"

"I'm not sure."

Debra fell silent again. Her brow was furrowed in thought. The silence lingered and Taylor was about to say something when she suddenly spoke up.

"Tranquilizers."

He looked at her.

"We have to use tranquilizers on him."

"You mean, keep him sedated?"

She nodded. "It's the only way to keep those things in check. I know it sounds harsh, but we have to do it. Otherwise—"

"I agree," Taylor said. "I've had the same thought." He paused for a moment. "But how? With sleeping pills?"

"No," she shook her head. "I was a nurse. I know what to use."

They were both silent. Although Taylor agreed that drugging him was probably the right course of action, it nonetheless made him uneasy. He scratched his arm and fidgeted slightly.

"I know what you're thinking," Debra said, observing him. "I don't feel real comfortable about it either. But it's our only option. These things are too dangerous. And I don't know if we can wait two weeks."

"But do you think it'll work?"

She stared out the window.

"God, I hope so."

Chapter 26

WHEN HE GOT BACK to the house, Kate was sitting at the kitchen table, dressed in her bathrobe and having a cup of coffee. A magazine was spread out on the table before her. She looked up as he entered, frowning.

"Where have you been?" she asked.

"Over at Debra's."

She nodded, but didn't say anything else, just took a sip. She dropped her head and stared at the magazine.

Taylor took off his jacket and hung it on the coat rack next to the door. He poured himself a cup from the pot and glanced over at Kate. He watched as with a slow, methodical movement she crossed her right leg over her left, glanced at her toe and then back at the magazine.

He sat down across from her. "Sleep well?" he asked.

She nodded again but didn't look up.

The silence lingered as they both sipped their coffee, and the kitchen suddenly seemed claustrophobic. Taylor wondered how he might break the uncomfortable atmosphere. But she seemed unwilling to talk. Finally, when the silence had grown to such unbearable proportions, he cleared his throat.

"You all right?"

She didn't say anything, didn't acknowledge him.

"For Chrissake, Kate, what's wrong?"

She lifted her head from the magazine slowly, as if the mere act of raising her head was a laborious task. The expression on her face, he noticed, wasn't angry; it was more one of exasperation, as if she'd reached the end of her tether.

"When is all this going to end?" she said.

"When is what going to end?"

159</>

She lifted her arms and swirled at the air with her hands, as if the answer was obvious. "This. All this. Your bizarre obsession with that old man and his daughter."

Taylor let out a frustrated sigh. He didn't want to have this argument all over again. It was pointless. And besides, he was beyond trying to convince her of anything. It was too late for that. The stakes were too high.

"Look, Kate," he said, trying his best to control his emotions, "it doesn't matter whether you believe me or not. This is the situation: We're dealing with supernatural creatures that Havelock created with his mind. And he's lost control of them. As he's retreated into a world of illness and dementia, they've become dangerous. We need to figure out how to get rid of them."

When he finished, she just looked at him, unblinking. Then, very slowly, she gathered the collar of her bathrobe around her neck and stood up.

"I don't even know what to say to that," she said, shaking her head. She turned and left the room, her footsteps echoing down the hallway.

A salty breeze blew cold against Taylor's face as he squinted at the horizon. The sun, a huge orange ball, was beginning to set over the water, and the sky was ablaze with color. Reds, yellows, oranges, and purples—an infinite variety of hues—mingled and intertwined, creating a lavish display. It seemed as if the sky was intent on staging one final burst of brilliance before settling into night.

In the impact zone—exactly where the waves were breaking—Taylor sat hunched over his surfboard, bobbing gently up and down with the swells. His eyes scanned the horizon carefully, looking for one final wave. He had been surfing now for nearly four hours straight and was beginning to tire. The muscles of his arms were sore, and his eyes were raw and scratchy from the salt water. And, despite the thick 5-mm wetsuit he wore, he was getting chilled. It was time to go in.

He turned his head and gazed back at shore. Atop the crumbling sandstone bluff that fronted the water, he could see his Jeep. He stared at it, imagining himself in the driver's seat, snug and warm, heading back toward home with the heater going at full blast.

Still, he wasn't altogether sure he wanted to get home anytime soon. The atmosphere in the house had been awkward and tense all day, and he and Kate hadn't spoken a word to each other since their argument that morning. Finally, when he had had enough, he had grabbed his board and headed for the coast.

A sudden splash made him spin around. A few yards away, a sea otter had just surfaced. It was flipped over on its back, floating casually, its tiny hands holding what appeared to be a shell. He watched the animal as it drifted slowly past. Above him, a lone gull circled, its white underbelly stark against the darkening sky. The atmosphere was quiet and serene, and Taylor took a deep breath, filling his lungs with the brisk, salty air.

A set wave suddenly peaked up on the horizon and advanced toward him. With a quick movement, he spun his board around and flattened himself on the deck. He began paddling. The wave drew up behind him, and feeling the drag of the bottom, began to arch forward. He felt himself lifted toward the crest, and he paddled even harder, hoping to match the wave's speed and momentum. Suddenly he felt the board move under him and he jumped to his feet, gliding smoothly and swiftly down the wave's face, spray whipping against his cheeks. He swept into a fast bottom turn and leaned into the wave, digging in his inside rail, a spray of water shooting out behind him in a long arc. He rode the wave nearly all the way to the beach and hopped off in the shallows, feeling his feet touch the sandy bottom. With his board under his arm, he jogged through the shallows and strode onto dry land.

He walked up the beach and then turned around, looking back at the water. It was nearly dark now and the stars were beginning to break through the pale fabric of evening, their lights reflected on the ocean's surface. The chill sea breeze stirred the coastal air, kicking up a variety of smells.

Turning back, Taylor readjusted the board to a better fit under his arm and hastily started up the bluff. As he neared the top, he suddenly realized someone was standing above him. He looked up and was surprised to see Tim Mahony standing at the edge of the bluff. He was wearing his sheriff's uniform, his green tie flapping in the breeze.

"Thought that was you out there," Tim said.

"What are you doing here? You're not going out, are you?"

Tim shook his head. "No, too late for that. I was driving by and saw your car." He paused and grinned. "Saw you get that last one."

"That was a beauty," Taylor said with a dreamy smile. He ascended the trail and came to the top of the bluff. He placed his board on the ground, with the fins up.

"Any news?" he asked.

"About rabid dogs terrorizing the county?"

Taylor nodded and peeled back his hood.

"No," Tim said, shaking his head. "But we did receive a complaint. A man was assaulted here yesterday."

"What happened?"

"He was assaulted by—"

"Let me guess," Taylor interjected. "A blond guy with glasses?"

Tim scowled. "If I ever catch that guy—"

"So, what happened? Is the victim okay?"

"Got the shit beat out of him. Had a couple of cracked ribs, broken nose and collar bone."

"Jesus," Taylor muttered, shaking his head. "How'd it start?"

"The victim said our 'blond friend' suddenly appeared while he was getting into his car. He started yelling and acting belligerent."

"What was he yelling about?"

"That's the crazy thing. The victim really didn't know. He said blondie started asking all these bizarre questions. When the guy told him to take a hike, blondie went ballistic."

"Any witnesses?"

"The victim's girlfriend. She tried to pull him off but got punched herself."

Taylor stood dripping in his wetsuit. All he could do was shake his head. Things were getting out of control.

———————

Taylor stopped reading and looked up, listening. The volume of the television from the living room seemed inordinately loud. He could hear the dialogue of a young Henry VIII—Kate was watching *The Tudors* on BBC America—as if it was coming from the adjoining room rather than from down the hallway. He sighed, shook his head, and then refocused his eyes on Havelock's meditation journal, which was open on his desk.

April 5, 2019

He reminds me of a dog—a small, needy puppy. He follows me around everywhere, as if the need to be in my presence is overwhelming and something he can't control. But like Dorje, he responds immediately to my commands. If I tell him to sit down, he does so without hesitation. This afternoon, I finally had to tell him to sit down and stay, because he was determined to follow me all over the house. He sat quietly for several hours, his hands on his lap, his eyes staring straight ahead of him. I told him he needs to blink his eyes once in a while.

His naiveté is both endearing and frustrating. I have to wonder whether this trait is a result of my own thoughts, however. When I think of Fletcher—the real Fletcher—I can't help but picture him as he really was, a curious mixture of intelligence and innocence, of boundless enthusiasm and social awkwardness. Therefore, I suppose, these traits are fitting in the Fletcher I'm creating.

April 6, 2019

I've been teaching Fletcher several small tasks, and he is learning very quickly. This morning, for example, I taught him to heat water up for coffee or tea. I taught him to fill the kettle with water and turn on the burner. I explained that the water had to boil before we could use it. As I said, he is a fast learner; much faster than I had expected. I only had to show him once before he got the hang of it.

There is so much I want to teach him. I want to teach him to read.

The next few entries were devoted to teaching Fletcher to read, and his general education. He learned quickly and soon progressed from children's books to novels and then to technical manuals. Havelock had him spend several evenings reading the dictionary and encyclopedia, and to learn as much as he could about a variety of different subjects, from chemistry and biology to history and literature.

May 11, 2019

I want Fletcher to go out and learn about and experience the world. There's only so much he can learn from books. He's so naïve and sheltered. He must try to gain as much knowledge about the world as he can. I told him that "there is so much in this world that you need to learn." I will propose he takes walks outside the house. He can start with short ones and then progress to longer hikes. I was thinking he should hike some of the more out-of-the-way trails in State Park. That way he won't come across too many people. But if he does, I told him to be polite and friendly, deferential even. Always ask permission before you do anything. If someone tells you "no," heed them. That is vitally important. By the same token, I told him to ask questions, and that he must be excited about learning.

Taylor finished reading and closed the journal. He glanced at his watch and noticed that it was well past midnight. He yawned, hearing the television coming from the living room. He was surprised Kate was still awake. He crept down the hallway and poked his head into the room. The television was on, but Kate was sound asleep on the couch, curled up and snoring softly, one hand resting underneath her cheek.

Taylor took a blanket from the linen closet and covered her with it. She stirred slightly as he pulled it up around her shoulders. Then he turned off the TV, switched off the lights, and left the room.

Taylor awoke later than usual the next morning. He noticed that Kate's side of the bed was cold, and her pillow had no imprint. She had obviously spent the entire night on the couch. He got up and got dressed, then went to the living room, but Kate wasn't there. The blanket he'd covered her with was neatly folded and placed on the side of the couch. He searched the house, but she wasn't anywhere. Looking out the window, he saw that her car was still in the driveway, so he figured that perhaps she'd gone for a walk.

He made himself a cup of coffee and some toast and when they were done, sat down at the kitchen table. He sipped the coffee and nibbled the toast, casting occasional glances out the window, hoping he might catch a glimpse of her coming up the back steps. But the minutes dragged, and he caught no sight of her. Feeling frustrated and anxious, he switched on the radio and listened to the news for a while, getting his fill of one depressing story after another—of wars, terrorism, government malfeasance and corruption, floods, famine, disease, and tragedy.

God, it was a crazy, screwed up world, he concluded, switching off the radio. He sat in silence for a time, wishing he could just snap his fingers and make everything go away—Havelock's creatures, the ill-feeling between himself and Kate, his feelings of powerlessness, the horrible situation he felt he was in...all of it.

It was then he heard footsteps shuffling on the steps outside. In seconds, the door opened, and Kate appeared in the doorway. She was dressed in jeans and a warm fleece jacket, her hair pulled back in a tight ponytail.

"Kate!" Taylor exclaimed, standing up. "I was beginning to wonder where you were."

She made brief eye contact with Taylor and then, without a word, came forward and sat down across from him. She looked down at the table, averting her eyes from him.

"I had a long talk with Debra," she said at length.

He was surprised, and for a moment studied her, trying to read her expression. But she had on her "lawyer face," so he just listened.

She gazed up at him and gestured at the seat across from her. "Sit down, will you?"

He sat.

"She told me some things about Havelock," she continued. "Some things about him when she was growing up."

This time Taylor opened his mouth to speak. He wanted to ask Kate whether Debra had told her everything, whether she had set her straight about the situation. But he soon realized the best course of action would be to keep quiet and just listen. So he clamped his mouth shut.

"It's nothing she probably hasn't told you already," Kate said. "But—"

He couldn't help himself. "But what?"

"She told me about his time in Tibet. And his strange behavior when she was growing up. All of it."

"Did you believe her?"

She paused, looking at him. "I don't know. I mean—"

Taylor waited for her to finish.

Kate sighed. "I can't believe I'm saying this," she continued. She shook her head as if the conclusion she'd reached was personally distasteful. "But maybe you're right. I mean, maybe there's something to what you've been telling me."

Taylor was too stunned to answer right away. He cocked his head and stared at Kate, as if he wasn't sure he had heard correctly. "Are you trying to tell me—"

"I don't know what I'm trying to tell you except maybe you're not exactly wrong."

"'Not exactly wrong?' What does that mean?"

She frowned. "Give me a break, Taylor. I'm trying to tell you that maybe you're not totally crazy."

He paused. "What made you change your mind?"

"I didn't say my mind's changed," Kate said. "I only said *maybe* there's something to all this. I'm just allowing the possibility."

Chapter 27

TAYLOR'S CELL PHONE STARTED ringing, jerking him from a deep sleep. He thought about letting it go to voicemail, but something in his gut told him to answer it. Sitting up, he fumbled for the device and glanced askance at the digital clock near the bedside. It was a little after two o'clock in the morning.

He put the phone to his ear and said groggily, "Hello?"

"They're here!"

He straightened, momentarily confused. His eyes darted around in the darkness, half expecting to see something lurking in the shadows. But then it dawned on him that he was listening to Debra's voice. And, as his mind unclouded from sleep, he knew immediately what she was talking about.

"Both of them? Where?"

"Outside. They're coming to the door."

Suddenly wide awake, he flung off the covers and bounded out of bed. He began to get dressed, frantically throwing on whatever clothes he could find lying on the floor. "Is the door locked?" he called into the phone, clamping it between his shoulder and cheek as he hoisted up his pants.

"Yes, it's locked." She paused. "I don't know what to do."

"Lock yourself in a room."

There was silence, though he could hear Debra's frightened breathing.

"Debra, are you there? Can you hear me?!"

"Oh, my God! They're at the door!"

"Lock yourself in a room!" Taylor repeated.

Taylor heard a loud bang on the other end and then the phone went dead.

"Shit!"

Kate rolled over and opened a bleary eye. "What's going on?" she murmured. "Who were you talking to?"

Taylor stuffed the phone in his pocket and bolted out the door, yelling behind him, "Debra. Something's going on over there."

His heart thudding in his chest, he clattered down the stairway and raced into the living room, where he snatched the shotgun off the mantel. He drew back the bolt to make sure the weapon was loaded, saw the metallic glint of shells in the dim light. He slammed the bolt shut and then dashed out the door.

A full moon drifted in and out of tattered clouds as Taylor sprinted up the street. The air was damp and cold, but Taylor didn't feel a thing as adrenaline coursed through his body.

Did he really know what he was getting himself into? he thought suddenly. He knew these creatures couldn't be killed. So, what the hell was he doing? The thought stopped him in his tracks. He stood panting in the cold air, his breaths coming out in puffs of condensation. His mind raced. What was he trying to do here? Was he trying to get himself killed? He waved off these thoughts with a shake of his head. The bottom line was this: Debra was in trouble; she needed help.

He tightened his grip on the shotgun, took a couple of deep breaths to steady his nerves, and then charged forward.

Through the trees ahead, he saw the front of Havelock's house. The porch was illuminated by an outside flood light, which cast hard, yellow light well past the porch and into the driveway. Two figures—Fletcher and Dorje—stood at the door. The dog was up on its hind legs, its front paws banging against the front door. The wood cracked and groaned under the animal's onslaught. Fletcher paced back and forth behind the dog, like a caged animal unable to get out, though in this case, the intent was to get inside.

Taylor skidded to a halt on the gravel driveway, his chest pounding, his mouth dry. He clicked off the safety and raised the gun to his shoulder, trying to quell the tremendous shaking in his hands.

"Stop!" he called out.

The dog continued to batter the door, oblivious, but Fletcher stopped pacing and turned around. The young man cocked his head, his eyes squinting into the darkness. He studied Taylor for a moment, and then, as recognition set in, his eyes narrowed. "I know you."

"I know you, too," Taylor said.

The two of them stared at each other. Dorje stopped pounding on the door and slowly lumbered around, facing Taylor. Taylor readjusted his grip on the shotgun, holding the butt tightly against his shoulder. His body shook with nerves and adrenaline.

"Where is my person?!" Fletcher bellowed, an angry scowl twisting his features.

"You have to leave," Taylor said.

Fletcher's hands balled into fists at his sides. He stood quietly, but there was a menace in his silence. The night was still except for the faint rustle of the breeze in the trees. Then he descended the steps, and strode out onto the driveway, his shoes crunching against the gravel.

"Get back!" Taylor shouted. The gun shook uncontrollably in his hands as he aimed it at Fletcher's chest.

Fletcher ignored him and strode forward.

"Havelock wants you to leave," Taylor said.

Fletcher stopped, the sound of his shoes against the gravel abruptly ceasing. He stood rigid, his arms at his sides, his glasses catching the flood light so that they flashed yellow. He stared at Taylor indifferently.

In the brief silence that followed, Taylor felt his heart pounding. Seconds passed. Taylor held his breath and shifted his weight onto the balls of his feet. The rifle quivered slightly in his hands, but he tried to control it, tried to hold it steady.

All of a sudden, Fletcher's face twisted into a wolfish snarl.

"You are a liar!" He rushed forward.

Taylor was unable to pull the trigger. He was suddenly paralyzed by the thought: what if he was wrong? What if this wasn't a tulpa, but a human being? He would be committing murder. But before he could ponder that train of thought any further, Fletcher's hand shot out and clawed at Taylor's throat, digging fingernails into flesh. Taylor wrenched free, stumbling backward with a gasp.

Fletcher rushed forward again. He swung a bony fist at Taylor that caught him against the side of the head. Taylor dropped to the ground with a grunt of pain. Fletcher stood over him and aimed a hard kick at Taylor's head. Taylor squirmed out of the way so that the blow landed against his shoulder. But it was a hard, vicious kick that sent shockwaves of pain coursing through him.

As Fletcher's leg pulled back for another kick, Taylor brought up the shotgun, aiming it point blank at Fletcher. He pulled the trigger. The roar was deafening, and the shotgun kicked in his hands.

Hit in the chest, Fletcher was thrown backward. He landed on his rear and sat for a moment, a blank expression on his face. And then, amazingly, he began to get to his feet.

Taylor watched, his mouth dropping open in utter disbelief. It was true; these things were not human. They were monsters. Taylor snatched the gun back into firing position as Fletcher gained his feet. Fletcher's shirt was torn where the bullet had hit but otherwise there wasn't a mark on him.

"I told you to get back," Taylor said, scrambling to his feet. He inched backward, and he had to fight the urge to turn and run.

Fletcher's face turned crimson. A vein in the middle of his forehead throbbed, his eyes blazing with a fury the depths of which Taylor couldn't fathom, couldn't begin to understand. But he knew it was really Havelock's anger—all the old man's frustrations, prejudices, and fears bundled together and unleashed in a volatile mix of raw emotion.

Fletcher charged again. Taylor pumped the shotgun and fired a second time. The blast caught Fletcher on the shoulder and jerked him backward, but this time didn't knock him off his feet. He stumbled but recovered his footing and came forward in a mad rush.

Before Taylor knew it, Fletcher was on him, wrenching the shotgun from his grasp and tossing it aside. It clattered noisily against the gravel and disappeared in the darkness. Taylor went down under a whirlwind of punches, boney knuckles hammering him. One struck him hard above the left eye, jerking his head back, and he felt liquid gush into his eyes, tasted blood. Another hit him in the mid-section. He grunted in pain and gasped for breath, covering his face as the blows rained down. He rolled over and tried to wriggle free, but Fletcher was on top of him, pinning him down.

He felt hands around his neck, fingers digging into his windpipe like a vise grip tightening. He gasped, desperate to escape, throwing punches of his own. But these did nothing to ease the pressure on his neck. Through a bloody haze that obscured his vision, he looked up. Hate-filled eyes blazed down at him, lips pulled back in a wolfish snarl.

He felt blood rushing to his head, his eyes bulging, his consciousness ebbing. Fletcher's hands tightened and Taylor's arms stopped punching and dropped like iron weights. Blackness filled his vision, followed by complete oblivion.

———————

The next thing he knew he was sitting up, coughing and wheezing, spitting blood and phlegm into the gravel. His head swam in a dizzying fog, his neck ached. His chest heaved as he gulped air.

He was suddenly aware of Kate. She was squatting next to him, her hand on his back, her eyes filled with tears. He reached a hand to his neck, felt the muscles and sinew, and was amazed he wasn't dead. Touching his face, he pulled the fingers away and saw blood.

He looked around, blinking several times, his vision gradually clearing, images emerging only slowly. When his vision had cleared, he saw his shotgun lying several feet away, the flood light glinting on the cold metal. There was no sign of Fletcher or Dorje. He cast a questioning look at Kate.

"W-what happened?" His voice came out in a croak, hoarse and barely intelligible.

She wiped away tears and stood up. "That thing," she said, "was choking you. I thought you were dead. Then he just let you go and stood up. He looked totally confused and bewildered. The dog, too. They both just wandered off." She shook her head, as if trying to dispel the images. "I don't understand it."

Taylor took a deep, shuddering breath and placed both hands palm down on the gravel to steady himself. He swallowed. Then he reached up his hand.

With Kate's help, he lurched painfully to his feet. At first, he remained doubled over, clutching his mid-section where Fletcher had hit him. He didn't think anything was broken but he wasn't entirely sure. At the very least, he knew he'd have some painful bruises tomorrow. Gradually he straightened. He stood unsteadily for a moment, feeling light-headed. His legs felt like rubber, but after a while he regained his composure.

"Where's Debra?" he asked, looking around.

Kate shook her head. "I don't know. In the house, I think."

Clamping a hand to the wound above his eye, he stumbled toward the front door. "We need to find her."

She grabbed his arm. "Wait a second. You need to go to a hospital. You're bleeding."

"We need to make sure she's okay."

"I told you, those things just wandered off. They're gone."

He shrugged off her arm. "We have to make sure she's okay."

"Taylor—!" She stopped herself and sighed. She knew she couldn't persuade him. She watched his back as he walked toward the house. Shaking her head, she reluctantly followed.

The door was a wreck; it was splintered and cracked. Dorje hadn't gotten through, but he had done considerable damage. It was warped and sat askew on its hinges. Taylor tried pushing it open, but it wouldn't budge.

He leaned his shoulder against the door, braced his feet and, with gritted teeth, shoved. This time, the door gave way with a splintering crack. Taylor lost his balance and almost tumbled headlong into the house but regained his balance. Kate followed him.

"Debra!" Taylor called out, but broke off into a gagging cough, his throat sore.

There was no answer. They stood in the living room and glanced around. All was quiet and nothing was disturbed.

Taylor stumbled on something underfoot and he looked down. It was a cell phone, presumably Debra's. Clamping his forehead tightly, he stooped down to pick it up.

"Debra's?" Kate asked.

Taylor nodded. He examined it and saw that it was still on. He pressed a button to end the call.

"Debra!" Kate called out. This time they heard the slow opening of a door from down the hallway. Footsteps reverberated against the floor and, in seconds, Debra appeared. She was dressed in a bathrobe and was holding a kitchen knife in her right hand. When she saw them, tension seemed to drain from her face. She dropped the knife and muttered, "Thank God."

"When that dog started banging on the door, I lost it," Debra explained. "I dropped the phone and ran to the kitchen to get a knife. I locked myself in the bathroom. Then I remembered the tranquilizers. At first, I'd forgotten where I put them but then I remembered. I injected Dad with enough to knock him out. I hid in the bathroom again. That's when I heard the gunshots. I didn't know what was going on."

They were sitting around the kitchen table in Havelock's house. Taylor was holding an ice bag to the side of his head. His lip was split, his cheek and chin were bruised, and his neck ached.

"At least we know the tranquilizers work," he said. "I'm convinced that was why he stopped choking me. When they kicked in, Fletcher stopped."

Debra nodded. "It's settled then. We have to keep Dad sedated. It's our only option."

Kate sat listening, looking from one to another as they spoke. They made it sound as if the whole thing was some strange experiment. She let out a frustrated sigh, which got their attention, and rose to her feet.

"This is crazy," she said. "We need to call the police."

"There's not much they can do," Taylor said.

"What do you mean? That man—that thing—tried to kill you," Kate said, exasperated.

"What we have to do is figure out how to get rid of them," Taylor said.

"And how do you propose to do that?" Kate said, glaring at him, crossing her arms over her chest.

Taylor pressed the ice pack against his cheek and winced. "I'm working on it."

"Well," she said, grabbing his arm, "while you work on it, we're getting you to a hospital."

Chapter 28

Taylor was awakened two days later by the sound of voices outside the window. Still on the threshold of sleep, he couldn't figure out whether they were speaking English. Rubbing a bleary eye, he sat up on his elbows and listened. As he gradually came awake, he realized the voices were definitely not speaking English. They were deep and thick, and to his ears, harsh and guttural. Then it dawned on him— they were speaking Tibetan.

He got up slowly and went over to the window, careful not to move too fast, clamping a hand to the stitches above his eye. His face was still sore from the beating he'd taken, and the stitches made his head throb if he moved too quickly. He pushed the curtains aside and peered out through the morning mist. A grinning, Asian face stared up at him from the flower bed below the window. The short, slight young man, dressed as a monk, immediately bowed in the Tibetan fashion. Though the window was closed, Taylor saw the man mouth the word "*Namaste.*"

Awkwardly, Taylor bowed back. Looking past the man, he noticed several other Tibetan monks emerging from the mist. They were milling about the grounds, each one dressed in a saffron and red-colored robe. He did a quick inventory and counted five monks in all. One of them was Lobsang. The old monk was standing at the far end of the yard, leaning on a cane and gazing up at the house intently. Under his other arm he carried what looked like several old scrolls. The man's face wore a grave and serious expression.

Taylor let the curtains fall back and stepped away from the window, quickly getting dressed. As he threw on a T-shirt and yanked up his jeans, he suddenly wished he hadn't been so adamant that Kate return to the city. After they had gotten back from the hospital, Taylor had told her in no uncertain terms that she should return to the downtown apartment. He told her he was afraid for her safety, and that it was dangerous to stay in Humboldt. She had at first refused, and they'd argued. But somehow he'd won out, so she had reluctantly left.

But now, as he thought about it, he wished he hadn't been so hasty. Debra had been using the tranquilizers on a regular basis and they seemed to be working. There hadn't been any incidents or any sightings of Fletcher or Dorje. And Kate was good at thinking on her feet; she might be able to help him sort things out.

Taylor went outside. A white minivan was parked in the driveway. Taylor noticed Norbu standing next to it, wearing a jacket against the morning chill.

Before Taylor could say anything, Norbu broke away from the van and came forward. The Tibetan smiled and put up a hand in greeting.

"My apologies for the early hour," Norbu said, "but Lobsang was anxious to get here as quickly as possible. We drove through the night."

Taylor didn't know what to say; in all the chaos of the last several days, he'd all but forgotten about the monks. The whole situation was overwhelming and had caught him off guard. He took a moment to collect himself.

"Would you like to come into the house?" he asked, gesturing toward the door.

Norbu's features broke into a bigger smile. "Yes, we would like that." He called out in Tibetan to the other monks. They turned and walked over to the front of the house, each smiling at Taylor self-consciously and bowing in greeting.

"Please," Taylor said, "this way." He stepped aside as the monks came up the steps in single file, like a small procession. They entered the house, their sandals shuffling on the wooden floor. Taylor led them down the foyer and into the living room, where he switched on the lights and gestured for them to sit down. He watched as the monks assembled in the living room in respectful silence and availed themselves of the seating. Each man did so with what Taylor might call a very considered formality, swishing aside robes and sitting down gingerly and quietly. Norbu and Lobsang sat down on the couch together. The old monk laid his cane and scrolls next to him and drew his robe tightly around his thin frame.

For a moment, Taylor stood quietly, awkwardly, not knowing what to say, shifting self-consciously from one foot to the other. He gazed around the room. All the monks were looking at him expectantly, their eyebrows raised, as if he was expected to say something. He fidgeted under their collective gaze and scratched his arm. When no one said a word, Taylor cleared his throat and asked, "Would anyone like tea?"

"Lobsang apologizes for the tardiness of his arrival," Norbu said, setting his teacup down on the table. "But he had to study the problem for some time."

"What has he learned?" Taylor asked. He was seated on the arm of the couch.

"That many of your suspicions are correct."

"My suspicions?" Taylor looked at Norbu. "What do you mean?"

"He says that you have correctly deduced that your friend's mental deterioration has created the problem."

Taylor didn't ask how Lobsang knew all this, but he didn't try to understand; it was obvious the source of the old monk's knowledge was beyond Taylor's comprehension. Instead, he said, "You mean, Havelock's mental state is responsible for the actions of the tulpas?"

Norbu nodded. "He is no longer in control of his emotions. He is reliving old memories, and many of these are painful and unpleasant. They are causing him great anguish. And great rage."

"The murder of Mr. Hsing and the attacks. Were they—"

"They were not deliberate, conscious actions," Norbu said. "They were created by uncontrollable fits of rage. The tulpas simply acted out what your friend was experiencing in his own mind."

Taylor was silent. He thought for a moment and then folded his arms across his chest. "Can he help me?"

Norbu translated Taylor's inquiry. Lobsang was silent for a full minute; his brow was furrowed in thought. He leaned over and said a few words to Norbu.

"Lobsang says, yes, he can help. But the process is difficult and fraught with danger."

Taylor paused, his mind flashing on the events of the previous night. He reached up to finger the stitches on his forehead and winced as he touched a tender spot. He drew a deep breath and cast a quick glance out the window. Low clouds hung in the sky. When he turned back to look at Norbu and Lobsang, his jaw was set and firm. "I understand."

Norbu continued. "He says the process is not only dangerous but one that requires the assistance of others to create the necessary amount of energy. That is why the other monks have accompanied us."

Norbu went on to introduce the additional monks. Each man bowed respectfully as he was introduced; all of them, except one, were older. The young monk, named Tenzin, was the man whom Taylor had encountered outside his window. To Taylor's surprise, the young monk addressed him in English. He studied Tenzin's face, noting the broad nose, wide mouth, full lips, and dark, intense eyes. The man was holding a Tibetan rosary, his long, slender fingers playing over the dark beads.

"What does this process entail?" Taylor asked.

Norbu and Lobsang conversed briefly, then Norbu turned to Taylor. "It involves intense mental acuity and concentration. Everyone needs to focus on the goal without distraction. All the participants must harmonize their thoughts. They must be in concert. Lobsang says that this is essential."

"How long does it take?" Taylor asked.

"A number of days."

"How many days?"

"Lobsang tells me that a harmony of energies must be created, and that takes time. It is difficult to predict."

Taylor had no clue what a "harmony of energies" meant, but he nodded. "I see. When does he want to start?"

The question was conveyed to Lobsang. His reply, even in Tibetan, seemed direct, to-the-point, and unmistakable.

"He would like to begin now," Norbu said. "He says there is little time to waste."

Taylor shook Norbu's hand. They were standing just outside the front door.

"I will return in a week to collect the monks," Norbu said. He zipped his jacket against the chilly mist that lingered in the air. "Hopefully by then these creatures will no longer be a problem."

"I thought you didn't believe in tulpas," Taylor said.

"I am still not convinced of their existence," Norbu said. "But—"

He paused briefly before continuing. "Lobsang is concerned, and I have over the years learned not to take his concerns lightly."

With that, Norbu clasped his hands together, bowed, and descended the steps. When he had driven off, the van disappearing down the gravel road, Taylor turned back and went inside. He proceeded to the study, where he had earlier settled the monks. The room had been transformed; the monks had pushed all the furniture up against the walls so that the middle of the room was empty. He also noticed that they had unrolled several brightly colored rugs on the floor and were using these to sit down upon. Lobsang was bent over and fully engrossed in a scroll that he had unrolled on his lap. The other monks were chatting quietly.

The young monk, Tenzin, looked up as Taylor entered the room. He smiled, showing brilliantly white teeth.

"Sorry to bother you," Taylor said, "but I'm just checking to make sure everyone is settled in."

"It is not a bother," Tenzin replied, "you are very generous to provide us with this accommodation."

"Thank you, I'm glad you think so. I hope you're comfortable." Tenzin just smiled and nodded.

The two men stared at one another for a moment.

"Does anyone need anything?" Taylor asked at length, glancing around the room at the other monks.

"No, thank you. I believe everyone has everything they need."

"I see." Taylor paused, nodding self-consciously. Before leaving the study, he grabbed an old laptop and a power cord.

He marched into the living room and sat down on the couch, setting up the laptop on the adjacent coffee table. Before long, he was checking *The Humboldt Courier* website. Emblazoned on the local news page was the following story:

Visiting San Francisco Couple Attacked by Crazed Man

A visiting couple, Gilbert Chu, 58, and his wife, Susan, 53, were attacked yesterday at State Beach by a man witnesses described as angry and crazed. The couple, up from their home in San Francisco, had just gotten out of their car to go on a hike when they were attacked by the man.

At least two witnesses were on hand to witness the vicious attack. One of the witnesses, Jason Wright, 25, of Oceanport, reported that the assailant, described as a young man in his twenties, started yelling racial epithets at the couple before he attacked them.

Mr. Wright and another witness, Ariel Sheldon, 19, watched as the attacker knocked Mr. Chu to the ground and began to stomp on his head.

Wright and Ms. Sheldon came to Mr. Chu's assistance, but both were then attacked by the man. Ms. Sheldon was knocked to the ground and suffered bruises to her back and right elbow. Mr. Wright was punched and kicked.

"He was surprisingly strong," Mr. Wright remarked to sheriff's officers in the aftermath of the attack.

When another car arrived, the attacker ran off into the adjoining woods. When sheriff's officers arrived on the scene soon after, they were unable to locate the attacker.

Gilbert Chu suffered multiple head injuries, including a fractured eye socket and deep lacerations to his scalp. He is currently in serious but stable condition at Arcata Hospital.

Police are investigating the possibility that the attack was a hate crime.

"My God," Taylor breathed. He stood up and began to pace the room. This was crazy. Absolutely crazy. Hadn't the tranquilizers been working? He thought they had, but after this latest incident, he wasn't sure. He stopped in front of the big bay window, thrust his hands into his pockets, and stared outside. It had been foggy all day and the branches of the big redwood outside dripped with condensation.

He turned away from the window and scratched his chin. What should he do? Call Tim and tell him everything he knew? But he knew his explanation sounded utterly absurd. He'd finally been able to convince Kate but that had only been after a lot of effort, and Debra's input. And even if he was able to convince Tim of the situation, what then? It certainly didn't mean the creatures would be caught. Hell, they couldn't even be harmed.

He continued to pace the room. Finally, he grabbed his cell phone and called Debra.

"The monks are here," he said.

"What are they doing?"

"They've just settled in."

"Are they going to be able to help?"

"They tell me yes, but I guess the process is dangerous."

"What's the process?"

"I'm not entirely clear," Taylor said. "Something to do with creating energy. But it'll take a few days."

"How many days?"

"I'm not exactly sure."

Debra was silent.

"How's Havelock?" Taylor asked.

"He's asleep."

"Has he been having any episodes?"

"Episodes? You mean, like angry outbursts?"

"Yes."

"No," she said, "because he's been drugged."

"Have you been using the tranquilizers?"

"Yes, of course." She paused. "Why? What's going on?"

"There was another attack."

"Another one? Where?"

"At State Beach. Yesterday."

Taylor heard silence on the other end. But then Debra spoke up again. "I've been using the tranquilizers religiously, I swear."

"No, I believe you," Taylor said. "But I don't think they're working anymore."

"What do you mean? Of course, they're working. Every time I give them, he—"

"No, I mean, I don't think they're controlling the creatures anymore."

She stopped talking for a moment. "What do we do?"

"I think all we can do is wait and see. We have to trust that the monks can help."

"What if they can't?" she asked. "What do we do then?"

Taylor sighed; he paused for a long moment. "I don't know."

Chapter 29

TWO DAYS LATER, TAYLOR stood by the window and glanced anxiously at his watch. It was a little after six o'clock. Kate was scheduled to arrive soon, and he was trying to think about what he was going to tell her. How was he going to explain the presence of five Tibetan monks in the house?

The monks had literally taken over the study in the last two days. They'd set up candles and burned incense so that the study became permeated with the smell of sandalwood. They'd started out by chanting on the first day, a deep, sonorous chant that had gone on for most of the morning; this was followed by a profound silence during the afternoon. Taylor hadn't known what they were doing, but he guessed they were in deep meditation or trance. He hadn't looked inside because he didn't want to interfere, but he was curious. The second day had followed the same pattern.

In the meantime, he felt like a caged animal. He hadn't left the house for the last two days—hadn't even surfed—because he didn't want to be away if the monks needed him. But they hadn't asked for any assistance. So while the monks had been ensconced in the study, he had simply roamed about the house with nothing to do, bored out of his skull, restless and agitated—sometimes perusing the Internet, sometimes reading, and sometimes simply sitting and staring off into space.

Turning from the window, he walked back across the room and slumped down in the sofa chair. In a moment he heard the soft pad of sandals from the hallway. He looked up and saw Tenzin. The young monk's face was drawn and haggard, as if he had undergone some physical ordeal, but there was nonetheless a look of serious intent in his eyes.

"I wonder if we might speak," Tenzin said.

Taylor jumped up from the chair. "Of course."

"Please," Tenzin said, motioning with his hand. "Let us sit."

Taylor sat back down and watched as Tenzin gathered his robes and lowered himself onto the couch. "The brothers are resting now," the monk said.

Taylor nodded, studying him. "You look exhausted. Do you want anything? Tea or coffee? Something to eat?"

"No, thank you. I am a bit tired, but not hungry or thirsty."

"What happened in there?

"We were creating *samanvaya*," Tenzin said.

Taylor furrowed his brow. "What does that mean?"

"It translates into—how do you say?—congruity, or harmony of purpose. It is very draining. That is why I am tired. But we must do this in order to achieve a cohesion for the task ahead."

"Which is?"

Tenzin cast him a questioning look.

"The task ahead," Taylor explained.

Understanding, Tenzin nodded and then said, "We will attempt to dissipate the creatures."

"Attempt? That doesn't sound too positive."

"The process is difficult, I am afraid. There are no certainties. Once a tulpa has assumed bodily form it becomes very difficult to dissolve."

"But it can be achieved, right? These creatures can be dissolved?"

Tenzin nodded dispassionately. "We believe that, yes, with the proper control of energies such a thing can be achieved. Unfortunately, your friend, Mr. Rowland, was quite a skilled practitioner. The tulpas he created are unusually solid and animated. They will be difficult to dissolve."

"I see."

There was silence between them for a moment until Tenzin spoke again.

"I do not wish to sound—what is the English word?" He paused briefly to consider. "A pessimist. I do not wish to sound like a pessimist, but it will take much effort to achieve."

Taylor opened his mouth to speak, but with nothing pertinent to say, clamped it shut. He studied the young monk's face. The man's gaze was steady and sober. The gravity of the situation suddenly struck him. What if they failed? What if they weren't able to dissolve the creatures? What would happen then? He rubbed his chin anxiously, then said, "Have you ever done anything like this before? Dissolved a tulpa, I mean."

"No," Tenzin said, shaking his head.

"What about Lobsang?"

"He tells me he has not, though he has studied the ancient scrolls. They describe what must be done."

Taylor was silent. "What can I do to help? I mean, I feel ridiculous just sitting here all day." He let out a frustrated sigh. "There must be something I can do."

Tenzin gazed at Taylor with a look of equanimity. "You have done much already."

Taylor raised his eyebrows, not understanding.

"You recognized the problem. And sought help. That is much."

Taylor studied him for a moment. "How old are you, if you don't mind my asking?"

"I do not mind. I am twenty-three."

"You seem older."

The young monk just gazed at him.

The two men were silent, and Taylor suddenly wondered why he'd said that.

"Anyway," Taylor went on, "there was something you wanted to tell me?"

Tenzin nodded. "Lobsang tells me that as the process continues, the tulpas will have to be summoned."

Taylor paused, and then his face dropped as comprehension set in. "Summoned? You mean here?"

Tenzin nodded slowly.

Taylor raised a hand to his forehead and instinctively fingered his stitches. "And when will that be?"

"When the preliminary observances are concluded. That is when the process is most dangerous." Tenzin paused and fixed his eyes on Taylor. "Lobsang will need your assistance then and wants to know if you are ready."

Taylor raised his eyebrows in surprise. "What does he want me to do?"

"He has not told me, except to say that you are needed."

For a long moment, Taylor didn't say anything. A million thoughts ran through his mind. But then he sat up, his back straightening.

"Tell him I'll be ready."

The sound of tires grinding on the gravel outside made both men look up. Taylor rose and glanced out the window. Kate's Prius rolled to a stop in the driveway. The lights switched off and Taylor watched as she stepped from the vehicle, carrying a duffel bag. She exited the car and made for the house. Her footsteps sounded on the front steps and soon the front door opened.

Taylor heard her coming down the hallway. He watched as she stepped into the living room and came to an abrupt halt when she saw Tenzin, her eyebrows raised in astonishment.

"Oh, hello," she said, staring at the young Tibetan. She paused to glance hesitantly around the room, as if waiting for an additional surprise to spring from the shadows. "I'm sorry, I didn't realize we had company."

"Kate," Taylor said, "this is Tenzin. He's from the Maitreya Monastery."

The young monk rose to his feet, clasped his hand together, and bowed reverently. "*Namaste.*"

"Nice to meet you," Kate said. She put her duffel bag on the floor and, adjusting her glasses, cast Taylor a questioning stare.

There was a moment of awkward silence.

"They're here to help," Taylor explained.

Her eyebrows raised even higher. "They?"

Taylor cleared his throat. "Yes, five monks from the monastery." He paused. "The rest of them are in the study right now. They—"

"What are they doing in there?"

Taylor was at a loss for words. He stammered out an incoherent explanation.

"Perhaps I can be of assistance," Tenzin said, stepping forward.

———

"I just wish I'd been warned," Kate said, dropping a soiled plate into the soap suds that filled the sink. "I mean, I don't mind, especially because they're here to help but, God, you should've warned me." She handed him a wet plate. "It was kind of a jolt."

Taylor took the plate and began drying it with a dishtowel. "I had no idea they were coming either," he said. "They arrived completely unannounced."

He placed the plate on the drying rack and turned to glance over his shoulder down the hallway and into the living room where the monks were gathered. They were talking quietly to one another.

"Do you think we have enough tea?" Taylor asked, turning back.

"I'll buy some more tomorrow."

They continued to wash the dishes in silence. Taylor listened to the monk's voices, but they were speaking in Tibetan so he couldn't understand what they were saying.

"Do you think they'll be able to help? To dissolve these things?" Kate asked. She handed him another plate.

He dried it slowly and methodically, his mind fixed on what Tenzin had told him earlier—about the danger involved and the uncertainty of success. Instead of answering her question, he asked, "Are you going back to the city tomorrow?"

"No, I have three days off." She knitted her eyebrows, frowning at him. "You know my schedule."

"I think you should go back."

She stopped washing the dishes and looked up at him. "We're not going to have this argument all over again, are we?"

"I don't want to argue, either. But I think you should go back."

"Why?"

"I think it'll be safer."

"That's not an answer." Her gaze bore into him. "Why?"

Taylor felt a sudden flash of anger and frustration at her stubbornness. But he quelled it and said calmly but firmly, "I'm not going to argue with you. You're going back to the city and you're going to stay there until this whole thing blows over."

Kate blinked in surprise at his dictatorial tone. "I'm not arguing with you. I just want to know why. What is it you're not telling me?"

"These things are dangerous."

"You think I don't know that?" Her voice was exasperated. "I watched while that thing tried to kill you, remember?"

Taylor sighed in frustration. "Look," he said, "part of the process—part of dissolving them—involves summoning them."

"Summoning them? You mean bringing them here?"

He nodded.

She was silent for a moment. "Shouldn't we both leave, then? And just let the monks do what they have to do."

"It's not that simple," Taylor said. "Apparently my assistance is needed."

"Yours? What do they want you to do?"

"I don't know yet. They won't say exactly. Lobsang simply says I'm needed and that I have to be ready. I told him I would."

"I see." Kate was silent again for several moments. Then she reached out her hand and touched his arm, transferring soap suds. "I'm not leaving you this time. Whatever it is you're supposed to do, I'm going to help you. We're going to do this together."

Taylor looked deeply into her eyes. There was a steely determination there that surprised him, and suddenly, the idea of sending her away seemed ridiculous. They *were* going to do this together.

After a moment, he nodded. "Okay."

Rain began to fall outside, drumming against the windows. Taylor stood looking out. From an earlier news report, he'd heard a big storm was poised to slam into northern California sometime later that night. By all accounts, it was going to be a bad one—with gusty high winds and torrential rain. In fact, an official storm advisory had been issued for Humboldt County, especially for areas immediately along the coast.

"I'm sorry I doubted you these past few months," Kate said.

Taylor turned away from the window and looked at her.

Kate began putting on her pajamas. "But I seriously thought you'd gone off the deep end. I just couldn't believe what you were telling me about these creatures."

Taylor couldn't help but chuckle. "Thought I'd gone off the deep end, too."

They were in the bedroom, getting ready for bed. "But when that thing was choking you," Kate continued, "it all became real. That wasn't a man, it was a monster."

Taylor sat down on the edge of the bed. "If someone had told me a year ago I'd be believing in mind demons, I would've thought they were nuts."

Kate went over to her purse, which was hung over a chair. She dug around for a moment and took out a small vial. She popped open the top and tapped a small blue pill into her palm.

"What's that?" Taylor asked, watching her.

"Xanax."

"Where'd you get that?"

"A colleague at work gave me some. I need it after everything that's happened."

"Be careful with those," Taylor said.

"Don't worry," she said. "It's only half a normal dose." She popped it into her mouth and swallowed. "But hopefully it'll help me sleep."

Kate crawled into bed and pulled the blanket up to her chin. She sighed audibly.

Taylor ran a hand through his hair. "Yeah, it's been a long day. For both of us." He stood up and went toward the door.

"Aren't you coming to bed?" Kate asked.

"In a moment, I'm going to turn off the lights and make sure the monks don't need anything."

He closed the bedroom door and went downstairs. Except for the rain outside, everything was quiet. There was so sign of the monks; they must have adjourned to the study for the night. Taylor went about turning off lights. When he had finished, he started back up the stairs.

He heard footsteps behind him and he turned around. Tenzin was standing at the bottom of the steps. The man's sudden appearance made Taylor jump.

"I apologize for the intrusion," the young monk said, bowing. "But Lobsang wishes to see you."

"Right now?"

Tenzin nodded.

Taylor followed the monk down the hallway and into the study. The room was dimly lit by a flickering candle that had been placed in the center. Its light cast moving shadows on the walls. Traces of incense lingered in the air.

As Taylor's eyes adjusted to the gloom, he noticed that the monks were seated lotus fashion on the floor so that they formed a rough circle around the candle. All were assembled, silent, waiting, looking up at him in expectation. In the flickering light, their well-lined faces seemed deep and cadaverous.

"Please," Tenzin said, gesturing down at the floor, to a spot across from Lobsang. "Lobsang wishes for you to sit."

Taylor crossed his legs and squatted down across from the old monk. Tenzin closed the door with a soft click and came over, sitting down next to Taylor. He leaned in close and whispered, "Lobsang says the time is now."

Taylor nodded, feeling a rush of anticipation. But he quelled it and sat quietly. He folded his hands in his lap, and waited, gazing across the room at Lobsang. The old man had closed his eyes. Taylor wasn't sure whether he should close his eyes, too. But he decided to keep them open until he was instructed to do otherwise. He studied the old monk's face in the dim light of the room. For a fleeting moment, he felt as if he might be gazing at the face of a Tibetan idol—the carved countenance of some deity or bodhisattva. But the feeling soon vanished, and as the minutes dragged on, he felt himself growing drowsy in the warm air.

Without warning, Lobsang's eyes flashed open, suddenly alert. He leaned over and said a few words to Tenzin.

Tenzin nodded and, turning his attention to Taylor, said, "He asks if you are ready?"

Taylor nodded. "Yes."

The monks began to chant. At first, their voices were low but, gradually, the pitch and volume rose. Soon the chanting filled the room until all other sounds disappeared—the rain outside, the gentle flicker of the candle. The words emanating from the monks' mouths reverberated in Taylor's ears like a living vibration. He closed his eyes, feeling each word course through his body.

All at once the chanting stopped. Taylor's eyes flashed open. He looked around, momentarily confused, half expecting something—some outside influence—to have caused the sudden cessation. But the monks were silent, eyes closed and brows furrowed in concentration.

Despite the deep silence, there was something different about the room. Taylor noticed it right away. A dynamic energy pervaded the air; it had not been there when he had first sat down, but it was here now. It was as if some invisible electric field now permeated the study. Taylor felt it in his chest, face, his arms—indeed, all over his body.

In the air above the candle, what looked like a thick gray mist began to form.

Taylor stared at it, blinked and stared again. It wasn't his imagination; a mist was rapidly forming. He watched in amazement as it thickened, enlarging and expanding, swirling about the room like a giant living creature. Taylor held his breath, barely daring to breathe, and for several seconds there was utter silence. Taylor gazed at the mist spellbound, then turned and glanced at the monks. They were continuing to sit in silence, eyes closed.

The strange gray mist rose, growing higher and thicker by the moment. It drifted around everyone, snaking about their head and shoulders, twisting sinuously upward. Taylor felt it inch up his chest, lips, and nose, covering his head. Soon the room was nearly filled with it.

All at once, in the center of the room, two figures began to materialize out of the mist, both hovering several feet above the ground. Taylor watched as they gradually manifested, taking on solid form, their outlines slowly crystallizing.

In seconds, Fletcher and Dorje appeared, standing side by side, hovering in the air. They both stood perfectly motionless, kept in place by forces that were beyond Taylor's comprehension. Fletcher's face was still and immobile. His eyes stared straight ahead, glassy and fixed. Both creatures didn't seem cognizant of anything; didn't respond to the monks' presence, or anything for that matter. They were utterly motionless, like figures in a snapshot, frozen in time.

As Taylor watched, both figures began to blur and drift out of focus. Within moments, however, they snapped back into focus again. He blinked, thinking his eyes were playing tricks on him, but as he continued to watch, the figures began to shift back and forth from blurry to clear and back again. Taylor turned to look at Lobsang.

The old monk's eyes were clamped shut, his brow creased. Taylor saw what looked like beads of perspiration on his forehead. His gaze shifted to the other monks. Like Lobsang, each man seemed to be concentrating with a fierce intensity. He turned back to the creatures. They continued this bizarre dance of fading in and out of focus.

Taylor watched with increasing anxiety. It was clear that the monks were trying to erase the creatures but, for whatever reason, the creatures were resisting. As soon as Fletcher and Dorje blurred they popped immediately back into focus. It was disconcerting and Taylor knew in his gut that something was wrong.

Then all at once the mist began to thicken and envelope the creatures. Soon, like images fading from a bad dream, they were gone.

Taylor spun his head around to look at Lobsang. The old man's eyes were shut tight, his lips compressed. He swayed slightly, as if under great strain. Then he dropped his head and muttered something in Tibetan.

Taylor looked over at Tenzin for a translation.

The young monk held Taylor in an intense gaze for a moment before saying, "He says, 'I have failed.'"

Chapter 30

RAIN PELTED HARD AGAINST the roof and windows, rattling loud as hailstones. The wind shrieked, and the branches of a nearby redwood tree scraped the window as another furious gust swept through.

Inside, Taylor paced back and forth in front of the fireplace, his sandals scuffing against the hardwood floor. He was at a loss about what to do. Their efforts had been a failure; the creatures had proven altogether too solid, too well constructed to be dissolved.

The monks, meanwhile, were sprawled on the couch and chairs, whispering in subdued voices. They were exhausted and drained from the ordeal; each man sat slumped, blinking back drowsiness.

Lobsang sat apart from the others. He was studying a scroll, holding it up close and squinting as he read the small text.

Tenzin stood and came over to Taylor.

"How are you, my friend?" he asked.

"I should ask you the same question."

Tenzin shook his head sadly. "I am greatly disappointed," he admitted, sighing.

Taylor glanced around the room and scratched the back of his head. "What do we do now?"

"We must not give up." Tenzin glanced over his shoulder at Lobsang. He stared at the old monk for a moment and then turned back to face Taylor. "I have faith in Lobsang. But he will need time to study the problem. He will need time to devise another plan."

"Do we have time?" Taylor asked anxiously. "It seems like the tulpas are getting increasingly violent."

"We think we do, but we must act quickly."

"I still don't understand what happened exactly," Taylor said. "Why weren't the creatures dissolved?"

"There is something about them that we do not properly understand," he said. "They seem to be much more powerful than we
suspected."

"You did tell me the process wouldn't be easy, as I recall."

"That is so. The process is indeed challenging." He paused, as if trying to formulate a difficult thought. "But there is an added dimension
in this particular case."

Taylor cast the monk a questioning glance.

"The creatures seem to be drawing energy from some undisclosed
source. I assure you that the energy we created was quite considerable.
In fact, we also drew psychic energy from you. That is why you might
have felt a drain of energy while the ordeal was occurring. All that
combined energy should have dissolved them."

"But it didn't."

Tenzin nodded. "Indeed, it did not. Each time we applied the necessary energy to dissolve them, the lost energy was immediately replaced."

"I don't understand."

"Think of a glass of water," Tenzin explained. "Each time one takes
away a tablespoon of water, that tablespoon is replaced. Thus, there is
no net gain in water loss."

Taylor nodded. "And you don't know where they're drawing this
from?"

"No, we do not."

"Where are the creatures now?"

"They are most likely in that place from which they are drawing
this energy."

The two men fell silent for a time. They stood by the fireplace,
warming their hands against the flames, and listened to the rain
against the roof.

"What is he reading?" Taylor asked, nodding at the scroll in Lobsang's hands.

"It is a text called 'The Way of the Ancients.'"

"Think it'll help?"

Tenzin shrugged. "I do not know. But we must not give up."

Taylor nodded. He continued to look at Lobsang. "He's tireless,
isn't he?"

"But it is not good for his health," Tenzin said, nodding. "He is not
so young."

Taylor grinned. "I have a feeling he might outlive us all."

Tenzin grinned back, one of the few times Taylor had seen the young man display such emotion. But his face immediately turned somber.

A strong gust of wind shook the house. This was followed by a clap of thunder, which reverberated like the crash of cymbals, rattling windows. Rain continued to pound against the roof.

Tenzin turned to face him. "Take my suggestion, my friend, and retire for the night. There is nothing you can do tonight."

Taylor nodded. He turned to the mantel and took down the shotgun. For a moment he fumbled in the cartridge box for a shell and then leveled it into the breech.

"That will not help against these creatures," Tenzin told him, observing.

"I know, but I feel safer with it. Even if it's only psychological." He turned and ascended the staircase. When he reached the top, he was suddenly overcome by fatigue. He'd been up for a while and he was exhausted.

He came into the bedroom and closed the door behind him. He looked over at Kate; to his surprise, she was sound asleep despite the violence of the storm. He knew, of course, that her deep sleep was probably facilitated by the Xanax.

He sat down on the bed beside her, gripping the shotgun tightly. He gazed out the window but saw only the steady deluge of rain through the curtains.

He sat and listened to the storm. The rain continued to pelt the house and the gusts of wind seemed to be getting stronger, more dangerous. Soon the rain and wind reached a crescendo, and the house was battered by the full fury of a storm unleashed. He heard the crack of a tree limb outside. There was a resounding thud as it slammed into the roof. A brilliant flash of lightning lit up the room for a brief instant, causing an almost painful afterimage in Taylor's vision. His mouth felt dry and there was a tightness in his chest, which he knew was the result of stress—that and the thought that these things were still, for all practical purposes, on the loose.

The thought sent a shiver up his spine. He wasn't sure he could face them again. The image of Fletcher's wolfish grin was fresh in his mind, emblazoned like a terrible snapshot. The feel of the creature's hands around his neck, bony fingers digging into his windpipe, was etched into his consciousness.

He took a deep, ragged breath and tried to compose himself.

Gradually, weariness got the better of him, and he began to nod off. He lay the shotgun down along the side of the bed and lay down. Soon he was fast asleep.

There was the sound of footsteps outside the door.

Immediately Taylor was awake, startled by the sound. He shot up, alert, his eyes roving back and forth in the darkness. Rolling to one side, he reached down and fumbled for the shotgun. He brought it up, pumped it once, and swung it around, leveling it at the doorway.

Taylor heard a soft click and the door to the bedroom began to creak open. A sliver of light spilled in from the hallway. It grew wider as the door opened.

Taylor held his breath. His finger hovered over the trigger, his heart pounding.

Tenzin stood silhouetted on the threshold.

Taylor breathed a heavy sigh of relief and lowered the shotgun. "Jesus," he muttered.

Tenzin looked at him, looked at the shotgun. "I am sorry," he said. "I did not mean to startle you."

"It's okay," Taylor said, setting the gun's safety. "What did you want?"

"Lobsang requires your assistance."

"Has he got something figured out?"

"He believes he does, yes."

Taylor stood up and glanced over at the clock. It was two in the morning. He followed Tenzin out the door. They went downstairs and into the study.

Lobsang looked up as Taylor entered the room. There was a curious expression on the monk's face. One that appeared to be, at least as Taylor interpreted it, a look of concern. Taylor was surprised to see it; he was so used to either inscrutability or what appeared to be insouciance. But this time the expression on the monk's face was decidedly different. As he continued to stare back at Lobsang, he also detected another expression. But this one was much more difficult to interpret; it gradually replaced the look of concern. He might have been influenced by the flickering candle, but he swore for a moment he saw a look of foreboding on Lobsang's face.

Tenzin said, "Lobsang would like you to close your eyes and, to the best of your ability, try to empty your mind."

"Empty my mind?"

"Yes," Tenzin nodded. "Try not to dwell on any thoughts. Breathe deeply and evenly and focus your mind solely on your breathing."

Taylor nodded and sat down, joining the circle of monks. He took a deep breath and closed his eyes. The candle flame left a bright afterimage on his retina, but this gradually faded. Utter darkness soon surrounded him. For a minute or two, he felt very self-conscious and awkward, trying to figure out what Lobsang wanted him to do. And his thoughts were racing. There was no way he was going to "empty his mind." But he followed Tenzin's instructions, drawing his brows together and concentrating on his breathing, inhaling and exhaling slowly and evenly, counting each breath. After several minutes, despite himself, he began to relax, feeling tension drain from his face and shoulders. He took another breath and felt himself beginning to relax even deeper. Although he wasn't in a position to analyze the feeling, it didn't feel like sleep, but like a very profound emotional calmness. The outside world began to fade, noises became fainter and less frequent.

The calmness deepened as he continued to focus on his breathing. Soon he was conscious of only one thing: the steady rhythm of inhalation and exhalation, inhalation and exhalation. He let this rhythm carry his thoughts away, until all that was left was an acute silence, an all-encompassing stillness.

He suddenly felt weightless, as if somehow he'd released from his body, floating in a dream-like state. The darkness dissipated, giving way to a hazy gray background. He soon felt as if he was floating in a thick gray fog.

Slowly, a figure began to materialize in front of him...

———————

He felt a firm but gentle hand on his shoulder, awakening him.

"My friend," Tenzin's voice said, "are you back with us?" The words seemed to come from a long distance away, as if echoing down a long tunnel.

Taylor's eyes fluttered open. Tenzin was standing over him, his face staring down anxiously and concern etching his features. He continued to shake him gently. "Are you awake?"

Taylor's eyes cleared slowly, and he glanced around. He was in the study. When Tenzin saw that Taylor was all right, the monk's face broke into a benevolent smile, his white teeth flashing. Taylor blinked several times and gazed with greater clarity around the room. It was still dark, lit only by the candle, which Taylor noticed had melted down nearly to its base. Looking at the circle of monks, he wondered how long he'd been out—and where he'd been. But he couldn't seem to remember. He felt tired—emotionally drained—and somewhat light-headed.

He rubbed his eyes and turned to look at Lobsang. The older monk was watching him with intense, probing eyes. Taylor turned back to Tenzin, a questioning look on his face. "What happened?" he asked.

"You must rest now," Tenzin said.

Taylor furrowed his brow, trying to remember what had happened. But his memory was hazy. He'd been floating in some kind of gray fog and a figure had begun to materialize. He thought it had formed into a man, but he couldn't be sure. After that, he didn't remember a thing, though he had a vague recollection that a conversation had taken place.

Still feeling groggy and lightheaded, he allowed Tenzin and one of the monks to help him to his feet. As he left the room, he felt Lobsang's gaze on him and he glanced over his shoulder. The old monk was staring at him, his eyes unreadable.

The two monks guided Taylor down the hallway, each one positioned at either elbow to steady him. He walked with them up the stairs, feeling increasingly exhausted, taking each step as if his legs were weighted down with lead weights.

As they walked toward the bedroom, Taylor turned to Tenzin. "What on earth happened? I don't remember anything, except—"

"You must rest now," Tenzin repeated, patting his arm gently. "Explanations must wait."

By the time the monks got him to his room, he collapsed on the bed in a heap, falling next to Kate.

The monks closed the door quietly and left him alone. He heard their footsteps disappear down the hallway, soft footfalls fading into quiet. Too tired to get undressed—indeed, too tired to do anything— he just lay in bed and stared up at the ceiling, his eyes gritty with fatigue. He racked his brains trying to remember what had happened. But he just couldn't remember. Everything was hazy and dim and getting dimmer. He blinked back sleep, trying to stay awake, but the effort was futile. Finally, he couldn't fight it any longer. His eyelids drooped and shut for good, and he drifted off, falling into an exhausted sleep.

Chapter 31

RAIN CONTINUED TO CLATTER against the roof the next morning. There didn't seem to be any let up, and Taylor wondered how long it was going to last. The official forecast had called for nothing short of a deluge, and as far as Taylor could tell that was exactly what they were getting—a deluge of Biblical proportions.

The main thing on his mind, however, was last night. He lay in bed for several minutes, trying to fathom what had happened. But it was futile. He just couldn't remember.

Finally, he crawled out of the covers and donned a bathrobe. He was about to leave the room but stopped and glanced down at Kate. She was lying with her eyes closed, breathing deeply in long, even breaths.

"Kate," he said softly.

For several seconds she didn't move, but eventually he saw her stir. Rolling over, she opened her eyes and looked up at him. He sat down on the edge of the bed beside her.

"How you doing?" he asked.

She rubbed her eyes. "Feels like I have a hangover. But I'm okay." She paused. "How long did I sleep?"

"All night. You slept like a log."

She sat up, continuing to rub her eyes. She glanced out the window at the rain. "It's really coming down out there, isn't it?"

"In buckets."

Taylor heard a soft rap on the bedroom door.

"Come in," he called out.

The door opened to reveal all five monks standing in the hallway. Each bore a grave expression, and Taylor could tell by the way they stood—with an air of solemn purpose—that a certain threshold had been reached in their preparations.

As if to confirm his thoughts, Tenzin locked eyes with Taylor. "Lobsang says the time is now. The final phase has begun."

———————

Taylor watched as Havelock's eyes fluttered open. For a moment they registered a look of astonishment as the old man gazed at the gathered monks. His head raised off the pillow as he continued to stare. The surprised look on his face gradually faded and was replaced by his normal expression—a sort of bewilderment and opacity. Gradually, his eyelids grew heavy, his head dropped back into the pillow, and the old man drifted off once again.

They were assembled in Havelock's bedroom. The old man lay supine, his head and shoulders propped up on pillows, a blanket covering his legs and torso. His breathing was labored and raspy. The monks seated themselves around the bed in the folding chairs Debra had provided. There was the sound of shuffling feet and the rustling of robes as the monks seated themselves.

Taylor stood at the back of the room, near the door. Debra and Kate were next to him.

When the monks were seated, Kate leaned in close and whispered into Taylor's ear. "What are they going to do?"

"I'm not sure," he answered, whispering back.

Everyone was silent. The monks sat with their eyes closed, their faces impassive. Nonetheless, Taylor could tell they were concentrating by the furrows that marred their brows. The room seemed to take on what Taylor could only call a denseness that was almost palpable, a denseness that seemed ripe with anticipation—and potential danger. The only sound was Havelock's labored breathing. Taylor felt himself almost unconsciously holding his breath. When nothing happened, he let it out with an audible *whoosh* and stole a quick sideways glance at Kate. Gone was any hint of suspicion, doubt, or disbelief on her face; she was as engrossed in the moment as everyone else in the room.

The monks began a low, guttural chant. Like the previous days, it was rhythmic and sonorous and consisted of a single phrase repeated over and over again: *O mani padme hum.* Taylor closed his eyes and listened until those four words seemed the sole basis of his entire existence, echoing in his skull and reverberating against the walls of the bedroom, like a wave sloshing back and form in perpetual motion. *O mani padme hum. O mani padme hum. O mani padme hum.*

When the chanting abruptly ceased—as if someone had flipped a switch—Taylor opened his eyes. The monks were deep in concentration, their backs rigid, their faces stiff and eyes clamped shut. The same dynamic energy he'd felt on the night they had tried to dissolve the creatures again pervaded the air. It swirled about them, filling the room, raising goosebumps on everyone's arms.

Taylor stole glances at Kate and Debra. Both women glanced back at him; from the look in their eyes, he knew they felt it, too. They looked anxious but alert, both apparently determined to see this thing through to its end.

In the center of the room, hovering over Havelock's sleeping body, Taylor noticed the same gray mist he'd seen before. It hung over the old man like a storm cloud. But gradually, the mist began to flow upward in a thick column, eventually bumping up against the ceiling and then expanding outward, filling the room.

Both Kate and Debra gasped, watching the spectacle.

Taylor felt Kate grasp his arm, her fingernails digging into him. "My God!" she whispered. "Look!"

The mist began to descend. But as it did so, it funneled toward Taylor like a snake advancing toward its prey, sinuously wrapping around him, enveloping him in a cocoon.

"Taylor!" Kate gasped. "What's happening?"

Taylor suddenly felt lightheaded and his vision blurred as the mist continued to wrap around him. The room and everyone in it began to disappear into an all-encompassing grayness, shapes and outlines growing fuzzy and indistinct. He blinked to regain his focus, but the feeling was overpowering. He felt his mind begin to drift as well, and he shook his head, trying to dispel the feeling. The mist only grew thicker until it had completely enveloped him. Then a new sensation struck him, like a jolt of electricity. It shot up through his body, from his feet to the top of his head. He staggered backward, his legs buckling. The last thing he heard was a gasp from Kate as he sank to his knees, his head spinning toward oblivion.

When he regained consciousness, he was still surrounded by thick gray mist. But he knew in an instant he was no longer in Havelock's room. Everything was different. He looked around, squinting, but his vision was unable to penetrate the mist. A shiver ran up his spine. Where was he? Was this a dream?

He reached down and grabbed his arm. It was real, no doubt about that.

Slowly the mist dissipated; vague images began to coalesce into solid shapes. Very soon the mist swirled into nothingness and vanished in the air, as if carried away on a breeze. To his surprise, Taylor found himself standing in the middle of a mountain meadow. Long-bladed grass rose to his ankles and wildflowers lay like a colorful carpet, vibrant and pulsing with a variety of hues. The air was filled with their sweet fragrance.

He looked around, bewildered. The surrounding vista was unlike anything he'd ever seen. It was breathtaking—green, rugged, and beautiful, and so vivid as to be almost surreal. The meadow was ringed on all sides by high, snowcapped peaks, as high as Himalayan Mountains, their crenellated tops falling in and out of shadow as gauzy wisps of cloud drifted overhead. There was a crystalline quality to the air that dazzled him, and every breath he took was like an invigorating tonic. He just stood quietly for a long moment gazing at everything.

In front of him was a path that led through the grass. Something in his gut told him to take it. He set off, but every dozen or so steps he stopped to look in all directions, still amazed by his surroundings, worried that suddenly everything might disappear. But, if anything, the surroundings seemed to get brighter, sharper, more vivid. Soon he was striding along the path, continuing to gaze around. Butterflies hovered over the wildflowers, flitting about, and the twitter of birds drifted in the air.

A slow-moving stream meandered through the meadow. Insects hovered over the sluggishly moving water, wings occasionally catching the sunlight and sparkling with brilliant flashes of iridescence. He crossed to the opposite side, using a series of irregularly spaced stones that stuck out of the water and formed a natural bridge.

Taylor soon discovered that the very act of walking, of striding along with his head up and arms swinging, was an unparalleled joy. He walked with an ease and rhythm that was almost akin to flying.

He felt neither fatigue nor strain, only a tranquility that he'd never before experienced.

The path led across the meadow and descended toward a stand of juniper trees. Eventually that ended and, before long, Taylor came out on the shore of a lake. He stopped, his jaw dropping. It was one of the most beautiful places he'd ever seen, and for a moment he just stood and stared. The surface of the lake was completely still, exquisitely reflecting the snow-capped peaks that thrust up into the sky like giants, their mantles of brilliantly white snow glittering in the sun.

In the distance, on the far shore, Taylor spotted what appeared to be a stone cabin with a thatched roof. It seemed incongruous in the rugged, mountainous landscape. From a short chimney smoke drifted lazily, rising into the still air in a thin plume.

He continued along the trail, which skirted along the shore of the lake. As Taylor approached the cabin, however, he felt an abrupt sense of dread. It was as if each footstep led him toward something it might be better to avoid. At the same time, he felt a sense of déjà vu, as if he had experienced this before.

A man suddenly appeared in the doorway. He was slightly hunched over and bowlegged, leaning heavily on a cane. Silver hair stuck out from underneath a beret, which was set at a jaunty angle.

"Havelock?" Taylor said, starting in surprise.

The old man's eyes were narrowed as he stared at Taylor. "I see you're back again."

Taylor was confused. "Back?"

"To persuade me." There was a sarcastic tone in the man's voice. "'To bring me to my senses,' as you put it last time."

Havelock was speaking as if they were continuing a conversation they'd recently had. But Taylor had no recollection of any such conversation. He searched his memory, trying to dislodge some shard that would bring everything flooding back. Havelock appeared lucid and coherent; there was no hint of dementia or physical illness in his demeanor.

"The last thing I remember I was in your bedroom," Taylor said.

"I don't know anything about that," Havelock snapped. "But I do know you've been hounding me. Why don't you leave me alone? I'm not going to get rid of my friends. No matter what you or the monks say."

"Friends?" Taylor didn't know to whom Havelock was referring.

Then, all of a sudden, it dawned on him; Havelock was talking about Fletcher and Dorje. And he suddenly knew why he was here. Lobsang had sent him—apparently more than once. When he had agreed to help, it was for this. For this very moment. He had to convince Havelock to dissolve the creatures, to let go of them.

"You know why I'm here," he said. "You have to dissolve them."

Havelock's gaze threw daggers. "I won't."

"Can't you see what they're doing?"

"They're my friends. You don't abandon friends."

"They're not real."

Havelock stared at him, his eyes ablaze. "Yes, they are! They're real." He tapped his chest. "I made them."

"You must let them go. They're dangerous. You've lost control of them."

"Lost control? What are you talking about?"

"Don't you see?" Taylor stared at Havelock. "Are you that blind? Dorje has killed."

Havelock was silent, just continuing to glare at Taylor.

"They're dangerous," Taylor said again. "You can't control them. Dorje killed Ed Hsing."

Havelock's face twisted in anger. "He deserved it. He was Chinese."

"My God, Havelock. He had nothing to do with any of this. He was innocent."

Havelock's fury burst forth without restraint. "They all deserve it. Every last one of them. They killed Fletcher. They shot him."

"The soldiers shot him. They're responsible. No one else."

"I think it's time for you to leave," Havelock said.

"You can't keep living in the past," Taylor said. "You have to accept that Fletcher is gone."

"No, he isn't! I brought him back."

"That creature isn't Fletcher. Fletcher is dead. He died long ago. He died saving your life." Taylor's words seemed to hang in the air between them.

Havelock's lower jaw moved, as if he was trying to say something but the words weren't forming. Taylor could see from the whiteness of his knuckles that he was gripping his cane tightly. Havelock's expression showed his inner battle as much as his fidgeting. He couldn't keep still as he shifted his weight and clenched his cane. It was obvious

Taylor's words had hit their mark.

"You must dissolve them," Taylor went on, pressing any advantage he could find. "Don't you understand the harm they're doing?" He paused. "You're not like this, Havelock. I know you. You're a good man. You've saved lives. You've helped many people."

"Shut up!" Havelock screamed. "You don't know anything! You don't know a goddamned thing about it."

"Then tell me what I don't know," Taylor said. "Help me understand."

"I told you to leave!"

"I'm not leaving," Taylor said. He glared at Havelock and steeled himself. "We're going to resolve this now."

Havelock waved an arm in the air. "This is my world. I created this and you're an intruder. You're not wanted here. Leave!"

"Havelock," Taylor said, "we're friends. I want to help. Tell me what it is I don't understand."

"If you're not going to leave, I'll have to force you," Havelock said.

A sudden, piercing howl tore through the air.

Chapter 32

THE SOUND STOPPED TAYLOR cold. He tensed, his heart thumping in his chest and his throat tightening. Two shadowy figures began to take form behind Havelock, one positioned at each shoulder.

Taylor took a step back as the figures crystallized. At Havelock's right shoulder Fletcher gradually appeared, standing calmly with his arms at his sides. Dorje materialized at Havelock's left shoulder, equally calm.

Both creatures stood silently, like statues. They stared straight ahead, their eyes glassy. They didn't seem cognizant of anything; didn't respond to Taylor's presence, or anything, for that matter. They were motionless, like figures in a snapshot, frozen in time.

Havelock snapped his fingers.

The two creatures suddenly sprang to life. Fletcher blinked and his face grew into a scowl. His hands balled into fists at his sides. Dorje began to growl, the low menacing growl Taylor had heard before.

"With one word I could have them rip you apart," Havelock said.

Taylor hesitated. He stared at the creatures, and then directed his gaze back at Havelock. He swallowed hard and steeled himself. "But you won't."

"Don't tempt me."

"Stop playing games," Taylor said. "This isn't the kind of person you are."

"You have no clue who I am!" Havelock roared. "You don't know the power I possess!"

"I know you're a person who has saved lives, not taken them."

"If I had the ability back then I have now I would have used it."

"To what ends?" Taylor asked.

"I would have killed all of them, every last one!"

"Then you would've ultimately been no better than they," Taylor said.

"They invaded Tibet! They were the ones who started it!"

"That's the past, Havelock. It's over. What's done is done."

"Nothing's over!" He tapped his chest. "I remember! Everyone else may have forgotten, but I remember. And I'll never forget."

"Then you'll never have peace."

"Peace? There's no such thing as peace," Havelock sneered. "This world is a miserable, evil place, filled with murderers."

"It's also a beautiful place. Filled with love."

Havelock glared at him. "If you saw what I saw, you would be singing a different tune. I saw whole villages devastated, men and women slaughtered like cattle. The bodies of dead children thrown together in a pile. Severed heads collected to form a pyramid. And starving Tibetans forced to eat their own dead! I saw it all!"

"I'm not doubting any of that. What you saw was real."

"You're damn right it was real!"

"But what does reliving it do? Can you change anything now? You can't bring the dead back to life. The only thing you can do is face reality and move on."

"You're going to lecture me about what I should do?"

"Call it what you like. I'm just trying to get you to see the futility of it all. None of this helps you or the Tibetans."

"It honors their memory. Someone has to remember."

"It doesn't honor anyone. All it does is mire you in grief and anger." He paused, looking at Havelock evenly. "And makes you a killer."

Havelock was silent, staring at Taylor with narrowed eyes. Dorje's growl increased to a vicious bark. The dog's canines flashed and drops of saliva glistened in the sunlight.

Taylor stepped back. He had to fight the urge to turn and flee.

"You don't know anything about anything," Havelock said.

"You keep saying that. And maybe you're right. Maybe I don't know anything. But what I see right now is a good man twisted by his own anger. Twisted beyond reason. What would your mentor say if he saw you now? What would Lama Tsering say?"

"That's enough!"

"Admit I'm right, Havelock. Just admit it and give all this up."

Havelock's face reddened and his eyes flashed. "Dorje, kill!"

The dog sprang forward, its powerful haunches propelling it into the air. All Taylor saw was a blur of fur and muscle. Instinctively, he threw his arms over his face and fell to the ground.

But nothing happened.

Shocked, he rolled over and uncovered his eyes. Dorje hung over him in suspended animation, completely motionless. The creature's sharp canines were inches from his face. Surprised, he looked over at Havelock.

The old man's face seemed suddenly drained of all emotion. His eyes were rimmed red, his skin ashen. He closed his eyes and shook his head. "I—I can't do it."

Taylor crawled out from underneath the dog and slowly got to his feet.

Havelock dropped his head. He took a deep breath that shook his entire frame. Finally, Havelock raised his head and opened his eyes, which were brimming with tears. "I can't do it," he repeated, the anger in his voice gone. He wiped the back of his hand across his nose in a careless gesture.

"It's time," Taylor said. "It's time to dissolve them."

Tears streamed down Havelock's cheeks. "I can't let go. My life—" His voice cracked, and he dropped his cane, covering his face with his hands, sobbing uncontrollably.

"You have to, Havelock. You have to let go of them."

Havelock shook his head. "No, it's not them. It's me."

Taylor stood watching the old man. It dawned on him, as he watched his shoulders shake that Havelock was truly at war with himself—at war with his own mind. The demons of his past had a firm grip on him. They had control of his emotions, his thoughts. They were the manipulators of the strings that, once pulled, made him dance.

Havelock dropped his hands and looked up. His face was red and puffy from tears. "My life—" he began again, but paused to swallow, his expression conflicted. It seemed to Taylor that Havelock was trying to articulate several thoughts at once. "They killed him. My life wasn't supposed to be like this. It was supposed to be different. They shot him in cold blood. All I wanted—"

"He saved you, Havelock. It was an act of love and sacrifice. He died so that you might live. You must honor that."

"Why did he have to die? Why? For what?"

"I don't know. I don't pretend to understand why those things happen any more than you do."

"He was the sweetest boy. A bright light in this insane world. A true innocent. And how did he end up?" Havelock's face twisted with anger. "Riddled with bullets!"

"All you can do now is honor his memory."

For a moment, Havelock didn't say anything. Then his face relaxed, and, awkwardly, he reached down and picked up his cane. He straightened back up and looked at the cane in his hand, as if pondering something. He wiped the tears from his eyes with the back of his hand. He took a deep breath, regaining his composure, and whispered, as if to himself, "The good do indeed die young. And the rest of us—"

Taylor watched him.

"Yes," Havelock went on, nodding. "They must go. It's time."

Taylor breathed a heavy sigh of relief.

"I've been deluding myself," Havelock continued. "And I've caused great harm. For that I am truly sorry." He looked at Taylor as he spoke, but his eyes were far away, as if he were gazing at something only he could see.

Havelock turned to look at the creatures.

Gradually, both figures began to fade. Their features grew dimmer and dimmer, their outlines less distinct, until each faded into the mist, leaving only a faint wisp of gray until that, too, merged with the swirling mist and was gone.

"It's done," Havelock murmured. His head dropped as if from great effort, his chin thumping against his chest.

Taylor awoke. He was lying on the couch in his living room, his forearm draped over his eyes. As he slowly regained consciousness, the first thing he heard was the soft murmur of voices. He listened as they grew sharper and more distinct. He lifted his arm and removed it from his eyes. His vision was hazy at first but as it unclouded, he saw Kate and Debra standing above him, concern etching their features. The monks stood behind them.

Kate dropped down next to him. She leaned forward and gently touched his cheek.

"Are you okay?" she asked.

He blinked his eyes, rubbed them, and then gazed around the room, as if trying to discern its validity. He felt light-headed, but unlike last time, he wasn't completely exhausted. He looked back at Kate and nodded.

She put her hand on his back and helped him sit up.

"How long was I out?" he asked.

"An hour or so."

He turned to look at Tenzin. "Where was I? What was that place?"

"A place created by your friend's mind."

"How did I get there?"

Tenzin hesitated, as if unsure how to respond. "Your essence was separated from your physical body. We call it the *linga sharira* in Tibetan. It is—how do you say?—your astral body. It was separated and sent there."

Taylor took a deep breath. He continued to look around the room, blinking repeatedly, as if to make sure it was real. The images were still vivid in his mind.

Kate touched his arm. "Are you sure you're all right?"

"Yes, just a little light-headed."

"I will get you a cup of tea," Tenzin said, observing him. He left the room with a soft shuffle of robes.

Taylor glanced out the window. It was gray and overcast but devoid of rain. The storm had spent itself. Broken tree branches lay scattered like driftwood on a beach and the gravel pavement was littered with standing puddles of water. Several bedraggled seagulls wandered about, looking dazed, apparently blown in from the coast during the storm.

A thought suddenly struck Taylor and he swung around on the assembled group. "Havelock? How is he? Is he okay?"

There was silence for a moment, the ticking of the clock on the mantel suddenly loud. When the silence lingered, Taylor looked expectantly from Debra to Kate and back again. "Is he all right?" he asked again.

This time Debra spoke. "He's dead," she said. "He never woke up."

Taylor swallowed and took a deep breath. He felt a pang of pity but also knew the outcome was inevitable. His eyes closed briefly and then opened.

"I see," he said, nodding.

Soon Tenzin came back with a steaming cup of tea. "Here my friend," he said, "drink this."

Taylor sat up straighter and took the proffered cup with both hands.

While Taylor drank his tea, Lobsang suddenly spoke up. Everyone turned to listen. The old man spoke calmly but his tone and manner,

Taylor noticed, were different. Although there was the normal serious-ness in his voice, it was a seriousness that was the result of deep emotion rather than concern or anxiety. When he had finished, he clasped his hands together and bowed in Taylor's direction. Tenzin translated what he had said. "Lobsang says that you have done well. You have achieved your goal. You are to be congratulated and he honors you."

In spite of everything, Taylor grinned. Every little sip of tea made him feel better, less lightheaded. There was a spice in it he couldn't identify but he had to admit it was sharpening his senses, bringing him slowly back to normal.

He turned to Tenzin. "The creatures just dissolved in front of me," he said. "They just faded into the mist."

"Yes," Tenzin nodded, "they reverted back into the energy from which they were fashioned. They no longer exist."

Taylor took a sip of tea and paused. "Where is Havelock now?"

"He has stepped back into the eternal," the young monk said.

"He was sorry for what he had done. But I don't think he really knew what he was doing. He was so clouded by anger and grief."

Tenzin didn't say anything.

"I can't believe he knew what he was doing," Taylor repeated, as if to convince himself. He looked over at Debra. There were tears in her eyes.

"There were brief moments of clarity," Tenzin said. "And in these moments, he knew what his creatures had done. But he was living in the realm of his own illusions."

"But he knows now?"

Tenzin nodded. "Yes, he knows now."

Chapter 33

TAYLOR WATCHED AS HAVELOCK'S coffin was slowly lowered into the rectangular-cut grave. It settled to the bottom with a slight thud and then sat silently, its polished surface contrasting sharply with the loamy soil. Taylor stood near the edge, looking down. There was a cold note of finality in the way the coffin sat, so silent and heavy it seemed immoveable, remote, and inaccessible.

Sort of like Havelock himself, Taylor thought. The man had been an enigma in many ways; he was likeable and generous, a lively companion, and a good conversationalist, but also arrogant, dismissive, secretive, neglectful, and irascible. Intelligent yet emotionally reactive. A scientist and yet a mystic. In short, a complex human being—in all the subtle and not-so-subtle intricacies those two terms, "complex" and "human being," implied.

Taylor gazed up at the bright blue sky, felt the sun's warmth caress his face. He could only hope that Havelock was now finally at peace. That his painful past had been left behind. That he had laid to rest all the ghosts that had haunted him for so long.

Dropping his gaze, he scanned the small group of mourners gathered around the grave. Most of them he didn't know. In fact, besides Debra and the contingent of monks from the Maitreya Center, he didn't know any of them. An older man with long white hair and a tie slightly askew stood nearby. He had the look of an academic about him and Taylor wondered whether he was a colleague of Havelock's. Near the older man was a young, professional-looking couple. Taylor didn't recognize them either, though he guessed they might have been Havelock's former students.

Off to one side were the monks led by Lobsang and Norbu. The older monk leaned heavily on his cane. His face looked especially haggard, as if the last several days had aged him immeasurably. Tenzin stood next to him, his hand on the old man's elbow.

Kate and Debra stood together, across from the couple. To Taylor's surprise, Debra had arrived with a puppy, a plump little ball of black fur. He thought it might be a Tibetan mastiff, but he wasn't certain. In all the preparations and chaos leading up to the funeral, he hadn't yet had a chance to speak with her.

When the ceremony ended, he walked over and stood beside her. The puppy was sitting on its haunches, looking thoroughly bored. "Who's this?" he asked.

She broke into a smile. "My new puppy."

"When did you get him?"

"Just a few days ago." She paused. "I felt it was somehow fitting. I think Dad would've liked him."

Taylor knelt and extended his hand. The puppy sniffed his fingers for a moment, and then licked his hand.

"What's his name?" Taylor asked.

"Fletcher."

Taylor nodded approvingly and stood back up. "Yes, I think he would've." He paused. "He's a mastiff, right?"

She nodded. "Hard to believe they grow up to be so big."

He scrutinized her for a few moments. "You okay? I mean, how are you holding up?"

"I'm all right," she said, but daubed at her eyes with a handkerchief.

Taylor was silent, contemplating what to say next, trying to think of something consoling and sympathetic. But nothing seemed to spring to mind. It was difficult to put into words the events they'd experienced.

"He did live an interesting life," Debra said suddenly, looking back at the grave. "I'll definitely give him that." She was talking to Taylor, but he felt she was also working something out in her own mind—trying to reach some definitive statement, some final testament to her father. "He achieved a lot in his life, but I don't think he ever achieved happiness."

"Perhaps—" Taylor began.

Debra looked at him when he didn't finish, her eyebrows arched, waiting.

Taylor put his hands in his pockets, gazed down at the dog. The little creature was panting in the sun, its pink tongue lolled out. "Perhaps happiness wasn't meant for him in this life."

"I'd like to think everyone can achieve at least some measure of happiness in life." She shrugged. "But I guess that's just the Pollyanna in me."

"I'd like to think that, too. But—"

"Once when I was a young girl," Debra said, "Dad told me about the night sky in Tibet. He said it was so bright up there in the mountains it took your breath away. He said the stars looked like diamonds glittering on black velvet. He used to say when he was looking at all the stars and planets, he was looking at eternity." She paused, a smile coming to her lips. "That made a big impression on me."

"That's a nice thought," Taylor said.

"It's things like that I want to remember about him. Not...not the other things."

Overhead, gulls whirled and swooped in the breeze. After a while, Taylor reached over and gave Debra's arm a gentle squeeze.

"Take care," he said.

She smiled at him. "I will."

Taylor turned and walked back to where Kate was standing. "I'd like to talk to the monks before we go," he told her.

She nodded.

As he approached Lobsang and the monks, Taylor clasped his hands together and bowed in the Tibetan fashion. The monks bowed back. "Thanks for coming," he said.

"We felt it was most appropriate that we attend," Tenzin said.

"I'm glad you did. I can't thank you enough—all of you—for what you did."

Tenzin looked at Lobsang and then back at Taylor. "Lobsang would like to say something," he said.

Taylor nodded. "Of course."

"Lobsang would like to remind all that we have greater control over this world than we think. With our thoughts we make the world. But our thoughts create waves that travel out and can affect others. We must therefore endeavor to think with a pure mind, because we are ultimately responsible for our actions."

Taylor gazed at the old monk and nodded. The man's eyes were dark and calm, his expression placid. He turned and was about to walk away, when he heard Lobsang's voice again. He turned back and looked at Norbu. "What did he say?"

"He says the things of the heart remain our greatest challenges. It has always been so."

Taylor left the monks and returned to Kate. He took her arm and together they walked back to the Jeep.

On the drive back Kate was silent for a long time. She sat in the passenger seat and stared out the window. Her brow was furrowed as she gazed at the passing landscape, her thoughts seemingly miles away.

"You all right, babe?" Taylor asked at length, observing her.

She didn't answer immediately but turned slowly away from the window. Her eyes, which had been distant and moody, now focused on Taylor. She nodded.

"Just thinking."

"About what?"

She shrugged, seemingly reluctant to answer.

"About what?" Taylor asked again.

She drew a deep breath and adjusted her glasses. "I guess I'm still trying to process everything we've gone through. I used to think everything made sense. That this world made sense. It might be totally screwed up but at least it made sense. When you dropped a rock from a height it fell to the ground. When you gathered all the significant and pertinent facts together you could make a logical argument. A low pressure system meant rain. Drinking three glasses of wine in rapid succession made you drunk."

Taylor was silent, just listening, feeling the Jeep's tires rattle along the road, the steering wheel vibrate gently in his hand.

"I guess I just don't know what to think anymore. What to believe." She gave him a searching look. "Doesn't any of this bother you?"

Taylor remained silent for a moment, and then he said, "'O brave new world that has such people in it!'"

She frowned at him. "That's Shakespeare, isn't it?"

He nodded.

She rolled her eyes. "My mom warned me not to get involved with a writer."

He chuckled.

"So what's your point?" she said after a moment.

"My point is, this world may not be the same anymore; it may be an entirely different place than we thought it was, but does that mean we should fear it? Isn't there cause here for celebration, too?"

"I'm not fearful. I'm just—" She hesitated.

He waited for her to finish.

"Okay," she said, "maybe I am a little fearful. I mean, look at what Havelock was able to do with his mind. He basically created monsters. Living, breathing monsters."

"The mind can also heal. It can create good things, too."

She laughed in spite of herself. "I'm married to the eternal optimist, aren't I?"

Taylor was about to say something when she stopped him. "And if you say, 'but that's why you love me, right' I'll kill you."

They laughed.

Taylor gazed out the window. Thick evening fog was rolling in from the coast, enveloping the surrounding hills like a slow-moving wave. He watched as it spilled forth, following the landscape's myriad contours. It rose up and over the high ground, wrapped around trees, and tumbled down into hollows, moving inexorably inland. Soon it would blanket the house. As it neared, Taylor smelled the faint but unmistakable scent of salt. He liked the smell but knew Kate would soon get cold, so he got up from the chair he'd been sitting in and closed the window. It slid shut with a quiet *swoosh*. As he settled back in the big leather chair, he glanced at her. She was sitting on the sofa, reading a book, a mug of hot tea on the side table. Her head was inclined slightly, her face etched with concentration, fully engrossed in her book.

Taylor picked up Havelock's meditation journal and flipped through it. He scanned several entries until he came to this:

> *I sometimes wonder whether I've violated everything Lama Tsering tried to teach me. I know he tried to warn me about the dangers of focusing exclusively on the siddhis; that it is easy to become seduced by them, and that ultimately they are distractions to one's true spiritual path. He said that they can easily become the focus of one's existence and that it is better to attend to one's own spiritual development. He said I must strive for enlightenment, for*

only can that blessed state bring me true peace and contentment.

As I look back over my life, I see now that he was right. I have spent a great deal of my life pursuing supernatural abilities, but have these given me happiness? Indeed, have those things I've pursued most passionately—career, reputation, scientific honors, even my philanthropic work—brought me lasting happiness and contentment? There have been moments, of course, but no, I can honestly say my life has been devoid of true, lasting happiness. In fact, in my mad pursuit of supernatural abilities, I have often overlooked and neglected those areas of my life to which I should have paid more attention. I am just now—at ninety-five years of age—finally realizing an idea the ancient sages have long propounded: The journey is more important than the endpoint.

When I think back, the happiest moments of my life were very simple things: Walking with Fletcher in the woods during a crisp fall afternoon, playing with my three-year-old daughter, or simply watching the clouds gather over the Himalayan peaks in the evening. Simple things indeed.

Why can't humans find lasting peace and happiness? Why are we so restless as a species? The Buddha was correct when he said that all life is suffering. For most of us, though, life isn't suffering on a grand scale. Our suffering is much more subtle; it consists of a general dissatisfaction, an all-pervading sense of disquietude at the transitory and imperfect nature of existence. We often find ourselves berating ourselves for things we did, or didn't do, or opportunities missed, or things said or not said—whatever it happens to be.

And yet now I am too old to change. I simply want a measure of love and companionship before I exit this world. Isn't that what any of us wants anyway? Love and companionship?

Taylor stopped reading and closed the journal. He glanced up, looking across the room at Kate. He smiled at her. She happened to look up at the same time, caught his glance, and smiled back.

Acknowledgements

IN WRITING *MIND FIELDS*, I am indebted to a number of different works, especially Alexandra David-Néel's *Magic and Mystery in Tibet* (1929) and Heinrich Harrer's *Seven Years in Tibet* (1952). While the latter, read in my teenage years, provided the spark that would ignite my lifelong fascination with Tibet, it was David-Néel's book that introduced me to the more esoteric aspects of Tibetan Buddhism. This gem of a book, the second of her many books about Tibet, remains her most popular. At turns bizarre, self-revelatory, and downright engrossing, *Magic and Mystery* takes the reader on a literary journey replete with events and opinions that challenge the reader's preconceptions. Other books that played significant roles in the genesis of *Mind Fields* include Peter Hopkirk's *Trespassers on the Roof of the World: The Secret Exploration of Tibet* (1982), Peter Matthiessen's *The Snow Leopard* (1978), Tsangnyön Heruka's *The Life of Milarepa* (2010), and *Freedom in Exile: The Autobiography of the Dalai Lama* (1990) by his Holiness the 14th Dalai Lama.

I would also like to acknowledge the wisdom, guidance and hard work of Catherine Oates, my literary manager. She was indispensable in setting me on the track to publication. There are times in life when people appear, seemingly out of the blue, to rekindle our inner fires and help us on our lives' paths. She appeared at one such time, and I am grateful.

Made in the USA
Middletown, DE
26 June 2021